MW01118181

NORTHERN EXPLOSION

A Laura Kjelstad Mystery

Andie Peterson

*[signature: Andie Peterson]*

Bloomington, IN Milton Keynes, UK

authorHOUSE™

AuthorHouse™
1663 Liberty Drive, Suite 200
Bloomington, IN 47403
www.authorhouse.com
Phone: 1-800-839-8640

AuthorHouse™ UK Ltd.
500 Avebury Boulevard
Central Milton Keynes, MK9 2BE
www.authorhouse.co.uk
Phone: 08001974150

First published by AuthorHouse   7/10/2006

ISBN: 1-4259-3197-9 (e)
ISBN: 1-4259-3196-0 (sc)

Library of Congress Control Number: 2006903508

Printed in the United States of America
Bloomington, Indiana

This book is printed on acid-free paper.

CHAPTER ONE

Canal Park
Duluth, Minnesota
11:00 a.m. - May 16

A thunderstorm moved over Lake Superior with a fury as Mark Brewster drove down Lake Avenue; the oncoming storm was building quickly. The heavens boomed loudly; the lightning was indistinct, being masked by a black canopy of low and swollen cloud. With each blast of thunder, Mark felt the car vibrate as the ground shuddered. From the windows of the van, the Lift Bridge was a spidery silhouette, the steel cross-hatching seemed something less than solid. A northeast wind possessed the lake, sending spectacular sheets of water flooding the parking lot as if a geyser had been born.

Motorists gazed through blurred glass and jigging windshield wipers as the storm burst into a torrential downpour. Pedestrians, their faces whipped by intermittent shafts of rain, ran along the pavement, blown litter assembling at their ankles and along the sidewalk edges. Rain persisted in a rhythmic drumming against the car as Mark pulled into a parking spot in an atmosphere of glowing shop windows and glaring neon.

Cars were parked in the lots near the ship canal, but most of the vehicles were empty. The few people huddled in their cars were watching the drama performed by Lake Superior.

A young man and woman burst from a camper-truck parked across the street. The driving rain made the pavement slippery and the man put a protective arm around her waist. They raced across the pavement toward one of the restaurants, water splashed around their ankles and along the sidewalk edges. The storm was in full force, but the young couple was laughing, clearly enjoying themselves.

Mark was in his mid thirties. He was handsome, with a lean body that women found sensuously appealing. His face was tan and his eyes, when they reflected his thoughts, seemed rather calculating. His hands were smooth, with long fingers, and his nails were cut close and were well manicured. Though he was in jeans, an Irish tweed fisherman's sweater, and nondescript anorak, there was something about him that gave the impression of wealth.

His cell phone beeped.

"You in Canal Park yet?" asked Wally.

"I am. In the parking lot."

"Good. I don't want my lessons wasted." Wally's voice was clipped and deadly.

"I keep my word." Mark's voice was strained. "Don't be so damn paranoid."

"I gave you a big advance. You mess up at all and you will lose your ass."

"Don't threaten me," said Mark. "I know enough about explosives to make your body dust and leave everything around you pristine. This is a business deal. It'll be your ass if you don't deliver the cash. With the money I'm getting it would seem your boss has assets enough to have someone watching you. I'd guard my damn back if I were you."

"Son of a bitch. I'll be there in five minutes. Leave your fuckin' cell phone on the front seat. You ain't callin' anybody until I make sure everything's in order." Wally hung up.

Mark had arrived early. Too much money at stake to be a fraction late. Besides, he wanted to get rid of the explosives in the back seat of the rental van. He'd packed everything in computer boxes, but even a minor traffic accident would bring him to the attention of the police. Wicked weather caused people to do stupid things with their cars. He inhaled deeply, cursed, and raked his fingers through his hair. He wanted the cash, simple as that.

Dealing with explosives came naturally to him. As a young man, he worked with his dad on construction projects blasting bedrock and clearing land. His dad had been in Vietnam and had learned all there was to know about grenades, bombs, detonation devices, triggers, and explosives. He had shared that knowledge with his son.

Mark had learned to handle explosives with a finesse that could rival anyone in the world. By the time he was sixteen, he could blow up a stump and not disturb the surrounding area. By the time he was eighteen, he could set a trigger device that would set off a chain of explosions. His dad taught him how to use clocks, weights, and pressure to set off the explosives. Mark had spent time at his parent's tree farm perfecting his trade. The original homesteaders had left some old vehicles and Mark quickly learned how to blow up part of a car. Front seat – driver's side. Back seat – passenger side. Trunk. Right front wheel.

"Some day you'll make triple the money I've made," said his dad. "Construction companies will bid for your expertise. You can write your own ticket."

His dad had been right about the bidding process for Mark's services. There was money in working the construction trade, but Mark wanted more. He had found his niche in the illegal weapons department. Then he'd expanded into training sessions for would-be assassins. He taught the crooks enough about explosives without giving them the expertise that he had. Always leave them at B level while he stayed the A plus expert.

A vague uneasiness rested on Mark as he watched the fog devour buildings in the distance. The air was heavy and foreboding, as if seized by a giant, malignant hand. He had been given instructions: keep the van unlocked, walk toward the lighthouse until someone contacted him. Now he had to leave his phone on the seat. Hell. He was dealing with a paranoid maniac. If he wanted the cash, he couldn't ignore the directions. Wally had been very emphatic in what was expected. Mark just wished to hell the wind and rain would stop.

His hand glided over his gun and the tension eased. It was always like this. Tension and thrills all rolled into one exciting, profitable life.

Wally Kaiser had appeared to be a successful businessman the first time they met, impeccably manicured beard, salon style haircut, white shirt and tie, expensive suit, and black rimmed glasses. They'd lunched at The Oslo House in Duluth, overlooking the lake, appearing to be two colleagues from one of the downtown firms.

The Oslo House – where he'd met Lisa.

"I got your name from a contact in Paris," Wally had said to Mark. "Your credentials are excellent."

"I know," said Mark. Maybe he was a little bit cocky, but he needed to keep Wally in the realm of the student. Never let anyone get ahead of the teacher. Give them exactly what they needed, no more. Wally was a big dealer in the criminal world, but in the world of explosives, Mark kept a step ahead of them all. He built the triggers and detonators to order. He would teach his customer how to use them, but he'd never teach anyone how to build one. Had to keep the field to himself. His wasn't the world of basic Internet devices, he owned the world of finesse and precision and never getting caught. The big buyers knew that. Why take a chance, when you could hire Mark Brewster to deliver the best?

The agreement was solid. Some cash up front, explosives and detonators to be delivered in two weeks. A few lessons on the best way to blow someone up. Then the rest of the cash would be paid. Period. No negotiations. Of course, Wally had never mentioned the word bomb or explosives while they were in the restaurant. Everything was in code and Mark knew the language. It felt good. The fact that he had helped invent the language added to his aura in the international explosives scene. "Walk in the woods" – Lesson on car bombs. "Window shopping" - Hit the house or blow up the car? It was his code, an extensive one, and if anyone wanted to talk to him, they better learn his language.

Wally had taken out a string of credit cards to pay for the lunch. He laughed as he showed them to Mark. One was made out to George Henderson. Another one said Miles Murphy. Richard Jamison. Ralph McNulty. Mark could see ten cards. All different. Not surprising. Wally was a chameleon. He changed his appearance every time they'd met.

Wally's hair was cut short, easier to put on various hairpieces. Glasses, clothes, beards, were all used to mask his looks. Sometimes he walked with a cane, other times he affected a slight limp. Always different. Never really him.

Except for the eyes. The eyes were cold. Disconnected. Cruel.

"Don't ever try to find me," Wally had said, his voice a vicious whisper. "Won't happen." His white teeth gleamed and he gave Mark a thin, brutal smile. "But I'll always know how to find you. You may be good at what you do, but I'm the best."

Mark let Wally believe in that myth. It was true; Wally couldn't be traced to the explosives in any way. Mark was his only contact and he didn't know Wally's real name or anything about him. Conversely, Mark could change identities quite effectively himself.

Mark had felt the adrenaline flow as they negotiated the transaction. He was part of an inner circle. This was what he'd worked for. He'd bought himself a nice resort in Ontario to keep his money laundered. Simple. Someone gets blown up was not his problem. There must be a reason for every hit. Someone pissed another someone off. Happens every day. Sometimes they get eliminated. But he did have rules. He never sold explosive devices to anyone that would hurt kids. Never to be used for schools or restaurants or hotels or malls. Never a hospital or nursing home. No public places, period. Always remember the rules.

His specialty was in making the explosion look like an accident. Right front tire explodes as the bad guy goes around a wide curve over a ravine. House, bank, whatever. He could make it seem like a tragic misfortune. A pinhole in a gas line, a little bit of explosive material and the cops rule it accidental. Eliminate the mobster for a mobster.

Right now his expertise was in great demand. The fact that he supplied weapons and explosives at high prices was masked by his youthful, innocent look. He loved the life of the rich and had found the way that would keep him a millionaire. He was part of an elite corps.

And he had Lisa. Just a few more big scores and they could live comfortably on legitimate businesses. Real estate was the way to go. Not selling, but buying. Making good investments on resorts and rental property. One corner of his brain always kept the thought viable, made him comfortable with the future.

He grabbed the gun from the seat, threw the cell phone down, and proceeded toward the lighthouse. The pebbles underfoot were slippery with the dampness of the falling rain and spray from the lake. He lurched into a boulder along the path and paused momentarily to see if anyone was coming to meet him.

A lightning strike was dangerously close. Hell. Explosives were one thing, a bolt of electricity from on high was something else.

The day had a profane feel to it. Earlier, the sky had been tinged with a deep blue, but rain and mist and cloud robbed it now of any suggestion of sunshine. The lighthouse was a solid, dark mass at the end of the pier, but it's features, like those of the nearby buildings, were under a giant shawl of haze.

Frowning, he scanned the parking area. Trusting Wally could be a big mistake, but Wally had paid him two-hundred-thousand dollars up front. That was just for the training sessions. The equipment cost more. Another hundred-fifty-thousand today.

Wally was smart. Two sessions and he could wire anything to blow up. The trigger devices, remotes, and small amount of explosives that could eliminate a person or two particularly intrigued him.

"For a bad guy in Jersey," Wally had told him. "Just one hit."

There were special sessions on car devices that Mark held on a two hundred-acre parcel of land he'd purchased in northern Minnesota. He'd built a large garage with shelves that held a variety of detonators, wiring, timers, transistors, trigger devices, C-4 plastic explosives, and every other type of equipment necessary for efficiently blowing up almost anything. He bought some broken-down cars and took them into the woods for Wally to practice on. Wally caught on fast. Wally Kaiser was also nuts. What was it the psychiatrists called people like him? Psychopaths? Sociopaths? Didn't matter. Wally was the monster under the bed.

When Mark wasn't teaching assassins how to eliminate the enemy, he enjoyed the property immensely. He'd started clearing a series of hiking trails, with benches and a few tables where he could relax, build a campfire, and pitch a tent. A large stream for fishing brook trout ran through his property and he would camp out for a week at a time.

No one had ever trespassed on Mark's land, but if they had, there was nothing to indicate the business being played out in the garage and surrounding property. Large garages and junk vehicles were part of the territory of northern Minnesota logging businesses. Nothing sinister appeared to the trespassing hunter, though Mark didn't have any sessions during deer hunting season. The hunters in this area were smart and expert marksmen so he made a point of being elsewhere when hunters were around.

Mark glanced at his watch, then looked out over the lake. The tempo of the rain had increased and the waves tugged dangerously at his feet. The backwash of waves had pulled people over the walls near the lighthouse in the past; he didn't plan to be one of them. Instructions or not, he was heading back toward the safety of the grass and high ground.

Mark scanned the area; no one around to witness the transaction that was about to take place. Lightning lit up the sky as Mark paced along the soggy grass near the canal. Thunder roared across the lake in deafening crescendo, the storm's intensity pelted hard rain, the wind sending waves into the parking lot, flooding it under six inches of water.

A couple had been standing near him for a while, but the lake was showing a possessive side and they had run for shelter. Best for everyone to be away from the lake's grasp. The Lake Superior

Maritime Visitor Center was open. It was well lit and people were staring out the window, tucked safely inside, watching the lake reclaim some land.

Hell, he was a damn sitting duck out here. The uneasiness he'd felt earlier returned. Besides, right now, the rain and wind were relentless. Time to go inside. He turned to check the parking lot when he saw Wally pull alongside the van. Mark moved closer to the museum. People were looking out the window and it eased his feeling of vulnerability, but he watched Wally.

Wally examined the contents of the boxes in Mark's van. All in perfect order. He transferred the load to his car and laid two packages of cocaine in the back seat of Mark's rental van. If the cops suspected a drug deal gone bad, they'd have no idea of the real work going on.

Mark continued moving slowly toward the museum. He couldn't shake the feeling that he'd been stupid to stand outside alone. Too cocky, perhaps. He had hoped for the usual crowds at the park, but the day wasn't cooperating. If everything were fine, Wally would just leave the money in the van.

The young man and woman from the camper-truck watched as Mark moved along the canal.

"Do you think we should call the police and report him out there by himself?" asked the woman. "It's really strange. Spooky. This is such rotten weather to be outside. Those waves are getting dangerous."

"There could be something wrong," agreed her companion. "Let's keep an eye on him. He's moving this way. Maybe he likes the adventure. The world is full of people who get their kicks out of challenging the elements. You have to admit it's impressive out there."

Mark fingered the gun in his pocket and watched for any signs of betrayal. Big money had made him too nonchalant. He reminded himself that Wally was deranged and he sprinted toward the museum. A rock caught his foot and he momentarily was off balance.

That was the edge Wally was looking for. Running low, he crouched behind a truck, pulled a Glock from an ankle holster and with one efficient motion shot Mark in the head. He fired another bullet into the heart. Mark hit the ground with his hand still holding the gun in his pocket.

"Stupid," said Wally to himself. "Everyone's expendable. Why in the hell did he think he could trust a paid assassin?"

When Mark fell, the woman screamed and a crowd gathered at the window. Several people ran outside to help; a number of people reached for their cell phones and dialed 911. Before anyone was even outside, Wally was in his car and headed up Lake Avenue toward Superior Street.

CHAPTER TWO

Lakewind Motel
Duluth
Morning - May 16

A crack of thunder banged menacingly, causing the windows of her car to rattle and the floorboards to vibrate. Overhead, the sky was powered by rain as the inky clouds burst, sending sheets of water off the roof of the motel. Lisa Sinclair ran across the parking lot, muttered greetings to the clerk as she strode down the hall, entered her room and started to shed her clothes.

"Hot shower and dry clothes," she murmured to herself. She pulled a bottle of wine from her suitcase, poured some into one of the plastic water glasses by the sink, and clicked on the TV.

She and Mark were going to be rich; she'd waited a long time to find a winner. Slept with too many creeps whose only motivation was in their crotch. Mark was different. He would always know how to make big time money. She wasn't interested in how he made the money that kept her in diamonds and designer clothes. In a month, she'd be in a million- dollar house on Lake Nemidjii. He let her spend funds any way she wished so why the hell should she worry about where it came from.

Tonight they'd drive to the Cities, stay in a first class hotel, eat at a fine restaurant, and enjoy a night of celebrating.

She had met Mark when she had been a waitress at The Oslo House. They'd had a steamy affair that turned into a deep love. Mark was totally committed to her; she returned his love and faithfulness.

"A match made in heaven," he said. "You can tell the gods have smiled on us." Strong words from a man who'd never been to a church.

When he'd kissed her this morning, he'd promised to bring back a suitcase of money, more than she'd ever seen before.

"I'm good at what I do, Lisa. Not many people in the world with my occupation."

She had believed him. He drove a Lexus, parked right now in the parking lot. He let her use it, while he drove a rental van. Not sure what he needed a van for, but she had agreed not to ask questions. Just believe in the money he brought in.

Thinking about the money, a smile slowly etched across her face. Money, enough so she could live like the rich ladies her mom used to clean house for. Mark had said they'd buy a huge house, she'd be the one with a maid. A realtor had shown her a lot of nice places and Mark put money down on a grand house west of Birch Bay; he could afford the best. An interior decorator was working on the house to make it a showplace. Big jobs over the last couple of months had brought in some incredible cash.

Mark had looked at a resort to buy in the lake country of central Minnesota. She had told him she didn't want to live in Ontario. The resort he had there was nice, but he'd be gone too much. They were both from Minnesota. Why not stay here?

"And what if we have kids?" she'd asked. "They need their daddy to be home."

"I need somewhere to deposit the money," he'd said. "Smarter to own a business out of the country. I have a good manager in Ontario. Most of the business can be handled by phone or e-mail. When I'm done today, we'll have enough money to buy that resort that we looked at near Birch Bay."

"How do you get the cash through the Canadian border? Don't they check all the bags and everything?"

"Private plane into the resort. It's really not that hard. I own the resort. Everyone thinks the borders are secure since the terrorist attacks. They're not. Too few border patrols, lots of water and forest. Float planes can drift in and out without anyone noticing. Everyone worries about illegal aliens coming in from Mexico so the concentration of border patrols is there. The Canadian border is quite penetrable. "

"Still. I want to live in Minnesota. Birch Bay will be a great place to raise kids."

"Nothing says I can't own a business in Minnesota, too. Even better for moving money around. Maybe a dog breeding enterprise. Lots of money there. Moving the money between selling puppies and owning the resorts will really bring in money."

"That seems like a lot of work."

Mark had laughed. "I wouldn't really have a dog farm. It would just show up on paper. The government doesn't have reliable checks on dog breeders. It's a big business without credible reporting to the government."

One thing about Mark – he was smart as anyone she'd ever known. Smarter than the nerds she'd known in high school. It was no wonder he'd bought a resort. He loved the outdoors. Played hockey in high school. Great skier. And he loved to garden. He was the only man she knew who could tell a lilac from a sumac and a primrose from a wild rose.

"My mom was a Master Gardener," he'd said. "When we have kids, we'll have the biggest garden in the neighborhood."

She had stripped to her black lace underpants and bra. Purposefully, her fingertips ran along the edges of her bra and then her hand dropped and her fingers carefully examined her stomach and butt. Bust was big and soft, nature's gift. The rest of her was firm and trim, thanks to the fitness center. Her face was good, too. She knew how to do her makeup and hair so that she always looked like a model. She kept her hair a light brown with blonde accents to give her the healthy, outdoors look. Men liked what they saw and she'd learned to use every inch of her body. The Oslo House was one of the finest restaurants in Duluth, but she'd learned that she could dress well and be classy and sexy at the same time.

The days of pleasing a multitude of diners were over. Knut and Emily Hansen were wonderful to work for, but she couldn't imagine working in restaurants for many more years. Young, nubile women and handsome, sharp young men were lining up for the wait staff jobs. She could compete with any of them, but waiting tables was difficult work. Now it was only Mark. He gave her a strong sense of love and care and she knew their marriage would last. Maybe Mark really would quit whatever it was he was involved in and make a good living off his resort businesses.

Mark was late. She'd wanted to take a shower with him. She made herself comfortable on the bed and started channel surfing. Sixty-one channels and nothing that she liked.

When the phone rang, she jumped. Mark must have been delayed and he always called if he was going to be late. He was her special sweetheart.

"There's been a problem." It was Wally's voice. "I need you to meet me at Lester Park right away. I'll explain when you get here."

"Why isn't Mark calling me? What kind of problem?"

"Just get over here right away. Mark needs you."

"I'm on my way. Where exactly in the park are you?"

"Parking lot. I'll watch for you."

Lisa dialed Mark's cell phone. She needed to verify Wally's words. No answer.

Five minutes later, Lisa was dressed and driving along London Road toward Lester Park. As she turned into the lot, Wally waved and motioned her to follow him. The tempo of the rain had increased, thunder and lightning shattering the air. An involuntary shudder rippled through Lisa's body.

"I didn't see Mark's car," she shouted. "Where is he?"

"I brought him. He's hurt and I didn't dare bring him to the motel. He's waiting for you on the trail." Wally's countenance had changed; he was the predator.

Wally watched her breasts move with the rhythm of her breath. Her nipples would be firm, her body taut when he took her, knife at throat, a wild look in her beautiful eyes. He felt the urgency between his legs. It was always a pleasure to take a woman before he killed her. Plunge the knife with the final violent thrusts of his body.

Recollections of the past few days penetrated through to the front of Lisa's thoughts, then retreated to become part of the great merger of impressions. Her mind rested on the matter at hand, walking over a muddy, slippery trail and wondering where Mark was.

"Why didn't Mark call me?" she asked.

"Cell phone's dead."

Lisa continued along the trail, now close to the cliffs over the river. She felt a strange wariness, a sense of everything out of focus.

"What's he doing up here?"

"Hiding." Wally's voice was wooden, the words clipped.

"Why?"

"Cops." His eyes were vacant. Frigid.

Lisa didn't believe Mark was here. It wasn't like him to hide in the woods. In the rain and wind. He would have come back to the motel. Frost crept up Lisa's spine.

"This is really weird. There's an outside entrance to our room at the motel. He knows that. Why here?"

Wally snorted a laugh. "Shit. How the hell am I supposed to know?"

"He wouldn't stay outside like this."

"There's a cave in the cliff up ahead. He's there. I built a fire."

A frisson of dread reached to the marrow of her bones. Lisa had grown up in Duluth. She'd hiked the Lester River trails with her friends. There was no cave. Something was crazy.

Wally was far enough ahead that he wouldn't notice that she'd turned around and started running down the trail, back to the safety of her car.

Memory slashed at her, memories of Mark saying he didn't trust Wally. He was a customer, but maybe a dangerous one. Lisa slipped and tumbled as she ran, grabbing tree branches, jumping over rocks. She didn't dare take the time to stop and look back. Just keep running.

No one had noted her journey up the trail overlooking the park. No one knew she was here except the person whose presence engulfed her in a cold, incomprehensible fear. Her foot caught on a gnarled root, and she was spinning, falling, digging her fingers into the earth as she bounced along the ground.

Wally watched her collapse and her attempt to get up. With a twist of her beautiful body, she shoved off from the ground, stood and began limping down the path.

It was time for the kill. He would like to use a knife on Lisa, feel her warm blood on his hands. The desire was strong. He would have done the killing slowly, watched the fear and listened to the pleading, felt the fulfillment as his body reached a climax.

His body tensed with excitement, a twisted smirk etched along his lips; the kill was the highest form of pleasure.

Lisa tried to quicken her steps, but her ankle was hurting badly. A spike of pain ran up her leg and she wondered if she had broken something. She turned around and saw Wally about a hundred feet up the trail. He was grinning down at her, a hideous grin that seemed dipped in poison. There was no one else in the park.

A groan moved through the branches overhead, from below she heard the rumble of water as the river raced toward Lake Superior. The stab of pain in her leg was incessant, draining her body of the adrenaline she needed to continue her escape. She grabbed a large pointed rock. If she could bolster enough strength, she would aim for his face.

He saw the rock and the helpless way she held it. Hell. He wasn't going to get close enough for her to throw the damn thing.

He shot her twice. Once in the head, once in the back. He kicked her body over the embankment into the swollen river.

She was a nothing.

CHAPTER THREE

Settende Mai Parade
Birch Bay, Minnesota
4:00 p.m. May 17

"Everything's set for the parade," said Emily Hansen. "Any last minute instructions?"

"We're set to go," said Laura Kjelstad. "I can't tell you how excited the kids were in school today. They were ecstatic. Every class has a presentation. Plus the puppeteers from the Puppet Barn have worked non-stop. They want to make this work for the kids."

Within half an hour, the entire Birch Bay Elementary School was assembled in the municipal parking lot. The high school band had practiced for weeks to become a true marching, precision unit. Knut and Emily Hansen had worked tirelessly as co-chairs of the first Settende Mai Parade in Birch Bay.

"Settende Mai, May 17," said Knut.

"Look at the kids lined up for Norway's Constitution Day," said Emily. "They look positively amazing. And the weather has cooperated."

"Mom, I can't tell you how much this means to the town," said Laura, giving Emily Hansen a big hug. "Everyone is so enthused. Dad, I need a hug from you, too. None of this would be happening if it wasn't for all the work you two did in making this a success."

"My parents would be thrilled to see a Norwegian children's parade springing up in their granddaughter's town," said Knut. "In Drammen, we had a parade every year. All the children marched in the parade and every single one of them carried a Norwegian flag. Look at the flags flying here. Flags from all over the world."

"The classes all made their own flags," said Laura. "Everyone chose a country and made the flag."

The flags were spectacular. Paper, paint, sticks, and energy all melded into one continuous sea of color.

"Any last minute words, Mayor Kjelstad? Or are you the teacher here?" asked Nancy Smith, reporter for the Birch Bay newspaper. "Which hat are you wearing right r.ow?"

"Both," answered Laura. "Mrs. Jackson is with my third grade class, but we worked on the flags and float in school. This is one instance when the school, town, and city council are all in agreement. I'll catch up with my class after I see that everything is set."

"I'd like to take your picture with all the color in the background. Could you get your parents over here, too? I'd like you all together. Then I need to hurry and get some pictures of the kids."

"Remember we need to circle the block and go down the street again," said Laura. "Otherwise it'll be over in ten minutes."

"Or less," laughed the reporter. "It's tradition to go around the block and march again. It doesn't take long to walk five blocks."

Laura waved greetings and stopped periodically to chat as she maneuvered her way through the crowd lining up for the parade. The street was filled with floats, bands, horses, fire trucks, and everything else that makes up a small town parade. The school children were in the front. Flags waving, the kindergarten class was first down the street. An eager murmuring rippled through the groups that were backed up in the parking lot, snaking around Third Street, a nervousness evident as they prepared to march in style.

Competition became keen as high school classes vied for best float, funniest ensemble, most creative entry, liveliest exhibit, and on through a list of fourteen prizes to be awarded at the end of the parade.

"How many high school groups will there be?" Knut had asked Laura. "Fourteen."

"Then I'll see that there are fourteen categories and fourteen prizes," he had said. "The adults don't get any. This is a parade for the children."

"And all the elementary kids will get ice cream treats during their milk breaks tomorrow," said Emily.

The puppets from the Puppet Barn were getting a lot of attention from the other groups lining up for the parade. Laura was entranced. Paul Bunyan soared above the ground held by six volunteers, all dressed in outfits that matched Paul's red and black shirt and blue pants. Four young women, each wearing a light blue T-shirt and blue jeans, held Babe the Blue Ox high in the air. Individuals using neck harnesses and arm rods maneuvered eagle, moose, and bear puppets.

"Quite stunning," said Laura to a giant fox whose huge green eyes, slathering tongue, and burnished red fabric was flowing in the wind. "Mike and Jason? Is that you under there?" she asked the two ten year olds navigating the puppet. They peeked from under the fabric and gave her a thumbs up.

Earth, wind, water, and fire had novice performers holding puppets aloft made of colorful Mylar, aluminum foil, and assorted textiles. Cardboard bird masks were attached to fishing caps and the young participants were waving feathery clouds high above their heads. A magnificent red fire beast jousted with an enormous blue and white water serpent. Laura was pleased to be a witness to such a fun production.

The air was lifted by a cool wind from Big Canoe Lake, caressing Laura's arms and whispering across her cheek. She watched her parent's faces as their eyes scanned the crowded streets. The parade was a great success thanks to their skill as leaders and creators.

Laura, Knut, and Emily walked beside the last group of puppeteers. A huge Viking ship had been built that was handled by ten high school students from the art class. A huge cheer went up from the crowd as the Viking ship passed.

"Laura. You've done everything perfectly," said Knut. "Quite a success story."

"Me? No. It's you and Mom. I can't thank you enough."

"This whole town has been a wonder," said a man standing nearby. "I've never seen such an event."

Wally Kaiser was dressed as a typical tourist. He wore a fishing cap with several lures attached and "Walleye Master" embroidered across the front. His sturdy boots and blue jeans were obviously new. Today his hair was pulled back in a brown pony tail, dark glasses hid his eyes, and his boots were fitted with lifts that gave him an extra two inches in height.

"Great parade," he said.

Wally looked appreciatively at Laura's sun-streaked brown hair, her thick, long lashes, and the beautiful luminescent eyes. She was slender, except for the rounded breasts that promised a man exquisite memories. Her lips were full, tinted a tasteful red; her whole being exuding a sensuality that grabbed at his crotch.

Birch Bay's mayor would be a pleasure to bed. They'd never catch him. He smiled and walked down the street toward Raspberry Point Inn.

CHAPTER FOUR

Birch Bay
Late Afternoon
May 17

Myrna Hanover was practically perfect in every way. At least that's what people said about her. Mary Poppins is what they called her. Her gardens were beautiful, her volunteerism was unflagging, and her house was the showcase of Birch Bay's society. The windows, upstairs and down, were washed regularly and her dirty dishes were never kept in the sink.

When her husband, Steve, walked in the door after work, he could expect coffee waiting for him and the newspaper placed on the dining room table. Steve was a prominent real estate broker. He owned the firm that was first to elevate prices on lake lots. The wealthy had a hunger for land and water and could afford his prices. Myrna was the office manager, which meant she could show up for work whenever she wanted to. Life was good for them.

Lance and Sheila, the two Hanover children, were exceptional students. All the teachers said they were charming in school and very bright. Polite, too. Of course, Myrna knew that already.

Sunlight was making a re-entry on the horizon, the sky a pearly opaque gray with bands of gold emerging in the west. Myrna stood watching the scattering clouds; the strength of yesterday's storm had become nothing more than a whimper.

She made a cup of Early Grey tea, caught sight of herself reflected in the cupboard glass, and slipped her fingers through her platinum hair, arranging wisps of curls down her forehead. She ran her hand over her butt, not too heavy, not too thin. A pleased smile played across her lips.

The kids should be home soon. The parade was over and they'd want a snack before supper. Myrna clicked on the television and did some channel surfing. Detective, crime, and reality programs weren't what she wanted to watch. Old black and white movies, her favorites, contrasted sharply with the frenzied undulating movements of living color music videos. She finally settled on the Andy Griffith show. In black and white.

Lance was home before Sheila. He'd stopped at the neighbors, but Lance had wanted some chocolate ice cream and the neighbor didn't have any.

"The parade was wonderful," said Myrna. "I'm so glad the weather cleared."

"Mr. and Mrs. Hansen did a great job," said Lance. "They made it lots of fun."

"How was your day, hon?" asked Myrna. "Other than the parade, of course."

"I asked Mrs. Kjelstad if I could have extra credit for memorizing all the states and capitals. I told her I could spell all the names, too, but she said I didn't need any extra credit. Besides, I know that states and capitals is in the fifth grade curriculum so maybe I should just wait 'til then. She gave me independent math to do. I really like Mrs. Kjelstad."

"I think Mrs. Ka-yell-sted is a good teacher," said Myrna. "Sheila liked her, too."

"Chell-sted," said Lance. "It's pronounced Chell-sted."

Myrna had trouble with the name. For some reason she couldn't grasp the pronunciation. It was Norwegian or Swedish or something. She didn't have time to respond though because Sheila slammed through the door shouting.

"Turn on Channel Four," yelled Sheila. "Pam's mom had on the news and there was a story about two murders in Duluth."

The hair on the back of Myrna's neck stood up. She clicked to Channel Four.

WTIK had interrupted regular programming with a news bulletin. The television screen showed a close-up of the Lift Bridge followed by a panoramic view of Canal Park in the background.

WTIK reporter Tim Rushton began: "It was along this beautiful lakeshore that a young man was shot and killed yesterday. There is no information coming from the police department, but an unnamed informant says there was a significant amount of cocaine found in the murdered man's vehicle."

The camera zoomed in on waves smashing against the rocks at the east end of the park, then slowly the camera moved to show the crime scene tape encircling a large area. Two police officers were measuring distances and pointing northward.

"The police chief is not commenting at this time, but there is to be a press conference in an hour." Rushton did a voice over while showing a close-up of a police van driving north on Lake Avenue.

"A source who wishes to remain anonymous has told us that a large amount of cocaine was found in a van rented by the victim. Now here's where the story has a strange twist. Our news crew is on hand at Lester River to give us the details."

The television screen showed a view of rushing water and cliffs. In the background, a police officer was walking on the trail above the river. Two police cars, an ambulance, and a crowd of onlookers were in the foreground.

News anchor Bruce Andresen introduced the story while the television camera zoomed in on the cliff above the river. Yellow crime scene tape surrounded the area and a police barricade barred vehicles from the parking lot. "I'm standing along the edge of Lester River," said Andresen. "Just an hour ago, a young woman was found on the rocks below the cliff. She was shot twice. A substantial amount of meth and cocaine was found in her vehicle. Now here's the twist. The car she was driving belonged to the man who was killed in Canal Park. Police aren't commenting, but it would seem there is a drug war going on in Duluth."

"Do we have any information on the identities of the victims?" asked Rushton from Canal Park.

"Not at this time. We don't have a time of death for the woman either. Yesterday's storm kept people away from the park so the crime may have been committed anytime over the last couple of days. We aren't sure exactly where the woman was killed. The water is high from the recent rains, so the body may have washed down stream. As you can see, the police are walking the area searching for clues. Speculation is that there might not be any evidence left. The rain may have washed everything away."

Myrna shut the television off.

"Both of you are staying close to home until this is settled," said Myrna. "Duluth isn't that far away."

Myrna rubbed her temples.

"We'll be careful, Mom," said Lance. "Birch Bay is a good town."

A chill slithered across Myrna's body. Her kids were smart. And good. The only trouble was they had no knowledge of the earth's sewers.

Laura Kjelstad's cell phone rang. It was her mom.

"Have you been listening to the news?"

"No. I'm still cleaning up after the parade. I won't be home for a while. What's up?"

"I wanted to call before you heard it on the news. Lisa Sinclair is dead."

"What happened?"

"She was murdered."

"How? Why?"

"The police don't know."

"Lisa worked for you quite a while."

"She was one of our best waitresses. I don't know how the press found out she had worked for us, but The Oslo House has been shown on all the local TV stations."

"Are the police sure it was murder?"

"She was shot. Twice. Once in the head and once in the back. Dad's on the phone with Gunderson right now."

"Do they have any leads?"

"No. But here's another thing. Do you remember Lisa's fiancé?"

"Sure. Mark."

"He was killed, too. Shot."

"At the park?"

"Not Lester Park. Canal Park. The news is talking about drugs. Maybe a drug war."

"You're still staying tonight aren't you?"

"I'm sorry, hon, but we won't be able to stay with you tonight. Chief Gunderson has been talking to your dad quite a while. He's going to meet us at The Oslo House first thing tomorrow morning. He wants to question us. Your dad says they'll probably ask us to give a statement."

CHAPTER FIVE

The Oslo House
Duluth
Morning – May 18

Police Chief John Gunderson sat in the dining room waiting for the crowd to thin out. There was no need to disturb the morning rush. The coffee was good, the waffles excellent, and the view spectacular. Gunderson often brought his wife to the restaurant. It was classy and his wife liked class and she liked the Hansens.

The Oslo House was at the top of a stone bluff with a panoramic view of Lake Superior. Floor to ceiling windows and a turreted observatory allowed diners a birds-eye-view of the Lift Bridge while enjoying some of the best food in northern Minnesota.

A barrel ceiling ran the length of the dining room and was draped with red and white sails replicating the old Viking ships. The hickory-planked floor was inlaid with intricate symbols from the ancient Norse calendar stick.

A full size Viking ship painting was a dramatic element on the north wall; thick-timbered ceilings draped with Norwegian flags and vimpler greeted the guests at the entry. Mrs. Gunderson liked the careful attention to details that suggested oldness and tradition. A sense of history resonated through the building, but Knut Hansen always said that if the food wasn't good, no amount of decorating would keep you solvent.

Knut. Gunderson's college friend. Knut had come to Duluth from Norway to study at the University, met Emily, and stayed. He'd worked at the Flaming Eagle restaurant during college, learned to cook, and used his business management degree to start his own restaurant.

"Why don't we go into the office?" Emily Hansen had appeared at Gunderson's side. "We can talk freely. There won't be any reporters eavesdropping."

Emily led the way through the dining room toward the kitchen. The office space had been planned well. The office was east of the restaurant, separated from the kitchen area by an intimate patio. A large expense of windows overlooked the lake and harbor.

They sat around a table in front of the windows, a table used by the Hansen family when they wanted to relax over a meal and not be disturbed by the bustle of the restaurant. Knut poured coffee, offered fresh blueberry scones, and sat across from the Chief.

"So what can we do?" asked Knut.

"Give us any information you can," replied Gunderson. "We're open to anything and everything. Start by telling me what you know about Lisa Sinclair."

Lisa's memory sent a feeling of bewilderment over Emily, like a frosty breeze slowly creeping across her body. She reminded herself that Gunderson was doing his job; that he was probably as incredulous as everyone else was. How do you explain two murders in a "Minnesota Nice" town like Duluth?

Gunderson watched Emily carefully. He wondered what thoughts had dimmed the usual merriment in her eyes, the swift smile that always greeted every guest to the restaurant. Did she have ideas about who was responsible for Lisa's murder or was she frightened with the dread of the unknown?

Knut wasn't easy to read. He sat across the table like a stereoptypical Norseman; his face showing nothing, his eyes taking in everything.

Emily started. "Lisa was always a very efficient, friendly waitress. Made really good tips. She knew how to get the customers talking to her. Exceptionally pretty. Great figure, but she dressed well. Seductive without seeming to know it. She did, of course, but the women all liked her, too. If someone had been here once, she knew their name the next time they came in. People didn't seem to be offended by her friendliness. She'd say, 'Hi, my name is Lisa. What's yours?' Then she'd go around the table and repeat everyone's name. She had a knack for remembering people."

"Maybe she remembered someone she shouldn't have," said Knut. "Duluth's not a high crime town, but we're close to the international border. Lots of highways going to Canada out of Duluth. I know what you told me, Matt. You said people would be uncomfortable if they knew who was driving through Duluth to get to a new life in Canada."

"Lisa also remembered what everyone liked to eat and drink," said Emily. "Annie Levitz was always iced tea and chicken salad in the summer and hot tea and soup of the day in the winter. Lisa would see one of the regulars walk through the door and she told the cook what the person would order before she even went to their table. She was almost always right. Then if someone changed their order, she'd sort of tease them and say, 'Well, I lost my bet with the cook. Sure you don't want the BLT?' "

"Good sense of humor," said Knut. "I wasn't sure of her choice in men, though. Mark seemed like a nice enough guy, but my money would be that it was one of his connections that got them both killed. Lisa graduated from school here. Her family is middle class, industrious, regular people. Lisa never showed any indications of being mixed up with drug dealing. Maybe I'm naïve, but I think there would have been some clue."

Frowning, Gunderson wrote in a little notebook. Typical comments. Nothing he wouldn't hear from everyone else he interviewed. Nice girl. Hometown kid. Never did drugs. Wouldn't get mixed up with drug dealing. Went to church. Good family. The dialogue never failed. Then why the hell did she get shot and thrown over a cliff into the Lester River? If her body hadn't been snagged on driftwood stuck in the rocks, she might have washed out into Lake Superior and never found. She would have been listed as missing. Last seen at the Lakewind Motel.

"Was she still living in an apartment in Lakeside?" asked Matt.

"Her parents would know that," said Emily. "Hasn't anyone questioned them?"

"One of our officers has talked to them," said Gunderson. "I wanted to know what you've heard?"

"I hadn't heard that she wasn't in the same apartment," said Emily. "But she quit a while back because she was engaged to Mark Brewster. She had talked about buying a house on Lake Nemidjii. I figured he must make good money if they were moving there. That's an upscale community."

"What did Mark do?" asked Gunderson.

"Not sure," said Knut. "All Lisa said was that he was into financial management. Managed people's personal accounts, that sort of thing."

"I presume you met Mark."

"Yes." Emily measured her words carefully. She had to remember she was talking to Duluth's Police Chief right now; he was much more than a long time family friend. "He was a regular customer. That's how he met Lisa. He used to come here with business associates."

"The men he came with were not regulars, though," said Knut, carefully enunciating the word not. "It seems like he came with someone different every time."

"I can't say I really knew him," said Emily. "Our relationship with Mark was very superficial. He was the fiancé of one of our employees. We didn't even know Lisa well. Her parents came in to eat occasionally, but we never saw them otherwise."

"Did Lisa ever mention anything about Mark's family?" asked Gunderson.

"Once in a while, she'd talk about how nice his family was. She'd spent time with them. I think Mark had a couple of sisters." Emily paused for a moment. "I think she said that Mark's dad worked in the construction business."

"Explosives," said Knut. "He made a good living."

"Explosives." Gunderson wrote in his notebook without looking up. He took a scone and spread it with butter. He held up his cup and Knut poured fresh coffee.

"That's not unusual, is it?" asked Emily. "Every time a road goes through in Duluth the construction crew is always blasting away at the rock. Straightening curves, leveling hills."

"No, not unusual at all," said Gunderson. "Duluth is rock. The whole north shore is rock. Lots of explosives used up here."

He flexed his arthritic hands. Since they'd taken some of his prescription drugs off the market, his hands had started to ache again. His expression settled into a blankness, never let the public know the police chief has arthritis. They'd worry about his ability to use a gun. Hell, he hadn't used a gun in twenty years. He was administration.

"Matt?" Emily offered more coffee.

"No. Thanks. I'm fine."

He had a murder case to solve and his hands were aching.

"Sorry we can't help any," said Knut. "We're at a loss."

Of course they were. Who would expect murders like this in Duluth? Usually it was a domestic situation that ended in death.

The conversation continued, but it was obvious there was nothing new. He'd learned about Mark's connections to explosives at midnight. Lots of construction companies with explosive experts.

Difficult case.

Mark Brewster was an ordinary guy. Polite. Successful financial consultant. Great identity to hide behind.

CHAPTER SIX

Birch Bay
June 25
Morning

Lawsuit pulsed through Laura Kjelstad's brain in flashing neon. There was a foot deep hole in the middle of Portage Street. Two feet wide. Three feet long. No orange construction cones. No barricades. It was bad. The situation had lawsuit written all over it. Where was the street crew? From where she stood, a block up the hill, she could see Leo Nelson on his daily walk, careening on a collision course toward the newly formed crater. He was oblivious, waving to people as they honked, not realizing they were giving warning signals.

Laura ran down the hill, veered around a garbage can, and imagined explaining to the townspeople why sixty-two-year-old, good 'ol boy, Mr. Nelson, was in the hospital. Broken hip. Possible concussion. There was still time to stop him, she thought. Only a half block to go. Her ears were making whooshing sounds and her breath became noisy gulps as she leaped over Timmy Swenson's tricycle, left on the sidewalk again.

Mr. Nelson was teetering on the brink of the chasm, his cane waving in the air where solid ground should have been. Laura could foresee disaster, the hospital image mingling with the courtroom scene. Everyone in town would have an opinion, blaming her for Mr. Nelson suing the city and costing the taxpayers a bundle of money.

And how would she explain it? The judge would find her guilty of allowing a dangerous cavern on a city street. Maybe worse. Cantankerous, just had a knee replacement, Mr. Nelson would tell everyone that's what happens when they put a young woman in the mayor's office. "Doesn't know shit," he'd say. And the heads would nod.

Laura grabbed him just as he began his header into the street. Only problem was, she overcompensated, sending them both backward. Her head whirled as she hit the ground, Mr. Nelson landing on top of her, his cane flying through the air and landing in Helen Gabler's rose garden. She'd broken his fall, but she wasn't sure that she hadn't broken in the process.

Mrs. Gabler's voice was shrill. "You're in for it if you wrecked my roses, young lady."

Mr. Nelson was spry enough to get to his feet, extending a hand to help her. Laura's body was not as cooperative.

"You going to get up?" he asked. "Doesn't look good for you to be sprawled out like that. On your back. Legs apart and all."

"Just give me a minute. I need to catch my breath." Understatement. She wasn't sure if anything was working. Her eyes did a scan of the clouds and sky; at least she could see through the wavy spots dancing across her brain. She pulled her legs together and rolled over on her side, hoisting herself on one elbow, trying to regain mobility. Mr. Nelson grabbed her under the arms like she was a bag of flour and lifted her up.

"Look at that hole," he yelled. "Where are the barricades? And orange cones? This city doesn't know shit. Good thing I'm light on my feet. Have to go to the doctor now to see if my knee went out of whack."

"And send the bill to the city," said Mrs. Gabler. "I watched them dig that hole. Then they just left it. Very irresponsible if you ask me. Somebody's going to get hurt."

Yeah. Like me. Laura kept the thought to herself.

"You've got dirt all over the seat of your pants." Mrs. Gabler gave her a pitying look. "Your head's full of straw and you've got grass stains on your T-shirt. Of course it's an old T-shirt from the looks of it."

"Looks like she's had a roll in the hay," said Mr. Nelson. They both laughed.

"Not appropriate for Birch Bay's mayor," said Mrs. Gabler.

"Who doesn't know shit," said Mr. Nelson.

"I hear she's having lunch with Governor Dahlberg and his wife." Mrs. Gabler rolled her eyes. "Something must be up."

"Dahlberg's a damn Democrat," said Leo. "Too bad he's not up for re-election this year. We could get rid of the governor and our mayor at the same time. A Republican governor for Minnesota could influence the balance in Washington."

"Charlie Dahlberg stands true to his principals," said Laura. "He's a giant in his passion to make this country better."

Leo huffed. "Firebrand liberal."

"He's been unyielding in cleaning up the Mississippi River."

"Damned environmentalist."

"The governor uses gas with ethanol. He's pushing for legislation to increase ethanol production dramatically over the next decade."

Laura stood her ground, Leo's face hardened.

"And he's created an Office of Children's Services." Laura continued drilling Leo. Helen was backing away. "Minnesota now has an accountable, effective unit for protecting the state's most vulnerable children."

"Giving our money away is what he's done."

"You can't find anyone across the country who's worked more diligently with tribal government."

"People losing their money to the damned Casinos."

"He focuses a hundred and ten percent on his job. Without...."

Mrs. Gabler interrupted. She knew too well that Leo was never one to shut up. "Would you like to come in for a cup of coffee and some of my cinnamon rolls?" she asked.

Laura was going to decline, but realized Helen only meant Mr. Nelson. The two of them cozied up together and left Laura standing in the middle of the street with cars honking and people waving. Over her shoulder, Laura could see Leo give Mrs. Gabler a pat on the rear. None of Laura's business. Two, sixty-something divorced people huddling over some hot buns.

"Hey. Mrs. Ka-yell-sted," shouted Myrna Hanover through the window of her blue Lincoln Navigator. "I thought this street was supposed to be fixed."

"Chell-sted," said Laura. "It's pronounced Chell-sted." Laura had had both the Hanover children in her third grade class at school and Myrna still didn't know how to pronounce Kjelstad. Give her a break, thought Laura. Her kids are polite and smart. Myrna must be doing something right.

"Yeah. Che-kell-sted." Mrs. Hanover's voice was loud enough to be heard down the block. "Someone's going to drive into that hole and the city will be in big trouble. Lawsuit. Then our taxes go up. You know we'll all end up paying for it. You're supposed to make sure we're protected."

"I was just going to call city hall," said Laura, waving a cell phone in the air.

"So where's the city crew? They can't jut leave a crater size hole in the middle of a town street."

"I agree. We'll have the situation under control as soon as possible."

"Before someone ends up in that hole and the town gets sued. Our taxes are high enough the way it is. I need to go. Can't stay around here waiting for some accident to happen. Don't want to be a witness. Can you imagine?"

Mrs. Hanover gunned the motor, spewing gravel as she maneuvered around the hole and headed downtown.

Laura clicked in the number for the city office and stood in the middle of the street directing traffic. The phone was answered on the third ring.

"This is Laura Kjelstad," she said.

"Good morning, mayor. What can I do for you?" Ruth Steiner, the deputy clerk, had answered.

Laura explained the situation and listened while Ruth called the street crew on the CB radio.

"They're not answering," said Ruth. "What do you want me to do?"

"Call the Viking Café and see if the crew is there. It's coffee time. Have Cliff round up any help he can get." Cliff Fredrickson was the city clerk.

"I'll call law enforcement."

Laura groaned. Sheriff Mikkelson was probably on duty. Sam Mikkelson entered her life three months ago. No one questioned his brilliance or his mesmerizing charm on all the women in town. Birch Bay, population 4,197, couldn't afford the sheriff's office Mikkelson wanted. Since Birch Bay and Nordland County had merged the police and sheriff's departments a year ago, the county had been pressuring the city for more than the seventy, thirty monetary agreement they'd made. The city's thirty percent was still a big amount for a small town.

Police Chief Burke was not part of the agreement. Burke had been a cantankerous blister to Laura and the county wouldn't hire him as part of the negotiations. The county felt that Burke was not only incompetent, but a major liability. Not wanting a court battle, the city had made Burke a constable with the understanding he'd take early retirement in two years.

Mikkelson had been an undercover homicide cop in St. Paul and was used to big city spending. Birch Bay didn't have the resources to cover his list of improvements.

"We need a new squad car," he said. "One with some decent technology."

"Not in this year's city budget," she had told him. "Ask the county commissioners." That was one of the big headaches she'd encountered when she became mayor a year and a half ago. The budget was restricted, the national economy was sluggish, and all the city departments had major projects coming up.

Arguing budget was an ongoing issue between Sam and Laura. He thought it was friendly banter, but it made her snappish. He is a very attractive, intelligent, capable guy. And eligible. Whenever he got close her bones liquefied and her heart raced. Maybe she was just desperate. Age thirty and no marriage prospects in sight.

Mikkelson, on the other hand, was a magnet for every single woman in the county. Even some of the fifty-something, single women were hot on his trail. It didn't seem to matter that he was thirty-two.

Five minutes later she was still waving vehicles around the hole, growing more impatient as the harshness of whistles and horns punctuated the air. Nobody from the city crew showed up. She dialed city hall again.

"Nobody's here," she said.

"Mikkelson's on his way," said Ruth. "Should be there any minute."

Laura gave herself a quick assessment. Blood drying on one elbow. Scraped back. Dirty sweats, T-shirt covered with assorted grass stains, stomach churning, and her self-esteem in the Dumpster. She was pulling grass from her hair when a red pick-up truck appeared followed by Mikkelson, cruiser lights flashing.

She recognized the two teen-age boys as they jumped from the pickup and started unloading the Birch Bay street department barricades and orange cones, placing them strategically around the hole.

"Happened to find these guys with the city equipment in the back of their truck. The dispatcher's calling their parents," said Sam, his hands pulling grass from her T-shirt, his breath blowing debris out of her hair.

Laura had a vision of Mikkelson running his hand along the curve of her back, caressing her cheek, and the thermostat in her body soared. Then an image of Eric appeared and her heart ached, shattered like splintered glass, altering her life's rhythm and leaving an emptiness she'd never imagined.

Mr. Nelson and Mrs. Gabler materialized beside Mikkelson, Mrs. Gabler cooing and Mr. Nelson slapping Sam on the back.

"Knew we could count on you to take care of the city screw ups," said Mr. Nelson. "You're the only one on the county payroll that's worth shit."

Mrs. Gabler patted Mikkelson's stomach. "Why don't you come in and join us for cinnamon rolls and coffee when you're through here? This has become such an unfortunate incident." She gave Laura a flinty look. "If our mayor minded to business instead of jogging around town dressed like a boy, this would never have happened."

Laura brushed off her Duluth Dukes baseball cap and put it on her head, pulling the brim down to shade her eyes.

"The Dukes moved to Kansas City." Mr. Nelson spiked his fingers through his hair.

"I was a staunch Dukes fan. I bought the hat for a momento."

"They've moved. Get over it." Mr. Nelson spit a hunk of phlegm onto the pavement. "Women don't know nothin' about streets and utilities. Damn shame what's happening to our town."

Myrna Hanover swung by again in her big gas-guzzling Navigator. As soon as she spotted Mikkelson, she was out of her rig flashing a smile and letting her eyes wander over his body. "Mrs. Ka-yell-sted was just standing here. I'm so glad you came to save the situation. If you need a witness, I'll be glad to do my civic duty."

Laura was ready to correct her again. Chell-sted. But she knew it wouldn't do any good. Mrs. Hanover just didn't get it. On the plus side, Myrna and Steve had two wonderful, polite, intelligent kids. Laura sighed; she needed to move on.

Mikkelson's eyes focused on something behind Laura. Cindy Snyder was parking her red sports car across the street. Cindy narrowed her eyes, ran her tongue over her lips, and dropped her voice an octave when she said hi to Mikkelson. Black spandex shorts and a body hugging pink tank top did everything imaginable to get attention.

Cindy was a study in seduction – from her long, blonde hair, to nipples protruding through her tank top, to the shiny red mouth that was breaking into a wide smile. Her large brown eyes were fringed with long lashes and artfully accented with a hint of eyeliner.

"Hero to the rescue again," said Cindy, touching Sam lightly on the chest. "And Mr. Nelson's here, too. I'm sure the two of you have everything under control. Nice to see."

"Nice to see you, too," murmured Mr. Nelson.

"Obvious plastic tits." Mrs. Gabler was muttering just loud enough for Mr. Nelson and Laura to hear. "Looks like a Holstein."

Who could argue?

"Always liked Holsteins," said Mr. Nelson

Laura's temperature index had dropped near freezing. Mikkelson was ogling and Nelson's breath was heaving. Brian and Judd, the two teenagers, had their eyes locked on Cindy's chest. Maggots, the whole lot of them.

Laura almost gagged. Cindy was a cat in heat.

"Keep up the good work, Sam." Cindy blew Mr. Nelson a kiss, thumped Brian and Judd on the back, and made a dramatic exit to her car.

"You will come in for some cinnamon rolls, won't you?" asked Mrs. Gabler.

"I'd be delighted," said Sam. "Let me call the dispatcher so she can take care of Brian and Judd and I'll be right in.'

Mrs. Gabler was so plumped up to have the sheriff coming for coffee that you'd have to stick her with a fork to return her to normal. Mr. Nelson said he needed to use the bathroom and Myrna Hanover clucked ever so graciously that Mrs. Gabler invited her in for refreshments, too.

Mrs. Gabler turned and looked at Laura. "I know you need to go home and change." As Helen opened the screen door, she patted Leo on his backside. "You've still got it," she said as the door banged shut.

Mikkelson handed the kids a ticket and explained what they needed to do. "The dispatcher said your parents will meet with all of us in forty-five minutes. My office. Don't be late."

"How did you find the kids and barricades so quickly?" asked Laura.

"I found the city crew as soon as I got the call. They said the street had warning signs and barricades, but they'd seen the kids watching them. Didn't take long to find the kids and the city equipment. The city crew knew who the kids were."

"I'm glad it was handled so efficiently. Enjoy your cinnamon rolls."

"Are you feeling excluded?"

"No. Typical Helen response. We're at opposite ends of issues. I figure if she's ticked off with me, that's a good thing."

Cars rolled by on Portage Street, people waved, and Sam plucked a leaf from Laura's hair.

"You have a big Saturday night planned?" he asked.

Laura did a mental head slap. He had to ask. O.K. Saturday night, she thought. And I have a date with my parents. Supper and a movie.

"You eating at your parent's restaurant?" he asked.

"Good food. Great view. The Oslo House is one of the best restaurants in Duluth."

Mikkelson gave Laura a smile as he went in search of the perfect cinnamon roll. Mrs. Gabler knew how to turn out a bun.

Laura started her morning jog without looking back. Mrs. Gabler and Mr. Nelson would be watching from the window, making snide comments that they'd repeat to her the next time they met.

Mrs. Gabler's politics were such that the facts were irrelevant to any situation. Leo Nelson fueled the fire. Third generation Birch Bay natives, they didn't like the intrusion of newcomers. Helen was especially incensed that a woman had been elected mayor.

"She's in her twenties," Helen had said during her telephone campaign for Laura's opponent. "And a woman. She should stick to teaching school." The age and gender issues had backfired on Helen. Laura had worked on specifics: protecting the lake, increasing jobs without harming the environment, and cutting spending. Combining the city police department with the county sheriff's office had saved both government agencies significant dollars.

Leo Nelson had spent his time with slogans that included, "She's not worth shit", "The town's going to hell", and "You'd be damn stupid to vote for Kjelstad".

Even after a recount, Leo wouldn't accept that Laura had claimed seventy-two percent of the vote. "Piece of shit," erupted from his mouth every time he saw her.

The news of her surprise defeat of the incumbent had splashed across the front page of the Duluth News Tribune, but was replaced the next day by a story of a moose walking along the shores of Lake Superior near the Duluth ship canal.

Laura's cell phone rang. "Hi, Mom. What's up?"

"I found out why my car smelled of gas. The cap wasn't screwed on all the way."

"Hmm," said Laura. "I've been telling that to Leo Nelson for a long time.

CHAPTER SEVEN

Laura continued her jog down Cranberry Lake Road, the Dukes baseball cap holding down her short brown hair, Oakleys covering her blue eyes, her pace slowed a little by the fall she'd taken. She headed downtown and then on to Raspberry Drive. The street names, derived from the Ojibwe language, still applied to the loveliest stretches of road in Minnesota.

Summer was easing into Minnesota lake country. School was out, softball fields were filled with kids, and local resorts had geared up for the busy season. Butterflies flitted, flower gardens were in full bloom, and the air was as clean as any you'd find in the country.

Birch Bay is a tourist town. It started out in lumbering and mining, but its beauty attracted the affluent from throughout Minnesota. Houses were single family dwellings, set on large lots. Garages were needed to hold the family boat, snowmobile, skis, ATV, and the kids' bikes. Cars are left outside. The people are mostly Scandinavian, but the mining towns nearby had held dreams for Polish and Czechoslovakian immigrants. Now Birch Bay had delis and bakeries specializing in Polish, Czech, and Scandinavian favorites and resorts with Nordic themes.

The shore around Big Canoe Lake had changed. One room fishing cabins had been bought, torn down, and replaced by immense second homes for the wealthy families from the Twin Cities and Chicago. No trespassing signs were prominently displayed, protecting the high-priced exclusive homes from anyone walking the road or beach.

There was a lot of money in Birch Bay. Affluent people from the Twin Cities had found the beauty of Big Canoe Lake, the solitude, privacy, and available real estate. Local amenities answered the needs of the rich: great restaurants, high-end retail shops, a thriving arts community, and good medical facilities.

Governor Charlie Dahlberg owned one of the expensive homes. He had claimed Birch Bay as his retreat away from the pressures of St. Paul. Charlie and his wife, Audrey, had become Laura's good friends. Conversations at their home were lively, Charlie ceaselessly pushing his agenda on environmental issues, education, jobs, and health care coverage for all Minnesotans. Charlie was charismatic and passionate; his voice energized labor unions and economists. He was outraged over air pollution from power plants and the amount of mercury accumulating in the waters of the state. He was truly a remarkable leader.

Sweat was pouring down the side of Laura's face as she finished mile number three. She smiled at the other joggers and walkers working their way along Raspberry Drive. The day was heating up and she was sharing the road with corporate executives, fitness fanatics, and young moms. Good grief. These women would have ten-year-old kids by the time they reached her age. And when would she have her 2.5 kids and become a stroller pushing soccer mom in search of a Dairy Queen fix?

She'd be the maiden aunt with two dogs, an aquarium full of tropical fish, and would send her nephews and nieces postcards from her travels all over the world.

The Dairy Queen fix sounded like a good idea, kids or not. Another half-hour and she'd be home, ready for a shower and that trip to the nearest ice cream shop.

Molly Berg pulled along side and shouted something from her window. Her car was in a state of disrepair, evidenced by the duct tape on the rear fender and the driver's side window.

"Ready for a cool, refreshing break?" Molly shouted from the car window that was only down halfway, probably why the duct tape was covering a section of glass. "I'm headed for the Inn right now. And guess what?"

"No idea."

"The Dahlbergs invited me to join all of you for lunch. One-thirty."

"Great. I'll be at the Inn in an hour. I need a shower."

"Of course you do. I'll meet you at the Inn."

"Why are you still driving that wreck of a car?"

"Can't drive the BMW. People would think I was showing off." Molly rolled up her window, waved, and did a U-turn. A U-turn in the middle of a street is not a big deal in Birch Bay.

Molly is fifty-nine years old, has short red hair, is on the plump side, and Laura's very special friend. The Inn is Raspberry Point Inn. Molly and her husband, Gary, own Raspberry Point Inn, a resort complex with fine dining, cafe, and hotel accommodations. They also own The Raspberry Patch, a coffee shop and bakery. Eric had been their General Manager.

Laura missed Eric dreadfully. He'd been struck by a drunk driver and she had become a widow at age twenty-nine. From that moment on, she had started shrinking inside. Eric had been assigned a special place in her mind, knowing that her life was now measured by the before and after of his death.

Laura gazed at the spectacular bulk of Big Canoe Lake, red pine and birch standing like sentinels along Raspberry Drive. When Eric was alive they used to come to the beach for picnics, sometimes with friends, but usually it was just the two of them. They'd throw rocks into the water, eat egg salad sandwiches, drink icy root beer, and talk about the children they'd have and the trips they'd take.

Two years ago she had the whole world in front of her, now she wasn't sure where she was headed. She often wondered if she would have run for public office if Eric had lived. Being mayor meant she had the likes of Leo Nelson stirring up trouble on a regular basis.

She slowed to a walk, finishing the last two blocks at a leisurely pace. As she entered the driveway of her house, Noah Sackett was unloading a couple of lawn chairs onto her new deck. Noah is sixty-three years old, a retired Admiral, former Navy SEAL, and is a consultant to the Navy. He's a widower and lives a couple of blocks from Laura's house and helps with projects around the neighborhood. The latest project was Laura's deck.

"Heard you saved Leo Nelson from cracking his cranium." Humor lit up his eyes.

"Lumberjack dot-com is doing its job."

Lumberjack dot-com was the name given to the local rumor mill. Since the advent of computers everyone thought they'd finally found a faster way for information to get around town, but they were wrong. The locals had always called the speed of rumors the lumberjack telegraph until someone called it lumberjack dot-com and the name stayed.

"You get defensive with Leo again?" asked Noah.

"No." Probably. Of course. She'd had a bad morning. Leo tended to set her on edge.

"Don't let him get to you."

Noah was good to have on your side. He was also a fantastic cook, gardener, and part time carpenter.

"Mikkelson found the barricades," said Laura.

"He's good," said Noah. "Former Navy SEAL. Good cop."

"I know. We're lucky to have him." She'd heard those comments from nearly everyone that had met Sam.

"I baked a fresh batch of caramel rolls and left some on your counter," said Noah. "They're a lot better than anything Helen Gabler puts out."

He was right. Besides, Noah was much better company. Eat your heart out Mikkelson.

"Thanks."

Noah's eyes were a striking shade of blue that crinkled attractively at the corners when he smiled. Tall and slender, he was energetic and fit, with a full head of white hair that gave his face a youthful look. He tended to get a few lustful looks himself.

"Call me if you need anything," he said. "I'm heading up to church to mow the lawn."

Within twenty minutes, she'd showered, put on clean jeans, white T-shirt, and a red denim vest. She applied a minimum of make-up, but she felt more presentable when she was finished.

Walking down Cranberry Lake Road, she turned west on Portage Street, and entered the business district, all eight blocks of it. Birch Bay is a mix of gift shops, restaurants, bait shops, and outfitters, mingling with banks, real estate offices, and hardware store of a more traditional town. Grocery stores and gas stations had been built along the highway a few blocks from the main section of town.

Molly was waiting in the sunroom that dominated the eastern side of the Inn, jutting at an angle toward Big Canoe Lake. She was wearing a bright flowered blouse with green fronds splashing across the white silk and a pair of pleated golf shorts in pale khaki. Her fingernails were long and elegant, done weekly at a nail salon in Duluth. An array of rings accented her fingers.

Molly's hands don't reflect the hard work she does. She's regularly in the kitchen cutting up veggies and washing dishes or cleaning rooms and vacuuming. She says keeping her hands looking well is an energy boost for her, lets her know that it's not all drudgery. Gary works hard, too, and his weekly tension releaser is Saturday at the golf course. They both attend church at Concordia Lutheran. Also an important part of their lives.

"Raspberry scones are fresh out of the oven," she said.

"Sounds good," said Laura. "I'll have some iced tea, too. Is Gary's mother doing all right?"

"Doing fine for someone who had knee replacement. His mother should be able to travel in a week or so and then he's bringing her here."

"The Inn is a wonderful place to recuperate."

"It is. We plan to take good care of her. She enjoys Birch Bay, all the activities, and the staff dotes on her. You leading the singing at church on Sunday?"

"I am."

"Everything okay?"

"I don't want to be the maiden aunt traveling the globe, sending postcards to the nieces and nephews and picking up trinkets that they'll throw in a drawer."

"Okay."

"I need to get married."

"Sure."

"I mean it."

"Anyone in particular?"

"No. But it will happen."

"Of course it will."

"How long does it take? After someone you love dies?"

"You never get over it, sweetheart. You move on."

Laura knew it had happened for Molly. Molly's first husband died of cancer. Then she'd met Gary and had four kids.

"So it happens."

"All the time." Molly smiled. She hadn't expected to ever be so happy again.

"I'm not getting any younger. Thirty. No prospects. I want to have kids."

"Don't push those buttons too hard, sweetheart. I was thirty-three when Gary and I got married. Had my first child a year later, had the second a year after that, and the twins two years after that. Four kids in four years. You'll find someone."

"Not Mikkelson, though. He tends to make me ..." She didn't finish. How could she explain that she found Sam desirable and that it made her feel guilty? "Just not Mikkelson."

That was taken care of. Sam Mikkelson would be assigned a place in the back of her brain. Sort of like a dream that never materializes because life becomes real and you get the 2.5 kids and go to soccer games and plan your daughter's wedding. Life was going to turn out just fine.

"There's always Jack Cummings." Molly tilted her head. "He's Minnesota's number one bachelor."

Laura gave her a dismissive glance. "The lieutenant governor? I don't think so. I've only met him a few times. He's in St. Paul and I'm here."

"And he comes to Birch Bay sometimes to meet with Charlie Dahlberg. Charlie actually gets a lot of work done at his home here."

"My relationship with Jack has been political. We're both public figures so I know that people are curious about us, but we're just acquaintances. He's probably not my type."

"You looked great dancing together at the governor's fund raiser last February. And what do you mean that he's not your type?"

"He's a city guy. Board meetings, big time politics. Fundraising. Speeches. There'd never be time to even get to know each other."

Jack Cummings was one of the few men that filled her with a feeling of anticipation. Their time together had been unplanned, dinner sometimes when he was up meeting with Governor Dahlberg. She put him in the same category as Sam Mikkelson. No future. Jack was engrossed in his life in St. Paul; Sam was a casual date.

In the two years since Eric's death, Laura had begun to create a new life for herself. She wasn't sure where Sam or Jack fit into things. It was important to take it slow.

"Mikkelson's here." Molly radiated gleefulness.

"I told you. It wouldn't work out. We always argue budget."

"I mean here –as in the sunroom."

"Am I too late to join you two?" Sam asked pulling out a chair and sitting down. "I'm ready for coffee."

Molly waved to a waitress who fussed over Mikkelson and brought out coffee, scones, raspberry jam, and fresh whipped cream.

"I figured these scones would be done about now," he said.

Sam and Molly sat chatting about fishing, while Laura listened. Her thoughts turned to the times she and Sam had gone fishing together. It was something they both had enjoyed. Then she tuned them out. Take it slow.

Laura admired the wonderfully decorated dining room, with large windows overlooking Raspberry Point and Big Canoe Lake. The rich texture of the canopies displayed hand painted plump raspberries hanging from lush bushes, boldly presented on sapphire blue silk fabric. Ornate crown molding rimmed the ceiling, displaying hand-carved raspberries of pine on oak.

Dominating the east wall was one of the largest stone fireplaces in the state of Minnesota. Built by a local Finnish stonemason using almost two hundred tons of Nordland County rock, it was the scene of many celebrations, including weddings, christenings, and significant anniversaries. It was where Laura and Eric planned on celebrating their fifth wedding anniversary.

"You not talking to me today?" Sam broke Laura's silence.

Sam's voice was deep and mellow with clean diction; Laura knew the dispatchers thought he was wonderful. When he stretched his legs out, Laura saw that he was wearing an ankle holster with a .25 caliber automatic pistol. Regulation.

"I'm just admiring this place," said Laura. "It's so relaxing here."

Sam exuded a quiet confidence and Laura had to admit that he was comfortable to be with. No pretenses, no stilted conversations. His brown hair was cut short and his blue eyes seemed to be taking in everything around him. He sat so straight and erect, that Laura felt herself pulling her shoulders back ever so slightly.

When Sam pushed his chair back, he gave Laura an intense, intimate look.

"Supper tonight at seven," he said and placed his hand on her shoulder. "I'm cooking. I'll pick you up."

And he was gone.

"Looks like you've got a date." Molly grinned like the Cheshire cat.

CHAPTER EIGHT

Wally sat at the counter of the Big Timber Café just down the street from the Birch Bay City Hall. The café had windows that faced east, west, and south, allowing people a panoramic view of Big Canoe Lake. Antique logging tools and old black and white photographs of Birch Bay covered the walls.

A busload of tourists had disembarked at Hook's Bait and Fish Market, buying smoked fish, cheese, and Kavli. Directly across the street, a group of children and adults were meandering along the beach. The day was warming up fast and the blue sky was touched by white clouds right off a postcard.

Laura Kjelstad walked through the door and stood by the coffeepots.

Ed Monroe, the cook owner of the Big Timber Café, appeared in the doorway of the kitchen, glanced around the room, and headed toward Laura. He was a muscular man with a thick chest, tanned body, and in-your-face attitude; the air around him seemed charged with energy. His black T-shirt was emblazoned with zigzag lines and it read: "My mind is like lightning, one brilliant flash and it's gone."

Third generation owner, Ed had run the café on his own for the past ten years. Laura stopped in daily to listen to the words of the locals. History. Gossip. Opinions. Voices clipped through the air from booth to table and out the door. If someone said they'd heard it at Big Timber, the locals figured someone was onto something. Lumberjack dot-com was connected.

"Hi, Ed," she said. "I heard you wanted to see me."

"Right. I thought I should let you know there's been lots of talk in here about you not signing the grant application for the marina project. The grant that Mr. Paxton wrote."

"That's true."

"Well, it's made some people upset. You know the big marina guys are hot under the collar about your opposition. They say you're not signing it, because you oppose the big marina."

"I didn't sign that application because the Parks and Marina group lied on the application form. They're being a bunch of jerks. Paxton lied, too. I'm posting the application on the Internet and highlighting the lies. But they're right in saying I oppose the big marina. The waters division of the DNR are quite deceitful. Corrupt might be a better word."

"Lies? Not inaccuracies?" Ed held her in a steady gaze.

"Lies. They said they need the new marina because of the number of deaths on the lake over the last three years."

"I didn't know anyone had died."

"That's the point. No one died. There hasn't even been a minor accident. They flat out lied on the application form. The DNR said they'd have a better chance of getting the money if they could show a real need."

"And you wouldn't sign."

"I won't sign anything that's not accurate. End of story."

"You can put the information on the booths and counter here, if you'd like," said Ed.

"I'll leave a copy of the state statute, too. Gossip is going around that the previous council had approved the big marina. People need to understand that Minnesota has a statute that says anything big like that has to have a four-fifths vote of the council. They went ahead and started working with the DNR with only three of the five council members voting for it. People need to know that the DNR is culpable, too."

"Bring anything in and I'll see that it's on the tables. The stuff about the former mayor voting for improvements to his own street, too. That was pure bullshit. And I have a master's degree in that. M. S. in B. S."

Ed's face clouded with fury. "And that damn Shinnler had the city pay for a fence and trees for his good friend at the Eagle Ridge Restaurant. Son of a bitch."

"Bruce Shinnler did a lot of things like that when he was mayor. The thing I never understood was how he won a second term. The corruption was obvious."

"Minnesota Nice became Minnesota Vice under Shinnler." Ed motioned the waitress to bring some coffee. "Locals started calling the place Shinnler's Shame."

"Shinnler doesn't get it."

"You're right. Let me know what I can do to help."

"Thanks. I'll run off copies of the application and bring them in later this morning. I've already written a report outlining my reasons for not supporting the big marina. I'll attach that to the info I bring over."

"Good. That bastard Paxton thinks he can take over this town just because he's got his Daddy's money. I hope you give him a political body slam that's going to keep him out of commission for a while. Maybe he'll move back to Colorado and he can take his frickin' wife with him. She's never liked it here anyway. I don't know why in hell they ever moved here."

"Probably because he thought we would all cave in when we saw how much money he has. He has no idea what this town is all about. And Birch Bay is where his dad grew up."

"I'll spread the word. You know the coffee crowd here. There's a different group every couple of hours. By the end of the day, I'll have them all set straight. None of them particularly like Paxton anyway."

Laura smiled. "Thanks, Ed. I appreciate you watching my back."

"Any time, all the time. I'm just happy you ran for mayor in the first place." Ed shifted his broad shoulders. "You're sure you don't want some coffee?"

"I'm sure. Thanks. I have to sign the papers for the fourth street sewer project."

"Jeez. The glamour of politics."

Wally watched Laura leave the building. A sense of power flooded over him. He knew the future. Knew what was going to happen. The rest of the dumb shits just sat there thinking everything was fine.

Laura walked through the alley and entered the back door of city hall. The building had been built in the 1950s, its architecture was unremarkable, small, and not constructed for the computer age. She was grateful for the efficient, dedicated city staff. The office was a welcoming, friendly environment, with every inch of space wisely utilized and the staff displaying an exceptional professionalism.

Cliff Fredrickson, the city clerk, had said there were some letters and forms ready for her to sign.

Hot, muggy air hit her as soon as she walked through the door. Air conditioning was not on the list of priorities in the city budget.

Ruth Steiner, the deputy clerk, was busy on the keyboard, a slight frown furrowed her forehead. Ruth always looked great. At five foot eight, Ruth had a sturdy build, but was certainly not heavy. She was wearing a crisply ironed, light blue shirt that had the Birch Bay logo on the left pocket. The logo consisted of sun, waves, and birch trees; a simple design that captured the essence of the town.

"Good morning, everybody," said Laura cheerfully. "Is Cliff here?"

He wasn't.

"I have the form for the fourth street sewer grant right here," said Ruth, holding it in the air. "Cliff had to go to the Rec. Park. Said you'd be by."

Cliff was predictable. You could follow his route out of the office like Hansel's bread crumbs. Utility folders on the secretary's desk, park board memo on the copy machine ready for the meeting, library budget on the front counter for the library director, street department work plan next to the coffee machine. Anything for the mayor was with Ruth. He always remembered where each person had said to put his or her papers.

"Mrs. Bayles left a message for you that her TV isn't working again. Said that since the city is in charge of the cable board that you usually fix it for her."

"I do." Laura smiled. "I've tried to explain how the TV works, but her eyesight is poor. Hey. She's ninety-one. If I can help her I will. She pushes the CATV switch to TV and loses cable. It takes me ten seconds or less. I'll take care of it right away."

"The lieutenant governor called," said Ruth. He's coming up the day after tomorrow to meet with Charlie Dahlberg and wondered if you would have lunch with him. He'll be here for a few days. He's working on some projects at the governor's lake house."

"Return his call and tell him I would be glad to meet him for lunch. Find out the time and place if you would, please?"

"You have to admit that when Jack Cummings walks into a room, the whole atmosphere changes. He is so charismatic. You can just feel the power around him. Not to mention his extreme good looks."

"I know." Laura left it at that. Any more words would lead to speculation on the part of staff. The rumor mill would start running soon enough. As soon as she had lunch with Jack, lumberjack dot-com would start churning. Having supper with Mikkelson tonight would only add to the chatter.

The door clicked open. A man in white shirt and chinos walked up to the counter.

"Hello," said Wally. "My name is George Henderson. I'm interested in buying a resort in the area and thought I'd stop in and visit the town fathers."

"In here, it's the town mothers," said Ruth. "We have a woman mayor and women on the city council and women in key staff positions. Welcome to Birch Bay."

Wally smiled and held out his hand. He had created himself once again. Gold rimmed glasses, short cropped dark brown hair, close shave. Dark brown contacts altered his blue eyes. A temporary, washable dragon tattoo slithered down his arm, partly concealed by the sleeves of the shirt. He carried a thin black leather briefcase. A slight southern accent flowed when he talked.

"You must be from Georgia," said Ruth. "At least it sure sounds like it to me."

"Guilty," said Wally. "George from Georgia. I always thought it sounded a little strange so I'm working on talking like a Midwesterner."

Wally was amused. It was so easy to distract people from who he really was. He'd perfected the Georgia rhythm, but he also could do a southern Iowa drawl, the Tennessee twang, and a strong German accent.

This was going to be an interesting project. There wasn't much left to do. His plans would be modified as situations changed. Of course he knew there was a woman mayor. He knew everything there was to know about Laura Kjelstad, Birch Bay, Sam Mikkelson, and all the other important players in town. He had the power.

Yes. Power was good. Knowing the future gave him more power than anyone else.

Wally chuckled. He was Lamont Cranston, The Shadow. He'd listened to his mom's old time radio tapes when he was a youngster. The Shadow... "knows what evil lurks in the hearts of men." Wally, too, had "the ability to cloud men's minds" so they wouldn't know him. Today it was the mayor and her deputy clerk who didn't have a clue who he was. He knew the evil lurking nearby, because the depravity was his and he controlled the demon.

Chapter Nine

Sam Mikkelson pulled his silver Acura into his garage and grabbed the groceries out of the back seat. His house was located a few blocks from the Law Enforcement Center. He liked being near his work. Better to keep an eye on things.

The house was small, but filled with life. A framed Eagle Scout badge hung in the kitchen. Golf clubs, pictures of his family, and a fishing creel were in the living room. The walls were a soft yellow; he'd painted them when he moved in a few weeks ago. No curtains hung on the windows yet, but some simple shades had been hung to give privacy. The polished floors were aged hardwood and Sam had placed a braided throw rug at the door. The smells of after-shave lotion mingled with coffee.

The bedroom reflected Sam's personality: pictures of him with his SEAL team, fishing trips, and one picture of Sam receiving an award from Governor Dahlberg. Mikkelson's body was healthy and toned and he looked quite dashing standing next to the governor. Whenever anyone commented on his good looks, he shrugged it off. He'd never thought of himself as good-looking. He thought of himself as a Navy SEAL, a former homicide cop, and a sheriff.

Sam's college diploma from the University of Minnesota hung next to the picture of his parents. He had graduated with majors in psychology and biology. There were also framed certificates showing his Navy and SEAL training.

There was a wide expanse of windows overlooking the town and lake, helping the plants around the house bloom healthily. He had picked up used furniture at various outlets and had the furniture recovered in a blue patterned twill. His desk was antique oak, with a matching chair, a family heirloom that was a gift from his grandfather.

Bookcases were filled with state codes and regulations, forensic science, psychological profiling, and standard law enforcement texts. Everything was orderly, files were well kept, and the couch comfortable enough for watching the Packers. The Minnesota boy had grown up a Green Bay Packers fan.

And there was a dog.

"Hey, Montana. Good boy. Sorry I was so long. I'll take you with me next time."

"Montana?" is what people usually said when they met the dog.

"It seemed appropriate at the time," he'd say. "I was watching a western on TV and the name sort of leapt out at me. Besides, he seems to like it."

It probably had something to do with Montana getting a treat when he heard his name. He was a well-behaved dog. Half Golden Retriever. Half Irish Setter. He definitely had the looks of the retriever, but his fur had the reddish glow of the setter. Mikkelson rubbed Montana's ears and gave him the good dog speech.

"If you're a really good boy, I'll scratch your belly. I missed you today, big fella."

Mikkelson changed from his uniform into tan chinos, a short-sleeved denim shirt, and Reeboks.

"I have the rest of the afternoon off," he told Montana. "We'll go for a walk, I'll take you to the DQ, and then we'll do some channel surfing. The Twins should be on."

Montana wiggled. He knew the word DQ and he was ready to go.

"In a few minutes," said Sam. He picked up the Duluth News Tribune and read through the sports page.

"And, we're having company tonight. I'm fixing supper and you have to be on your best behavior."

Montana's tail was thumping, nostrils twitching as he listened to the joyful tone of his master's voice. He sprang forward and licked Sam's face, his whole body quivering as he recognized familiar words.

Mikkelson felt more relaxed than he had in months. Bad divorce, tough job. He had taken a good look in the mirror one day and saw the emptiness in his eyes. His ex-wife had been a chaser. Everyone's girlfriend. Undercover cop and homicide detective had left wounds. It had been time to move. When the sheriff's job in Nordland County was offered to him, he felt like he had been reborn. When he looked out the windows at Big Canoe Lake, the thoughts of the brutal St. Paul street gangs left him.

He was looking forward to supper with Laura. Grilled salmon, asparagus, spinach mandarin salad, and strawberry shortcake for dessert. He made a note to make some iced tea and he'd brew some freshly ground coffee to go with the shortcake.

It wasn't a date. Both of them had agreed they were friends. Nothing more. Laura tensed up whenever they talked business so they'd challenged each other to playing board games. They both won their share of Mexican Train Dominoes. Laura usually won Scrabble. Mikkelson won when they played Boggle. It worked.

A failed marriage had left him wary. The marriage had fallen apart before it even began, but he hadn't noticed. He forgave his wife the affair she'd had when they were engaged, but by the time she'd had a third affair, they'd divorced. He hadn't spent a lot of time grieving, but to the very center of his soul, he felt hollow and broken beyond repair.

His attraction to Laura was troubling. Being hurt again wasn't part of the agenda. A relationship now could be a disaster, but there was such a wholesomeness about Laura that he knew, no matter what, that she could be trusted. He had been a homicide cop and a Navy SEAL, but another emotional attachment was downright scary.

The phone rang. It was his mother.

"What did you have for supper last night?" she asked.

"Popcorn and root beer."

"You've got to be kidding."

"I had some ice cream, too."

"What are you doing tonight?"

"I'm fixing supper for Laura Kjelstad. Salmon, asparagus. All the fixings."

He knew she was smiling. Probably doing a little triumphant dance, too.

CHAPTER TEN

Governor Dahlberg's Lake House
Birch Bay
Afternoon - June 25

Molly looked stunning as she and Laura began the drive to the Dahlberg's house for a one-thirty lunch. Molly was wearing beige silk slacks, white blouse, and lots of gold jewelry. Her makeup was perfect and her red hair glimmered in the sunlight. A hint of a smile lit up her exquisite green eyes.

Laura felt her outfit was less striking, but she thought it looked good. Black slacks, gold colored blouse, and a necklace that had been a Christmas gift from Eric. The necklace hung along a silvery chain with stone, glass and metal beads in varying shades of browns, blues, and reds. She thought it had a rather exotic look. Matching earrings shimmered when she moved her head. The jewelry gave her an air of confidence, a gift from the man who was the love of her life.

They took Raspberry Drive, headed east, and followed the scenic road along Big Canoe Lake. Minnesota's wild side is clearly displayed on the shores of this spectacular bulk of a lake. Laura had watched the shoreline explode like thunder as the wind sent water lashing against rock, trees, and asphalt. Witnessing the glistening splendor when the sun touched water with golden needles of light always seemed like a celebratory gesture from nature.

Big Canoe Lake was an ongoing drama. Hiking across the glaciated rocks, she'd faced the open water and felt wild surf pelting a drenching spray so rejuvenating that she didn't care that she was dripping wet and shivering. Some days, curtains of fog presented visual displays so lovely that she would forget the grayness of the day as she watched stunning visual tricks of fog touching earth.

"Reminds me of the Hardanger Fjord," said Laura. "I think this area reminded people of Norway. That's why so many Scandinavians came to this part of Minnesota."

The exclusive Dahlberg estate had a curved driveway with immense gardens on each side that led to the main house. Trees hugged the periphery of the property on three sides and the majestic water of Big Canoe Lake beckoned to the south. A slight wind had kicked up, sending waves lapping along the rocks.

Charlie met them at the door. He was looking remarkably handsome and greeted them with hugs and a vigorous shaking of the hands. Governor Dahlberg was a striking man. He was tall, slender, athletic, and always congenial.

There was something in his demeanor, a relaxed friendliness that seemed to put people at ease. He had smooth skin, with just a few wrinkles in the corners of his blue eyes, and a warm, gentle smile. He was wearing khaki chinos and a pale green polo. His light brown hair was cut short and his intent look gave a feeling of intelligence.

Audrey Dahlberg came from the kitchen, wiping her hands. She was irrepressibly good-humored, her smile flashing with just the right combination of warmth and geniality. She knew Charlie was on the fast track to the White House, but she remained as honest and sincere as the farm girl from Ortonville who had married the rich guy on campus.

The governor's wife was pretty in a refreshing sort of way. Wholesome, refined, blonde, slender, and confident. She never compromised her beliefs because her husband was governor. She spoke her opinions and people listened. The press loved her.

The Dahlberg's lake house shouted wealth. Laura didn't remember the square footage, but it was huge. The flow throughout the house was on an east-west axis, permitting a grand view of Big Canoe Lake. A south facing patio, accessible through French doors from the dining room, was filled with flowering plants, and a stone path led to the water's edge. Off to the east was a tennis court. A gazebo was nestled amongst tall pines on the west edge of the property. The lake was a commanding presence in the whole design of building and yard.

"I have some new LeTourneau paintings in the living room," said Charlie. "Rick had a show at the Hollingsworth Gallery and I couldn't decide which ones to buy, so I bought all the Lake Superior watercolors. I'm sure you'll agree that they're quite stunning. I only bought the lake images. He had lots of woodsy scenes, too, but with the setting of my house I couldn't resist these paintings. Anyway, I have a weakness for watercolors."

"Me, too," said Molly. "I did a series of watercolors of downtown Birch Bay a couple of years ago."

"You'll have to show them to me," said Charlie. "I'd love to buy some."

"I sold them all. I hang my watercolors at the Inn and they sell in a few days."

"Let me know when you have some more ready to sell."

"We should show you the whole house," said Audrey. "We've had some interior design work done since you were here last, Molly."

The Dahlbergs led them on a tour of the remodeling job. Stained glass windows had been added to the north walls of the dining room. Shaker ladder back chairs and a six-foot pine table were arranged in the center. Draped over the second-floor balcony, a silk and taffeta quilt commanded attention.

An intimate living room, anchored by a stone fireplace, had bookshelves flanking the back wall. A lovely copper horse weathervane, green with age, pranced atop an early American doughboy used as an end table.

Gloria Minot, of Minot's catering, came through the kitchen door and began talking to Audrey. Gloria has bouncing blonde curls, huge blue eyes, and an infectious smile. She was Birch Bay's only caterer and kept immensely busy.

"Sorry to be in such a rush," said Gloria," but I have another delivery. Everything should be set."

Ten minutes later they were seated at the table enjoying grilled lake trout with a maple glaze, wild rice with leeks, roasted potatoes, and brown sugar glazed baby carrots. A spinach and strawberry salad with raspberry poppy seed dressing was served on the side.

"Dessert is macerated berry and crème fraiche parfait," said Audrey. "Plus good coffee and heavy cream."

"And I'll clear the table," said Charlie. "That's what I love about this place. I can do whatever I want to without a herd of reporters asking for verification."

The phone rang. It was Anne Bradley.

"Let me put you on speaker phone," said Charlie. "Laura and Molly are here."

Anne was Charlie's executive secretary. She'd been coming to Birch Bay since the Dahlbergs had purchased the house. Usually she stayed at Raspberry Point Inn at the Dahlberg's expense so the taxpayers wouldn't have to pay for his secretary being out of the St. Paul office.

After a brief conversation with the governor on routine matters, Anne asked Molly about affairs in Birch Bay. It was five minutes of chitchat before Anne had to terminate the call.

"I've so enjoyed getting to know her over the years." Molly was animated; her eyes sparkling with remembrance. "She's so conscientious and personable. I wonder if the people in this state know what a gem she is."

"I know the legislators do," said Charlie. "Her word is golden and she's brilliant. She's trusted by both political parties."

"Nothing gets better than that," said Molly. "Especially after the last administration when no one got along."

"Anne was a miracle when my campaign got started." Charlie was silent for a moment and he reached for Audrey's hand. "As we were heading into the early stages of feeling out the political waters, Anne stepped in and energized the campaign. She handled reporters, political friend and foe, and organized the schedule so I could cover more of the state. I often wondered if she ever slept. She didn't work by intimidation, she moved forward on charm and diplomacy and the gift of discernment."

"She was as perceptive as anyone I've ever met," said Audrey. "Anne could spot a phony right off."

"Anne gave me exposure with the general public," said Charlie. "She grew up middle class and hardworking. She wasn't flamboyant; she was in your face honest."

"We covered more radio shows, county fairs, and quilt shows than I even knew existed," said Audrey. "Anne was in touch with the population that was hard working and industrious and worried about their kids' education and health. She touched painful nerves and told people that Charlie could make it better."

"Kept a notebook that detailed every fraction of an hour. Hired staff that would follow through on whatever it was they were scheduled for. With her talent and energy, I've thought she would make a great governor. Minnesota's never had a woman in the top office and I'd sure like to see her reach for it."

"Being from a rich family worked against Charlie," said Audrey. "Anne turned it around and made it a plus. She put the story out about Charlie's grandpa going from poor immigrant to entrepreneur and philanthropist. From anybody else, that wouldn't have worked, but Anne made it a keystone. And she shook up the good 'ol boys."

"Tell us about the presidential possibilities," said Laura.

"I've been talked to by the party," answered Charlie. "All the usual stuff. Money raising. Platform. I have to tell you that I'm not interested. There's so much pressure to do the fundraising and make promises, that really good people have lost sight of the needs of this country."

"You'd be a truly great president," said Molly.

If Minnesota ever had a viable presidential candidate, thought Molly, it was clearly Charlie Dahlberg. He was a hard working risk-taker with incredible charm. His credentials were impeccable. Friends and family used similar adjectives when speaking of Charlie: Honest. Confident. Trustworthy. Focused. Intelligent. Generous. Great sense of humor. Passionate. Devoted. Patriotic.

Audrey sighed, sat back in her chair, and brushed her hair with her fingers. "So what hot button topics are at the top of your list, Laura?"

The presidential discussion was clearly over. Audrey was the governor's greatest asset, becoming protective when she knew he was uncomfortable with the conversation.

Laura took the cue. "People grumbling about streets, taxes, and why the library isn't open on Sunday. Next to what you do every day, my life seems very tame."

"Except for Leo Nelson, of course," said Molly.

"He sure doesn't like my politics," said Charlie. "He's a racist, sexist, misanthropic, contrary man. If he doesn't like what you're doing, Laura, then you're doing things legal and right."

"Lots of people are thrilled with Laura's abilities," said Molly. "She's done more in the last year and a half than any mayor before her. She's promoted jobs, secured the conservation easement for the park land, and trimmed the budget without hurting services."

Charlie reached for a file and placed it on the table. "Which brings me to the question of the day, Laura. I'm looking for a new commissioner for the education department. I'd like you to consider taking the job."

Laura's face went blank. "You've caught me completely off guard."

"Part of Charlie's persona," said Audrey. "Always has been very straightforward."

"I certainly hadn't anticipated this," said Laura. "I enjoy my life here. Birch Bay is comfortable. It may not be the pinnacle as far as politics is concerned, but I've accomplished lots of things I set out to do. I'd like to follow through on my campaign issues."

"You've only a few months left in your term," said Charlie. "By the time all the wheels turn in St. Paul, everything will be ready for you to start in January. You won't be quitting your mayor position, your term will be up. You need to find someone to run for mayor who has the same beliefs you do. Face it, Laura. The conservation easement was your major issue and that's done. I don't expect an answer today. I'll have Anne send you all the information about the commissioner's job; you can come down and visit the office, talk with our staff, and get a feel for what's expected. Please consider it."

"I wasn't prepared for this," said Laura. Anxiety and surprise tripped the thought process in her brain. "I don't have enough experience."

"You have exactly what I'm looking for. You're a successful classroom teacher and you've proven yourself in the political arena. I've heard you handle reporters and watched you at city council meetings. You're exactly what this state needs for an education commissioner."

"I'll think about it," agreed Laura. "Have Anne send me the information. I have the time right now to make a visit to St. Paul."

Laura had the feeling that despite all the chaos in St. Paul, life might just get simpler for her.

Her gaze caught Molly's.

"How would you like to run for mayor, Ms. Molly?"

CHAPTER ELEVEN

Strolling along Raspberry Drive, Wally appeared to be an athletic young man. Grey jogging pants with a white stripe down the side, a white T-shirt, running shoes, and a Chicago Bears baseball cap were carefully chosen. Bleached blonde, short hair added to the impression of a regular person out jogging. There was nothing that said disguise. Wally was too smart for that.

His arms were swinging as if he was just preparing to take a run or had just finished one. He did some stretching exercises along the edge of the road and pulled his sunglasses to the end of his nose, peering over them to see more clearly. To an onlooker, he would appear to be another of the many hikers and runners in the area. Instead, it was another distraction; let people look at the jogger, not at him.

His concentration was intense. Today would be an interesting day. Excitement moved through every cell in his body, anticipating the day's events. The unknown heightened his excitement.

Wally didn't bother looking down the driveway; he didn't need to. His work had been precise, perfect in fact. He touched the device in his pocket, looked up and down the road to make sure no one was near and walked into the woods.

A chipmunk scampered noiselessly across the road, disappeared, then chattered from a vantage point somewhere overhead. Chipmunks had been the targets for his gun practicing when he was a kid. He'd enjoyed such target practicing since the first time he'd blown a little critter apart.

He moved rapidly through the woods and paused where trees and beach met. Using the trees for cover, he made it to the house in less than a minute. His practice runs had made everything flawless.

Strains of "Dixie" emanated from his cell phone. His anger was palpable.

"What the hell. I told you not to call me."

"I'm the boss, remember?"

"You hired me to do a job. Don't fuck it up."

"Call me when it's done."

"I will." A blazing anger slithered through Wally's teeth, the predator emerging once again.

"As soon as it's done," the voice was hard. "I have to make sure people notice me today. In the office, a restaurant, coffee shop."

"I thought you were a couple of hundred miles away."

"I am. It doesn't hurt to solidify an alibi."

"Don't call me again."

"You don't give the orders, remember?"

"Go to hell."

"Did you forget to put your phone on vibrate again? Is that what the anger is all about?"

Wally clutched the phone with an uncontrollable passion. He was silent until he was in control again. There was laughter on the other end.

"Stupid mistakes get people killed," said the caller. "There's nothing to link us together so don't think I'll come to the rescue if you're caught." The phone clicked off.

"Fuckin' jerk," said Wally, but he knew he had made a mistake. He'd be sure never to make strike three. "Fuckin' cell phone." He pressed the off button and looked around the area. This was private property; no one would dare penetrate it. He relaxed and moved into the shadows of the forest so he could watch the house.

Like other buildings along the shore, this house was of significant size, well constructed, and built in the last five years. The façade had substantial beams dominating the exterior, with a three-tier deck wrapping around the house and angling toward the beach. Windows spanned the full two stories, reflecting water, sky, and beach.

There was movement in the house and he moved further into the darkness of trees. Wally focused on the people coming out of the house; they were obviously having a good time. He fingered the simple mechanism designed for this moment. It was going to be a good day, but the aftermath would be completely new for him. It would be a pinnacle for everything he'd ever done.

His smile was cold; he was thinking of the aftershocks. It would be most enjoyable.

CHAPTER TWELVE

Charlie and Audrey Dahlberg followed their guests out the door, walking up the driveway to where Charlie had parked the car alongside the garage. Audrey had a dental appointment and Charlie had scheduled a talk with the county commissioners for the same time.

"Next time we'll make a day of it," said Charlie. "I'd like to talk to you some more about the state commissioners job, Laura. And Molly, we'd like you and Gary to come sometime soon. I'll take everybody sailing. The lake is perfect this time of year."

"Please take some of the flowers for the Inn," said Audrey through the window of the small Chevy Malibu. "We have so many. Enjoy the beach if you have time. We want people to use this place."

Molly moved toward the huge beds of flowers, then leaned down to pick something from the ground. Laura followed her and then turned to wave good-bye.

Wally inhaled deeply. The device had been built by a genius, but he'd destroyed that intellect. Mark had told him exactly what to do. Follow directions, he'd said. Now it was test time. Wally clicked the detonator.

The explosion stunned Molly and Laura beyond words and they gasped in horror as the car became a fireball reaching for the sky. Their attention was locked on the grotesque scene and everything around them seemed to melt into a tormented moan as they watched the bodies of Charlie and Audrey become human torches.

The heat was intolerable. The wind gusted, sending flames licking at their faces. Molly was on the ground, debris falling all around her. Laura threw herself over Molly's body, protecting her from big chunks of burning rubble. She felt her back heating up.

"It's raining fire," said Laura. She rolled over on her back, letting the ground squelch the heat.

Molly didn't respond. She jerked Molly to her feet, and began running for the house dragging Molly with her. She searched frantically for a fire extinguisher, looked back at the flames devouring the car, then grabbed Molly and pulled her toward the lake.

"There could be a second explosion." Laura's voice was drowned by the sounds from the car. Catastrophe swept over her in a frightening arc.

At the edge of the water, Laura dialed 911 on her phone and reported the explosion.

"Who did you say was in that car?" The dispatcher's voice was strained as she tried to comprehend the power of what had been said.

"Governor Charlie Dahlberg and his wife, Audrey."

"Were they both in the car?"

Laura was yelling, focused on what was happening. "Yes. They're burning. We need help now." Her voice was shrill.

The dispatcher switched to methodical, no hysteria, every bit of her training called into use. Laura could hear the town's fire whistle wailing.

"You're at Governor Dahlberg's house. 5609 Raspberry Drive."

"Yes."

"Are you still by the water?" asked the dispatcher.

"Yes. There was nothing we could do. Everything exploded. It was instant."

There were sirens in the distance.

"I hear the fire trucks. And police," said Laura listening to the distinct differences in the sirens of the two agencies.

"Just stay on the line with me until someone is with you."

"All right." Laura took one of Molly's shaking hands and held it in a strong grip.

Soon the sounds of sirens were louder, and then quiet; ambulance, fire truck, and squad cars pulled into the driveway and parked along Raspberry Drive. How long had it been since the explosion? Laura didn't know. There were medics running toward them, equipment swinging from both hands. Two sheriff deputies were sprinting along the water's edge, talking into the radios attached to their shoulder straps. Behind them, the fire was as intense as the corona of the sun.

"There's help here, now," said Laura, her voice flat. She felt like a scarecrow filled with ice, frozen and stiff.

"Let me talk to one of the deputies," said the dispatcher.

Officer Howard Wickstrom ran to Laura's side. Laura handed him the cell phone. "Mikkelson's here," he told the dispatcher and gave the okay to hang up.

An EMT was talking to Molly. They walked down the beach, away from the crowd of medical and law enforcement personnel. Fire engines were in position hosing down what was left of the Malibu.

Laura froze as she watched the tableau unfold. Mikkelson, projecting the confidence of a man clearly in charge, was in animated conversation with the deputies and fire chief. He wasn't missing a thing as he surveyed the scene, giving directions, and taking in every aspect of the devastation.

The medical team had been sent to tend to Laura and Molly who had been moved down the beach, out of sight of the carnage, but Laura could hear the agitated shouts of the emergency teams.

"The EMTs want to talk to you, Mrs. Kjelstad." Deputy Wickstrom's voice seemed far away and her legs felt rubbery. The tension in her body was overwhelming and she sat on a large boulder that jutted into the lake.

"I need an aspirin," she said. Understatement. Her head was swelling, her spine felt rigid, and her mouth was cotton.

"We're going to have one of the EMTs stay with you."

A nurse was at her side, taking her blood pressure and holding her wrist.

"I'm cold." Laura ran her hands up and down her arms; her muscles quivering.

A blanket was wrapped around her shoulders. Laura wanted to see the rescue workers face to face and talk to Mikkelson. She wasn't sure how bad the situation was, but she looked toward the house and saw flames shooting from the garage. Either there had been another bomb or the fire had spread. A dreadful certainty moved through her brain, a realization that her world was forever changed.

Molly was wrapped in a blanket and being helped to a gurney. "I'm not going anywhere until I know what's happened," snapped Molly. "Don't even think of wheeling me out of here on one of these things. Give me some details."

"Can't," responded the nurse. "We don't have any information. Not yet anyway. It's chaos."

Laura's eyes rested on the dreadful scene at the house. Images of human terror, of betrayal and fear. Image by image, she felt her soul being drained.

Images of death condensed into one inferno. Images of terror that would be translated around the world.

Unfathomable.

Inconceivable.

Laura opened her mouth, closed it, and watched with a strange fascination as the law enforcement teams did their work. The fire chief was shouting non-stop, but the fire was still out of control. Two medics stood nearby with gurneys ready to extract the bodies of Charlie and Audrey, but they couldn't get near the car.

Mikkelson was talking on his phone and giving orders to his deputies spontaneously, eyes constantly scanning the area. His movements were automatic; the trained response of someone with black belt fighting skills.

A crowd was gathering on the lakeshore and people were walking through the woods to get a better look at the terrible wound ripping across the state. Several people were on cell phones, snapping pictures and sending them off to be received by unbelieving friends and relatives. Laura stiffened as she realized some of the phones were aimed at her, pictures traveling to points across the country.

Mikkelson sent deputies to detain the crowd, asking for identification, and recording the information in their little notebooks. A look of horror spread across the faces of the people as they suddenly comprehended that they were seen as suspects. The deputies confiscated cell phones and matched cell phones to driver's licenses. No, the phones would not be returned. They were logged into evidence bags.

Wally wasn't among the onlookers. He had left the woods as soon as the explosion occurred and was on his way to Duluth.

"I'm taking a walk along the beach," Laura told the deputy. "I won't go far."

"Stay where I can see you," he said.

"Of course."

Walking along the edge of the lake, she tried to erase the sight of Charlie and Audrey in the burning car. She watched as yellow crime scene tape was suspended between trees, then fastened around rocks and boulders. Mikkelson was gesturing and more yellow tape reached far into the woods and down to the water,

The tenseness in her body hadn't lessened and she walked faster, pacing back and forth, trying to ease the strain her body was experiencing. She followed the beach to the east, picking up rocks, examining each one carefully before she threw it into the water. At the edge of the tape, she squatted beside the lake, plunging her hands into the cool depths, patting water onto her face and neck.

More squad cars and emergency teams pulled into the driveway, units from the nearby towns of Swendell and Laketon. An EMT from Laketon brought a thermos of coffee to Molly and offered her a Styrofoam cup. Her hands were shaking, but she took the coffee and began sipping, letting the caffeine begin its march through her body.

Laura didn't move, but a moment later she was drinking hot coffee and feeling the warmth soothe her throat.

Reporters emerged on the scene to cover the tragedy. Accident. Laura didn't think so. Murder. Assassination. The words were forming in her head. The car hadn't moved; there was no collision, nothing near it that would cause such an explosion. She watched Mikkelson move toward the media and saw two deputies escort them from the property.

Laura's cell phone rang.

"Mom?"

"Your dad and I were wondering if you're still planning to meet us for supper at The Oslo House tonight. Maybe take in a movie."

Laura's brain slid into overdrive.

"Mom. I need to talk to you, but right now I'm in the middle of a catastrophe."

"What is it, hon?"

"I love you, Mom. Tell Dad I love him, too." Tears streamed down her face.

One of the deputies took the phone from her hand and walked down the beach, talking into the cell, but out of Laura's hearing.

Laura's mind was rushing along at warp speed. The blur in her brain had cleared and she focused on the immediacy of the situation. She swallowed the last of her coffee and moved purposefully toward the sheriff.

Mikkelson was talking tactics and strategy to his deputies. They made a formidable team. Her intensity level was rising exponentially with the remembrance of Charlie and Audrey's flaming death. The buzz she was feeling caused her muscles to tense. She wanted to scream, but she pushed the feeling aside. Adrenaline would make her impulsive, not thoughtful.

Fire fighters were finally controlling the burning car. Outrage and dread were fighting for control of Laura's mind. She'd use both to energize her thoughts, to hang on to her logic. Irrational people often ended up dead.

She watched as a cloud of smoke moved over the tranquil lake. Big Canoe Lake, edged by tall, elegant pines, glistened in the afternoon sun. Prisms of light danced playfully across the shimmering water.

This wondrous place had suddenly become enemy territory.

Chapter Thirteen

Two hours later Molly and Laura sat in Sam Mikkelson's office. Sandy Freemont, the dispatcher, made some fresh coffee, but they both declined. Laura moved to the back door and started outside.

"I'm going to get some fresh air," she said to Molly. "Want to come outside, too?"

"You can't leave the office," said Sandy. She moved toward Laura with a no-nonsense look on her face. "Sam said you're to stay here. He'll be here as soon as possible to get your statement."

"All right." Of course. They'd both have to give statements. Probably be taken into separate rooms and interrogated more than once. She knew that the FBI was already on the scene. So was the Bureau of Criminal Apprehension, CIA, and officers from the Department of Homeland Security. Helicopters had been landing in the high school parking lot and mobile investigative units had set up stations in the elementary school lot. Extra rooms in the hospital were filling up with forensic scientists.

Law enforcement had undergone a transformation. A full contingent of staff was manning telephones and talking to citizens as they came to the office with worried questions. The media was invading the streets taking pictures and interviewing anyone who would give them as much as a sentence.

A uniformed presence was felt throughout the stricken town. She watched as another crime scene van and sheriff's car left the parking lot and headed for the headquarters set up at the school. There would be so much ground to cover, so many people to question.

Laura's mind was reacting like a kaleidoscope. One simple twist and a new image appeared. She took some deep breaths. The prismatic images wheeling through her brain weren't new. She'd experienced a similar reaction when the police told her that Eric was dead. There were times when she knew Eric's death was influencing a reaction.

Memories of Eric surged over her. She was making vegetable soup when Eric went out the door that day. Chopping vegetables, bread rising on the counter. It was all so comfortable. Eric had commented on the smells filling the house; he wouldn't be long. Just a two-mile run and he'd be home for supper and they'd watch the evening news. When the police came and told her that Eric had died, she felt exposed. Raw. Naked. There was a hurt deep inside that never went away.

Laura moved to Molly's side. "How are you doing?"

"Trying to put together what happened so I can answer questions."

"Did you come up with anything?"

"Nothing. You were there. One minute I was looking at flowers and saying good-bye to Charlie and Audrey. Then there was the explosion and I was on my face in the dirt. The ground rumbled and the air was stifling. I didn't see any warning signs. Nothing. Zilch. Do you think all these cops are going to leave us alone after they hear what we say? They're not going to be satisfied with a we-didn't-see-anything answer."

"They'll have to be. There's nothing else to tell."

Absently, Laura moved across the room. Mikkelson's office had windows overlooking the town. Laura could see people on the street chatting and pointing toward the lake. Usually, Birch Bay was a lively community with people laughing and enjoying the camaraderie of a bustling tourist town. The faces she saw now were blank, not worried, not tearful, just empty. It was like the expression you'd have if your best friend slapped you, then turned and left.

Laura's body was tense; she could feel her muscles contracting and her eyes didn't seem to be focusing that well. The world was broken. How long would it be before life had a semblance of order?

"Do you have any idea how much longer Sam will be?" she asked.

"No idea," said Sandy. "I'm sure Mikkelson doesn't either. He's very considerate so I know he'll be here as soon as possible."

"How is the public taking the news?"

"They're numb. Lots of phone calls, but no one has any answers. Who knows what the talk around town is? You know the way gossip goes."

Laura felt Sandy's quiet calmness settle over the room as if a beneficent presence had walked through the door.

Sandy continued. "We're under a code silence." She shifted in her chair. "That means the scanners aren't picking up any messages."

"Doesn't make any difference. Stories will fly."

"I know." Sandy came around the desk and reached for some coffee. "I've never figured it out. I was at the hospital once because I'd tripped and I was afraid I'd broken my wrist. Stupid accident. I was alone in the house and drove myself to the hospital. I was sitting in the waiting room to see the doctor when my cell phone rang. It was Lucille Barken wanting to know if she should pick the kids up after school. Never did figure that one out."

"That's what I mean."

"Are you getting lots of phone calls?" asked Molly.

"Dozens. They were coming in immediately after the explosion. I had a couple of calls before your 911, Laura. People reported that a blast was felt around the area. The fire and smoke could be seen across the lake so some were just reporting that there was a fire. Of course, your phone call let us know exactly what had happened."

"There was probably quite a lapse between the explosion and my call," said Laura. "We were dealing with the situation. I have no idea how much time went by before we got to the lake and I talked to you."

"Not much," said Sandy. "Your call came in rather quickly. Good work on your part."

"Thanks to cell phones." Laura shifted, did a neck roll, and started massaging her temples.

"Do you have any milk?" asked Molly. "I need something to calm my stomach."

"There's a carton in the fridge. I'll be right back."

"Milk might help," said Molly. "I figured they wouldn't have a bottle of Scotch handy."

Sandy was back quickly and handed Molly a mug filled with milk. She placed a plate of cookies on the desk.

"Milk, Laura?"

"Sure. Rule number one when she was a kid: Never refuse a chocolate chip cookie. Rule two was to dip them in milk. Mom and Dad said it was a great way to reduce stress." Laura grabbed her phone. "Good grief. I forgot to call Mom. I'll bet she's hearing all sorts of things on the news."

"Didn't she try to call you?" asked Molly.

"I shut my phone off so I wouldn't have to answer to every person in town. This is the phone I have listed on the city's web site."

Laura hit the cell phone's speed dial, watched the encoding function blink with a green luminescence, and waited for her mother to pick up.

Mikkelson had already called them. "Don't worry about us," said Mrs. Hansen. "Sam said if we came over to Birch Bay, it might cause more entanglements. Too many reporters, tons of law enforcement. We're here when you need us." Sending lots of love, Emily Hansen ended the phone call.

Molly kicked off her shoes and thought about a bottle of wine, candles, and a hot bath. "Doesn't work," she said.

"What?"

"Visioning. Thinking of something else to take away the tension. All I can see is the car in flames. Do you think Charlie and Audrey knew what happened?"

"I'm sure they didn't," answered Laura. "It happened too quick. There wasn't time for their brains to register what happened. They had to have died instantly."

"You're right."

Laura moved to the edge of her seat and listened to the deep motor and thubthubthub of another helicopter.

"How many choppers have come here so far?" asked Laura.

"I'm out of the loop," answered the dispatcher. "They're setting up posts in the high school gym, every governmental agency has a separate unit on site. Right now, the FBI is gathering all the information and disseminating that info. Since no one knows who planted the bomb, FBI is taking over jurisdiction."

"Any interagency squabbles yet?"

"None. I think this is too big to start arguments over. The media's already perched all over town, around the lake, all the restaurants. You name a place, there's a camera crew. My educated guess is that the FBI will control every detail. Loose lips will probably end a career or two."

From the window, they could see Mikkelson wheel into the alley and park in an eerily empty lot. He grabbed a cup of coffee and motioned them into his private office.

"I wanted to let you know what you could expect from now on," he said. "Questions. Statements. Plural. My office will do some of the work, but the FBI may talk to you, too. Right now, they're at the site. There's no press conference yet. The FBI spokesperson will talk to the media within the hour."

"We don't know anything," said Molly. "I was picking flowers and then the sky was on fire and the ground was moaning."

Laura finished her glass of milk and rubbed her aching head. "There was no warning. It was instant."

"We'll question you several times," said Sam. "You may not remember anything now, but there's always the hope that something may come to mind. Clues aren't always brilliant flashes. Sometimes they're part of the everyday that may become part of a larger picture."

"Don't you think we would have noticed someone standing in the yard ready to blow up the governor of Minnesota?" Laura's voice had a caustic edge to it.

"Sometimes your mind blocks out images until something makes them click in."

"Not likely," said Molly. "That's the way assassins work. Surprise and shoot."

Laura's eyebrows arched, but she remained silent.

Mikkelson reached for a recorder.

Chapter Fourteen

The Kjelstad House
Late Afternoon
June 25

Noah Sackett was standing on Laura's doorstep when she pulled into the driveway. His black Durango was parked near the deck. Mikkelson had followed her home, waved to Noah, and proceeded to drive Molly to the Inn.

"Let me guess," said Laura. "Mikkelson called you."

"He did."

"How much did he tell you?"

"Probably everything."

"Figures."

Laura closed the door and clicked on the kitchen lights.

"You may want to consider locking your doors for a while." Noah's voice had the penetrating tone of an Admiral with edges of the Navy SEAL showing through. "Too many people know that most doors in Birch Bay are unlocked. I came in to make sure you're secure for the night."

"How long are you staying?"

"Until Mikkelson tells me otherwise."

"I'll make some coffee," said Laura. "Or would you prefer to have tea?"

"I'll have whatever you're having."

Laura looked in the refrigerator. Oranges. Grapefruit juice. Colby cheese. An assortment of leftovers. Noah's caramel rolls were neatly stacked in the freezer.

"Hot tea and warmed up caramel rolls," she said. "I'll make a pot of coffee for later."

"Perfect. I made lasagna. It's in your oven and should be done in an hour."

Noah made the best lasagna she'd ever had. A man of many talents.

"Anything I can do right now?" asked Noah. He was sitting at the kitchen table, reading the Variety Section of the Minneapolis Star Tribune.

She sighed, then a broken breath escaped. "No, thanks. I'm going to throw in a load of laundry. I need something to do."

"Then I'll read my newspaper, do some Sudoku, and keep out of your way."

For a moment, Laura looked out the window as the wind whipped across Big Canoe Lake. White caps skimmed across the surface, waves began an assault on shore.

Laura did a quick inspection tour of the house, making sure it was clean and picked up. The house was small, built as a cabin by Laura's Grandpa Anders for a weekend vacation retreat. Logs were used for the main structure, choosing purlin roof construction for its unique design. Purlin roofs consist of full-size logs that stretch across the entire length of a building: a ridge beam dominates the center with small logs descending from gable to gable down the roofline to the edge of the walls. Grandpa Anders kept the integrity of the light color of the logs intact. When he built a similar, larger cabin closer to Duluth, he had sold the Birch Bay cabin to Laura and Eric.

Built on a hill, the house has a great view of Big Canoe Lake three blocks away. In the living room, a large bay window dominates the south wall that overlooks the town and lake. To the west of the living room is the small kitchen. The dining room juts out from the main house, with floor to ceiling windows on three sides, giving a stunning panoramic view. Along the back of the house were two bedrooms, one of which she had converted into an office.

The rhythmic sound of the washing machine wrapped the house with the comfort of everyday. Laura put tea and the caramel rolls on the table.

"I told Mom I'd call as soon as I got home. They must be inundated with news reports and media."

"Mikkelson talked to them and sent some federal agents to guard their house. They're going to stay home and let the staff handle the restaurant. No one will get past the FBI. If anyone can handle the media crush and nosy onlookers, it's the feds."

"Good."

"You okay?"

"I'll be fine. You must have seen terrible things during your years in the Navy. How do you get rid of the images shuffling through your brain?"

"Never do. You learn to put them in a remote corner of your brain and shut the door, but you know they'll come bouncing out sometimes."

"Then what?"

"You shut the door again."

"I thought that wasn't good to do. Stuffing things."

"There's no other way. Once you've been through the ravages of war, the memories are there forever. The Navy shrinks have you talk about it, ask how you're doing, offer you some therapy, but in the end, the memories are always there. I was an officer so I had the preparation. It's really tough on the enlisted personnel. For tonight, you'll do other things. When you're ready, you'll talk about what happened a little at a time. And when you talk, you'll put a little more of the memory in that back closet in your mind."

"Isn't that just kidding yourself into thinking things will be normal again?"

"No. It's called being realistic and you will move to a new normalcy. Never the same, but day-to-day life will go on. Now's when your faith really kicks in."

"Have you ever questioned your faith?"

"Of course. But faith is part of every cell of my being. Laura, faith goes to the very core of existence. We may lose some battles here, but we know who wins in the end."

"Like when I lost Eric."

"Yes."

"Faith of our fathers. Faith like my moms. I need to call home."

Laura grabbed her cell phone and hit speed dial. Her mom answered on the first ring.

"We're fine, hon," said Emily Hansen. "The agents are parked on the road and there's one in the driveway. No one is getting near the house."

"Even with all the woods around?"

"We're very safe. The neighbors are sending over food. We've let some people in to visit. One of the agents gives us a call and reports who wants to come in. It's actually sort of nice to have company because otherwise the time would drag. We're playing Mexican Train Dominoes right now with the Simpsons."

"Could you call the Dahlberg family for me? Give them my condolences and tell them I'll contact them as soon as I'm through with law enforcement here. Let them know I'll do anything I can to solve this case."

"Of course I will, hon."

"Good. I'll keep you updated on anything I find out."

"And Noah told me he's spending the night at your place. Your dad and I feel relieved about that. Of course, as we understand it, you were just in the wrong place at the wrong time. Whatever the motive, it's obvious the killer was after the governor, not you. We're thankful you're safe. Dad wants to talk, too."

Knut Hansen gave his love, then chatted briefly with Noah.

Noah hung up and gave Laura a reassuring look. "There'll be agents around your parent's house tonight. This whole area around your house is sealed tighter than a drum."

"And I'm to stay here, right?"

"For now. There's no place you'd want to go anyway. Media everywhere."

"And friends. Neighbors. People wanting to talk, ask questions," Laura reached for a roll, but her mind was still on the beach watching the flames. She shivered, rubbed her arms, and sipped her tea. "I don't want to see anyone right now."

"I unplugged your phone and answering machine. I told your parents I'd make sure your cell phone was plugged in or to call me any time. They're not going to call after ten o'clock so you can try to get some sleep. Mikkelson knows our cell numbers."

Noah's calmness settled like a warm shawl over her shoulders.

"When Eric was killed, a jury found the driver guilty of vehicular homicide. He's serving time in prison. I thought it would help to have the man behind bars. It doesn't. After the jury verdict, I went to the scene of the accident thinking that it might give me some closure. I have images in my head that don't go away. I've tucked them in that closet you talk about, but today, they're swimming through my brain. Stupid. Drunk. Driver."

"Stupid drunk driver," Noah repeated, understanding what Laura hadn't said. The loneliness, nightmares, questions.

Laura went to the oven and peeked inside. She rummaged in the cupboards for glasses and plates. Silverware was in a drawer. Silently, she set the table, poured milk, and handed Noah a couple of hot pad holders.

"Start with a little milk," said Noah. "It'll help calm the nerves."

"But sometimes there are never answers."

"Humans can be quite arrogant; we forget that our minds are finite. The creation of the world is not perfect. Look at Genesis. Adam and Eve sinned; Cain killed Abel. Noah had to build an ark because society, the very fabric of life on earth, had deteriorated so badly that God set out to destroy his creation. Noah accepted it and built his ark. Our species continues to be haughty, smug."

"Could be you're reading too much Old Testament."

"Could be my name is Noah. I've always been fascinated with the ark builder."

"The Old Testament is quite brutal."

"It helps give a perspective on life. Everything is there, every inhuman act, evil, greed, corruption, immorality. Nothing we see on TV is new. But good people still do good deeds. It's amazing." His gaze held her eyes. "And no. You never get over some things."

"Forgive me, Noah. I know how horrible it must have been for you when your wife died."

"She was the love of my life. Tell me this. Why do they spend millions of dollars to discover a drug like Viagra, but they can't get the funding to find a cure for breast cancer? Some things are out of focus, Laura."

An hour later, they had finished their lasagna, and settled into a game of Scrabble. Noah was winning. They had decided not to watch the news. Not yet.

A gentle tapping at the deck door caught Laura by surprise. She looked out the window and saw Mikkelson standing in the dusky light. Noah opened the door and Sam stood in front of her, smelling of smoke, his eyes red and his hands raw and bleeding. Montana wiggled beside him.

"I'd like to wash up a bit, then we can talk," he said. He moved casually to the kitchen sink, reached underneath and pulled out the dish soap, and washed his hands without saying a word.

"Sam needs someone to watch the dog," said Noah. "I told him we'd be glad to take care of Montana. Sam's going to be too busy to give him food, water, and potty breaks."

Mikkelson gave them a thumbs up and sat down at the kitchen table. Noah poured coffee and put some lasagna in the microwave.

"I'm assuming you haven't eaten yet," said Noah.

"Not for a while."

"What happened to your hands?" Laura's eyes narrowed as she apprised the damage. "Do you want some bandages? Antiseptic?"

"They don't feel as bad as they look. A chunk of the garage roof came down. I heard it moving overhead, caught sight of it as it was falling, and deflected it before it hit my head."

Mikkelson gave her a dismissive look. He was quiet until he finished eating, then went to the sink and rinsed his dishes.

"How's Molly doing?" asked Laura. "Is someone with her?'

"Most of the staff," said Sam. "They're taking turns playing Scrabble with her, bringing food from the kitchen, and generally seeing that she's not alone for a minute."

"I wish she would have stayed here, but she thought she'd sleep better in her own bed. Besides, she was going to talk to Gary; maybe for hours on end is what she said. She told her kids not to come up either, said to wait a few days to see what happens. She might go the Cities to be with family instead of them traveling to Birch Bay. We'll have a better sense of what's happening tomorrow."

Sam moved across the room and sat down beside Laura. He accepted a cup of coffee from her and reached his hand across to gently rub her shoulder.

"The good thing is, you and Molly don't know anything. The bad thing is, nobody else knows that."

CHAPTER FIFTEEN

Evening
June 25

"How did the press conference go?" asked Laura. Montana had his head in her lap and she gently rubbed behind his ears. A look of contentment swept over him and he wagged his tail, licking her hands and doing a little wiggling.

Sam smiled, reached across and petted Montana on the back. "FBI handled it in their usual way. Very organized, orderly, took questions, and said they'd keep everyone apprised as things moved along. Of course when it was over, all the media had was superficial news, but the press was taking notes."

"Feds are great at saying a lot of nothing. Whatever they learn needs to be kept confidential," said Noah. "No leaks until someone lets something slip and then it's on all the news shows."

"Perfection is expected from every agent," said Mikkelson. "The units will produce solid work. Everyone's hoping the conclusion will come quickly."

Laura clicked on the TV, found one of the all-news channels and watched the highlights of FBI Agent Dean Beckwith's report to the public. TV stations, radio, and newspapers were represented in the audience. Beckwith gave an intelligent, concise update, confirming the identity of the two victims and the time of death. Reporters gripped their notebooks like video, combatants looking for the words that would sail into headlines and sound bites. TV news services were asking questions, scowling, making assumptions, pointing their microphones like sabers; the camera crews scrutinizing the town with probing lenses.

Birch Bay had spun into the national spotlight.

Beckwith listened patiently to each question, repeated it into the microphone, and answered precisely. At times he said there would be no comment on that particular phase of the investigation, other times he said that BCA would be analyzing data for a very long time; he assured the media that he could keep everyone updated as the information became available.

"What about general safety in the area?" asked a woman. She looked calm and professional, assessing every word that came out of the agent's mouth.

"It's quite safe," answered Beckwith. "Sheriff Sam Mikkelson has secured the whole area. Deputies from adjoining counties are maintaining road blocks on all routes into Nordland County."

"Are they stopping everyone?" asked the reporter.

"They're showing a presence," he replied. "People need to know that it's safe to continue their day-to-day activities. Law enforcement is doing intermittent vehicle checks."

"What assurances have you given local authorities?" shouted a young man, his transparent earnestness being captured by the cameras. "How many uniformed law enforcement do you need to protect residents?"

"Several agencies are assisting in the investigation. Homeland Security, U. S. Marshalls, Minnesota Bureau of Criminal Apprehension, Nordland County Sheriff's Department, and anyone else we need to capture the people responsible for this horrific deed. At this time we don't feel there is any danger to the community."

"Why so many agencies?" asked a reporter from Channel Twelve in Duluth. "Who's doing the coordination between all the units?"

"My team is systematically categorizing all data," said Beckwith. "Each agency is being assigned a certain part of the investigation. All the information is turned over to the FBI with copies to all the other groups. We're not letting anything slip."

"Who responded to the explosion? Fire department? Sheriff?" The voice came from the back of the assembled reporters.

"The fire department, sheriff and deputies, and ambulances were on the scene in minutes."

"Any general sense of how soon you'll have some leads or answers?" asked the reporter.

"For every deadline given, our response has been that it's not fast enough. This investigation has the highest priority; we've given it the ultimate speed. All the agencies will be working twenty-four hours. Be assured it will be around the clock."

Beckwith pointed to a reporter in the front row.

"Have the bodies been recovered?" asked the young woman.

"The forensics team is on site. They are doing a complete analysis of the crime scene; that includes recovery operations."

"You didn't mention the mayor of Birch Bay," persisted the reporter standing in the back.

Beckwith turned from the microphone and spoke to Mikkelson who stood beside him, stepped aside, and let Sam continue.

"We are not commenting on any of the specifics of the case at this time. Tomorrow morning at nine o'clock we'll give you the next update. Thank you."

Sam Mikkelson had a forceful way of ending the news conference. His eyes narrowed, scanning the crowd with a no-nonsense look; there was unflinching confidence in the way he walked and the impressive breadth to his shoulders added to the control he was emanating. To the camera's eye, he looked all business, a tautness pulled at the muscles just below the skin and he stood on the balls of his feet as if in a fighting stance.

Laura was fascinated watching Mikkelson's TV persona. He was magnetic in front of the assembled crowd. The cameras were having a great time; his strength and good looks would be picked up by TV stations across the country. She was sure the story would make it into the international market.

The camera focused on the crowd, then the lens turned toward Big Canoe Lake. Network reporter Josh Maxwell did a voice over while the camera continued an examination of the shoreline.

"Birch Bay is experiencing a nightmare of unparalleled proportions for the state of Minnesota. It's a state brought to its knees with grief." The camera centered on Maxwell. "The positive thing going for this town is the caring they're showing to each other."

"We're returning to the swearing in ceremony that took place in St. Paul earlier," said the news anchor. "Jack Cummings has become Minnesota's new governor."

The anchor did a voiceover while the camera zoomed in on Jack standing in the rotunda of the capitol building. Staff members, friends, and family stood at his side followed by a time of meet and greet.

Jack's energy and charisma and penetrating blue eyes held people spellbound. When Jack Cummings walked into a room, it was his. His intelligence was evident, too. The media was entranced.

"Is that guy FBI?" asked Laura. She pointed to the one person who stood out from the rest, the person whose gaze was constantly moving, watching the crowd, always mindful of the menace that could be near the governor. "The guy in the dark blue suit and red tie isn't shaking hands. He has his eye on the crowd."

"He is," said Sam. "FBI is doing all the right things on this one. They don't want any screw ups. You can see the earpiece he's wearing. Typical FBI or Secret Service."

Next a picture of Governor Dahlberg filled the screen.

"Charlie Dahlberg has spent his adult life serving his community," said the reporter. "He began service when he was in college and volunteered for numerous campus and church projects and continued volunteering as he rose through the political ranks in Minnesota."

A voice interrupted. "Gary, we are going live to Wesley Forsberg who is speaking on the steps of Minnesota's capitol building. Wesley is Speaker of the House in Minnesota."

Representative Forsberg was surrounded by hundreds of people, many of them holding flowers, some waving Bibles in the air.

"Losing Charlie and Audrey Dahlberg is a national tragedy," he said. "It hurts deeply. They were inspiring leaders, whether in the realm of environmental concerns or education of the state's children. He was a populist governor who always talked of bringing integrity and honor to the political arena. Charlie was a giant in trying to protect the environment. He was committed to making sustainable living a reality in the state and an example to the rest of the nation. Charlie warred with corporations who tried to pollute at will. He was a spellbinding speaker with an irrepressible energy and charisma.

"A few days ago, Charlie and I were meeting to discuss how we could better serve families with increased funding for child care and making sure all child care facilities were well regulated and taking the very best care of children.

"He was devoted to helping veterans, finding them jobs when they returned from service, and making sure they were all treated honorably.

"Audrey was a role model for all the people involved with the state's schools and spoke with intelligence and conviction in championing the causes of teachers. She shared Charlie's passion for health care coverage for all Minnesotans. Something that most people don't know is that Audrey worked with small communities to gain funding to build soccer fields, playgrounds, and parks in their small towns. She went to corporations and government agencies to raise money for areas that had a limited tax base so these communities could have parks and after school programs for their kids.

"Our thoughts and prayers go out to their family members. Tonight, beginning at nine o'clock, there will be a candlelight service in honor of the Dahlbergs. It will be held right here."

Forsberg began walking through the crowd shaking hands, but was soon out of camera range as he moved down the stairs.

"Would you mind turning to one of the local stations?" asked Sam. "I'd like to see their perspective."

Duluth's TV stations were united in their coverage of the tragedy. A picture of news anchor Margaret Jones was in the upper corner of the screen as the camera did a sweep of Birch Bay and Big Canoe Lake.

"Sid Lovell is on the scene by Big Canoe Lake. What is the latest news on the Dahlberg assassination?" she asked.

"It would appear that law enforcement agencies are working together in an unparalleled cohesiveness. I attended the press conference earlier today and was able to see the professionalism of this investigation."

Sid stood in front of the high school, various law enforcement vehicles crowding the parking lot. Two helicopters were visible in the adjoining soccer field.

"Let's hope they've learned the essential lessons of other national tragedies. I'm experiencing only the most visible signs of federal, state, and local government, but those signs tell me that these agents came to Birch Bay prepared to move quickly to find the person or people responsible for this horrendous tragedy.

"I've interviewed some people that have expressed how difficult it is to talk with a broken heart. The people of this community loved the governor and his wife."

Interference stopped the reporter for a moment.

"I'm having trouble with the microphone because of wind from a helicopter overhead." Sid was shouting. "It's another symbol of the gravity of this situation. Charlie Dahlberg's name has been in the forefront of discussion about a possible presidential candidacy."

"Besides being broken hearted," asked news anchor Margaret Jones, "how have the people been responding to the situation?"

"There have been rumors of people driving around with guns, but I have to tell you, that they seem to be just rumors. Nordland County's sheriff, Sam Mikkelson, runs a very tight ship. He's well liked by the people, deeply respected, and he keeps order. I've watched him move through the area and he's a no nonsense guy. I get the feeling he's having a 'take no prisoners' kind of day."

"Damn right," said Mikkelson. He snapped his fingers and Montana thumped his tail and put his head in Sam's lap. Sam stroked the dog's head and Montana looked happy as any dog Laura had ever seen.

"Sid." The camera focused on the anchor who was holding up a sheet of paper. "I just got this off the wire. It says there may be a dead body floating in Big Canoe Lake."

"I haven't heard anything of that nature," responded Sid. "They're keeping all the information classified, but I do know that rumors are running rampant. Not all the stories are being told by locals. There are a lot of people from out-of-town who are getting pretty psyched up. Mikkelson has deputies walking the streets to keep order, but you can't control people's mouths."

News anchor Margaret Jones looked straight into the camera. "Remember that folks. Help local law enforcement by keeping a lid on rumors. Any real information, tell the authorities. Keep the speculation and rumors to yourself."

Laura clicked to the Canadian Broadcasting Network. Pictures of Charlie Dahlberg and Birch Bay filled the screen. "I imagine this story is the lead for every news service around the globe," she said.

CNN, Fox, and MSNBC were running similar stories. The Dahlberg family had received enormous television, newspaper, and magazine coverage over the years. Once speculation began about Charlie's presidential prospects, the media frenzy increased.

Pictures of the Dahlbergs in Oslo, Athens, Geneva, and London showed an upbeat, photogenic family. The press had obviously staked out the family for some time. A short synopsis of Charlie's quick rise in political circles was followed by a similar story about Jack Cummings. There were pictures of Jack carrying boxes from his lieutenant governor's office to the temporary office in the State Office Building. Charlie's office had been sealed tight until the investigation was complete.

Laura picked up the newspapers that Noah had brought with him.

"Have you seen any of the tabloid coverage?" asked Laura.

"The King of the media beasts? Didn't bother to look," said Noah. "They want a face to blame and they don't care which face they throw to the lions."

Laura shuddered. "Even mine?"

"Especially yours."

Chapter Sixteen

The Dahlberg's Lake House
Morning
June 26

Laura focused on the scene around her. They had passed some people as they turned onto Raspberry Drive, but barricades were across the road and law enforcement had officers patrolling the site. A roadblock was set up on the other end of Raspberry Drive making it impossible for anyone to get through without official approval.

A U. S. Marshal's pickup, a sheriff's car, and a BCA unit were parked alongside the road. Three FBI vans were at the end of a walkway. Pulling into the driveway was a dark blue SUV, with Nordland County Search and Rescue written across the side.

Dr. Hess, the county coroner, was writing in a file folder and talking to a sheriff's deputy. Dr. Hess was a tall, broad man, with silver hair that stood on ends and blue eyes that usually sparkled with good humor. Right now his gaze was intense. He looked like a cross between a Biblical patriarch and a hurried Einstein.

The house was under twenty-four hour security. FBI agents were carrying boxes and computers to their vehicles.

Officer Howard Wickstrom was on the beach, looking intently at the ground and speaking into a tape recorder. BCA agents were photographing the scene, "one more time", she heard a woman say.

"Show me where you were when the bomb went off." Mikkelson lifted the crime scene tape while Laura ducked underneath and walked toward Charlie and Audrey's house.

Laura stared at the aftermath of the bombings, then silently turned away from the burnt-out shell of car, and followed Sam to the edge of the house.

"Is this where you were?" he asked, pointing to the large gardens west of the house.

"Yes. Molly was a little ahead of me, but then she bent down to pick something up."

"Do you know what it was she saw?"

"No. You'll have to ask her."

"I already did. She wanted to come out here early this morning."

"You didn't want us together. Afraid we might influence each other's testimony."

"Yes." Businesslike. Precise. Never missing anything.

"I imagine the political pressure is screaming for answers. Now."

"Everyone's working together in a very formidable, unified unit. We're going to catch whoever is responsible for this."

"You're probably the one that everyone should be thanking for the smooth work. That usually doesn't happen. Agencies get territorial."

"Beckwith's a good man; served as a Navy SEAL. Admiral Sackett has worked with him in the past. Helps to have a man like Noah in the neighborhood."

Laura pointed to a piece of debris. "I knew stuff was falling, but I didn't realize how big some of the metal pieces were."

Sam did a mental assessment of the distance from the car to where Laura had been. "Any closer and you and Molly may have been killed or seriously injured. Show me where you made the phone call from."

"I don't know if I saw as much as I felt. The earth was vibrating beneath me, gyrating like a carnival ride. Heat was moving across my back and I grabbed Molly and ran."

Laura led him down the path to the beach.

"You're walking in a rush," said Sam. "Are you okay?"

Sam's voice brought her back to reality. She hadn't realized the adrenaline buzz that was flowing through her body; that she was once again fleeing the burning car dragging Molly behind her. Yes. Dragging Molly. She couldn't remember if Molly was fully conscious or not. She remembered dialing 911, that Molly was on the beach and then the ambulances were there and the EMTs were wrapping a blanket around her shoulders. And giving her hot coffee.

She had seen the explosion and watched Charlie and Audrey become torches.

"I didn't go to help them," she said.

"There was no way anyone could have saved them. They died instantly, Laura."

"That's what I heard."

"We'll keep this visit short. Just a few more questions."

Tiredness swept over Laura in waves, sending the message that she probably hadn't slept as well as she thought. Every movement she made seemed brittle; her voice thin. She let out a breath, slowly and deliberately calling forth all the skills she'd learned getting her brown belt in Tae Kwon Do. Her voice was stronger now when she spoke.

"I'm fine, Sam. Really. I want to do whatever possible to capture these murderers."

"Did you see anyone else on the beach when you and Molly got here? Any movement of any kind?"

Memories slashed at her, feelings that needed to be controlled. Sam watched her with grim clarity, his mouth a thin line, shadows were under his eyes from lack of sleep.

"No. I didn't see anyone. The only thing I saw was the fire, smoke, rubble lying around the yard. I know the mind can go blank when something like this happens, but I don't think anyone was here. If there had been, I would have run to them and asked for help."

She was seized by a nightmare, but Mikkelson was by her side, giving her assurances of safety. And Noah was at her house.

Mikkelson led the way to the garage; the men with the evidence bags looked battered. They gave a nod and continued toward the BCA van. Sam stopped to talk with Deputy Roger Parks, Dr. Hess, and Don Collins from BCA. Laura shook hands and greeted them warmly, but she kept the comments to herself.

"The FBI agents just left for a coffee break," said Dr. Hess. "It's been a long night. These guys haven't been to bed yet and I ordered them all to take a mandatory eight-hour break. Another BCA crew just arrived at the high school and will continue the work here. Roger was told that another deputy would be here soon to keep watch over the crime scene."

"And the FBI will have two more men out here in fifteen minutes," said Parks. "I'm heading to town for some breakfast. Then I'll be back."

"Follow the doctor's orders," said Sam. "We have a strong team from each agency so we can do twenty-four hour work without abusing any staff. Rested people are much more productive. There's an assignment board at the high school gym listing all the agencies, staff, and when each person is expected to report for work. It's twelve on and twelve off. Go home and get some shut-eye."

"I should be here," insisted Parks. "All I need is a little food and I'm set."

"Twelve off sounds good," said Hess. "With a high profile case like this we need as much staff as we can get. Rested, alert staff."

"Be back here in twelve hours," said Sam. "We'll need a fresh look at everything then. If you're rested and well fed you'll be a much bigger help to me."

Parks nodded and headed toward the squad car.

"People make mistakes when they're tired." Hess looked intently at Sam. "When are you going home?"

"Not for a while. I need to be here to keep everything moving smoothly. We don't want any territorial disputes."

"Sounds like all the government agencies are cooperating."

"So far," said Sam.

Sam pressed his hand against the small of Laura's back and maneuvered her past the burnt out shell that had been the Malibu. Laura hesitated, then ducked under the crime scene tape circling the garage. She felt emotion tightening her throat, tension pulling at her neck, and she slowly exhaled.

"The garage doors were closed," said Laura. She stepped through a gaping space that had once been a garage door. Most of the roof was gone as were the two walls next to where the car had been parked. The north wall had been sheared off like a power saw had attacked it. "They were going into town."

She stared at the blackened skeleton of the Malibu, then turned abruptly away. Violence had prowled this land, shattered the peace, and the phantom shadows would haunt these shores for decades.

A locker had been blown in two, one part of it outside, the other half tipped crazily against a remaining support post. Cement had been blown from the floor and lay in various sized chunks among the ruins. The double garage door was somewhat intact, but the opposite wall was shredded. A disorienting contrast.

Mikkelson was following her, but she didn't turn around. She wondered where she would find the words to explain what she felt about the bomb.

"Some of the windows aren't broken," she said. "Bizarre. Kill the people, but spare the glass."

In a hushed voice, Sam asked, "Were you ever in the garage?"

"No. There would be no reason. It was utilitarian; nothing to show guests. The house, gardens, and the beach were the showstoppers of the property. Charlie and Audrey enjoyed sharing what they had and they had guests here sometimes. Staff, too. Did you know that Charlie paid for the staff to come here? He didn't want state taxes covering his time here. Of course, the employees loved it. They often brought their families."

"Did he bring staff here often?"

"No. There were times, though, when the legislature was battling, that Anne Bradley would come here and fill Charlie in on all the happenings in St. Paul. Charlie could think things through without the rush of the media and legislators putting pressure on him. I think that's what made him a great leader. He had a keen intelligence, meditative. He'd walk the beach or the trails through the park system and think things through very logically. Then he'd return to St. Paul energized and full of ideas and the legislators would get caught up with his enthusiasm. He was very passionate about this state. No matter which side of the system you were on, Charlie could get you excited about his ideas."

"Which is why the party wanted him to run for the presidency."

"Absolutely. I don't know if he would have made the run. He and Audrey were doing a lot of talking, but I think they were happy with life in Minnesota." She stepped over wreckage strewn across the floor. "Campaigning is brutal. Both of them had impeccable backgrounds, but the rumor mill can be designed to destroy really good people. And they were the good people."

Laura wanted to cry, but she was afraid she wouldn't be able to stop. Good people. The world was insane.

She walked back outside and moved toward the beach.

"I need to get away from here." That was all she could say.

Her whole body was too heavy.

Out of focus.

Memories knifed through her, slicing to the core.

She stumbled, but Mikkelson put his arm around her waist. He called something to the deputy and he was beside them in an instant. One was on each side of her putting her in the squad car.

"I'm taking her home," said Sam. He looked at Laura. The color had drained from her face, giving her a frosty look.

Anger spread icy fingers over Laura's skin, a rawness creeping up her chest and clogging her throat.

Her voice was frigid. "This is obscene."

CHAPTER SEVENTEEN

It was eleven o'clock before Laura was able to meet Molly for brunch at Raspberry Point Inn. When Sam had brought her home, Noah had given her a couple of aspirin, a cup of coffee, and made her sit on the sofa and watch a segment of the old Andy Griffith Show.

The town was a frenzy as they crossed Portage Street. FBI, U.S. Marshalls, BCA, and the Office of Homeland Security were all making their presence known. There were no accommodations left in the area. Schools and the hospital were filling with staff from the various agencies.

FBI agents gave the all clear for Noah to drive into the alley by the Inn. A clearly marked law enforcement vehicle led the way. Noah drove to the service entrance and followed Laura inside.

"There's plenty of law in this place," said Noah. "The media have been told this is private property and there will be no interference with anyone involved in the case or with any of the guests. I'll take Montana for a run and be back in an hour."

"Sounds good," said Laura.

Molly was waiting in the kitchen.

"Do you want to eat in my apartment or in the dining room?" asked Molly.

"Dining room. All the activity gives me a sense of normalcy; maybe it will take my mind off what happened."

"It may take a while to get a table. We can sit in the sunroom until Hal clears a place."

Hal Marshall, tall, thin, and a starting player for his college basketball team, was one of Molly's nephews. Blonde curly hair, strong chin, enormous brown eyes, and an engaging smile made him an asset to the Inn's dining staff.

Molly walked briskly through the Inn, brushing the short-cropped red hair from her high forehead and sticking sunglasses atop the curly mass. Her glance was swift and appraising as they made their way through the dining room. Molly's milky skin and the prominence of her cheekbones gave her a theatrical look. Her temperament, which was cheerful and abundantly optimistic, added to the success of the business. Looking at Molly, everyone would agree that there was one attractive, put together woman.

"Laura." Clara Hixson was on a mission, moving through the crowd with a determined look. Clara, sixty something, gray curly hair and short round body, was eternally interested in everything.

A sheriff's deputy was by Clara's side in an instant.

"Oh my." Clara pursed her lips and made a clicking noise. "I see you're being watched. For your protection, I'm sure."

"It's all right, Melvin. Clara can stay."

"Of course." He moved to the far end of the room.

"Have you read the papers this morning?" asked Clara. "The news about Governor Dahlberg is the headline in every paper I've looked at. All the TV channels, too. It must have been awful. Everyone is so worried about you. Lots of prayers."

"I've been keeping up with the news," answered Laura. "Thank you."

"Well, it's just the whole thing is an awful experience for the whole town to go through. An assassination of a national leader. Right here. Having to be afraid on the streets for fear of some nut killing us. It's downright frightening."

"Lots of law enforcement agencies in town right now," answered Laura. "We have the best investigative team in the world here. Other than that, I'm not allowed to make any comments."

Clara wrinkled her forehead. "Something needs to be done."

Not wishing to become involved in a long-term conversation, Laura asked, "And how is your daughter Roxanne doing since she moved to the West Coast?"

The subject of Roxanne silenced Clara momentarily.

"I talked to her last night. She married that fellow Greg Wilson, but she still goes by Hixson. So what do I know? After all, I'm only her mother. I thought after they got married she'd change her name, but no. It's not the modern thing to do."

"Your group is waiting for you to order, Mrs. Hixson," said Hal.

Clara followed Hal to her table, then she turned and called, "You'd think she'd at least hyphenate."

Molly was standing with arms folded, looking across the dining room. "I'll check on things in the kitchen. Back in five minutes," she said.

Laura decided sitting in the sunroom wasn't in her best interest. "I'll be outside," she told Molly. "I could use the fresh air."

Outside, Laura watched a television camera crew taping for an on the spot news coverage. They were wearing red shirts with WKTP emblazoned across the front. The oldest, a young man of about twenty-four, was dripping with sincerity, dreams of the CBS news beating in his heart.

"Damn it," shouted the young reporter. "What do you mean you didn't get it? That was a winner. My move to the Cities. Maybe even Chicago. Fix the damn cable connection."

"That was hardly Emmy caliber," shouted the cameraman. "Besides, it wasn't my fault. It's this second rate equipment the station gave me. Okay. Here we go again."

The camera focused and the reporter underwent an immediate, if not permanent, transformation.

"This broadcast is brought to you from the scene of a ghastly explosion in which Governor Charlie Dahlberg and his wife, Audrey…"

"Aw, shit."

"Now what?"

"You tell me what. The damn wire is loose again."

Loose wires did nothing to improve the young reporter's verbal skills. Laura left the television crew spitting profanities and went into the dining room.

"Molly had a phone call," reported Hal. "It's her husband. She said she'd be here in a few minutes. You can be seated now if you like."

"Great."

Hal escorted her to a table overlooking the lake.

"Do you know where the WKTP news crew is from?" asked Laura. "I've never heard of it before."

"Media is coming from all over," said Hal. "It's becoming a carnival out there. Sheriff Mikkelson is keeping a tight net around the town, but Molly hasn't chased that crew off the deck, yet."

"I thought the Inn wasn't open to the media. Only the guests."

"That's the trouble. Those guys paid for a room and now they're waiting for a table. That won't slow Molly down once she sees what they're up to. She'll boot them out of the place. I'll bring you some coffee."

"Thanks. With cream, please."

The weather outside was glorious, one of those halcyon days of summer; the translucent cool greenness of the birches that lined the shore caught the gentle waves splashing aimlessly over the pebbles. Pine scent mixed inextricably with the smoke from the campfires in the municipal campground. The externals of life seemed so unchanged and the earth had such a before-Eden look that it contrasted sharply with the events of the last two days. Actually, quite like Eden, thought Laura. Evil thrusting it's way into paradise.

The young quartet at the center table, garbed in sneakers and T-shirts, spoke in deeply shocked tones about the events of the previous day. It was evident that the dramatic images of an assassination were the main topic of conversation as they devoured Bunyan Burgers, lumberjack fries, and raspberry pie.

At the round table next to her, the party was commenting on the horrors of the explosion. "There was nothing left of the bodies to examine," said a middle-aged man. "Nothing left but some bones and ash."

Reminiscence and exchanges passed in muted tones from table to table.

"I was at the tennis courts with Mrs. Dahlberg that morning. Just a few hours before it happened."

"I saw her at Minot's catering checking on a lunch order."

"Such an amazing governor. Attractive. Honest. Worked well with the legislature. That doesn't happen often."

"I understand they were good friends of the local people."

Laura knew the stories would take on a life of their own. In the fall, when the leaves were crimson and the days turned cold, they would speak of these days to their fellow Fitness Club members or golf buddies: "We were there, you know. In Birch Bay. We actually got to know the governor while we were there. Wonderful fellow." Selective memory and vivid imaginations would feed the story of tragedy, flame new stories of Charlie Dahlberg's legacy, and Charlie and Audrey would have a bevy of new friends.

A waitress appeared at the same time Molly arrived. The conversations around the dining room became more animated when people realized who Laura and Molly were. "They're the last ones to see the Dahlbergs alive." "Except the killer silly." "Not silly. The bomb was hitched to the starter of the car. Bomber's probably in Cancun by now." "How is the mayor involved do you think?" "Involved?"

Hal moved to the archway of the dining room entrance and ushered a paunchy, middle aged man and a long-legged slender woman of about forty to a center table. The man looked around the room with a total lack of expression, complained about the heat, and summoned an unfortunate waitress.

"It' so exciting," gushed his companion. "I love it. We were so lucky to get a table," she explained to the waitress. "We were vacationing in Duluth when we heard about Governor Dahlberg's murder and I said right away that we should visit Birch Bay. I can't believe our luck. We're actually here."

"The curious, the bizarre, the bored," said Laura.

"And the vulgar," said Molly.

The faces and conversations shifted, but the topic was the same. Laura gave the couple a sidelong glance. They obviously had more money than she'd ever see and they were having fun. One of them was anyway.

A few tables away, Clara Hixson was entertaining some out-of-town guests. She looked at Laura and gestured with her index finger. "That's our mayor. Mrs. Berg is with her. Mrs. Berg owns this place. They were almost killed, too."

Laura gave them all a friendly look and waved.

"You sure you want to eat in here?" asked Molly.

"Actually, I think we should go to the apartment. Or the kitchen. You have a family table in there. People in the dining room will want to talk to or about us."

"Kitchen it is. That'll give you some activity with privacy at the same time. My staff knows to leave us alone."

"I didn't realize how sheltered I was at home. Noah watching out for me. Sam stopping by. Hal was right. It's a carnival atmosphere around here. The media honing in on everything that moves."

"Sam took me out to Dahlberg's house this morning. Early. I wanted to leave before things started moving around here."

"So what time were you at the house?"

"Five o'clock."

"Did you sleep at all last night?"

"Fitfully. I might be able to nap later. Sam didn't get any information from me, I'm afraid. Being out there didn't trigger any memories. All I remember is leaning over to pick something up and then the explosion."

"Did you remember what was on the ground?"

"A penny. That was all. I think Sam thought it might be a clue. It wasn't."

"Mrs. Kjelstad." Lance Hanover walked through the dining room carrying a bouquet of flowers. The bright blue shirt he was wearing accented his blue eyes; his blonde hair was wet, slicked back like he'd just finished a shower. His smile was filled with the good will and excitement of a ten-year-old. "This is from all the kids in our class. I collected the money. Everybody gave something."

"How kind," said Laura, taking the flowers in her hands and returning a smile. "These are delightful."

"There's a card, too. We all signed except Jeffrey 'cause I didn't have a pencil when I brought the card to him, so he said to be sure I tell you that he gave money."

"Thank you so much." A lump was swelling in her throat and she could sense tears brimming to the surface. She gave him a gentle pat on the back. "This really means a lot to me."

"I have to go now," he said as he gave her a hug. "My mom said not to bother you much and she has lunch waiting."

"You're no bother at all, Lance. I am very grateful for the flowers. Please tell everyone how thrilled I am."

"Mrs. Kjelstad, are you good at keeping secrets?"

"That depends on the secret."

"Why?"

"Sometimes, a secret needs to be told if telling helps the person. Things change. I always try to do what's best for the person who told me the secret."

"But if the person wouldn't be safe if you told the secret, then would you tell?"

"I'd do whatever necessary to keep the person safe."

"Mom has lunch ready. I better go."

"Isn't he a sweetheart?" said Molly after Lance had left. "Makes me wish my grandkids were around all the time. I wonder why he asked you about keeping secrets."

CHAPTER EIGHTEEN

Conference Room
Raspberry Point Inn
June 26

Dean Beckwith, the man assigned to head up the investigation of the Dahlberg's death, sat at a conference table in Raspberry Point Inn. The meeting room was designed for seminars with kitchen facilities, tables, fireplace, and a grouping of comfortable chairs in one corner. The wall overlooking Big Canoe Lake was composed of glass; the other three walls were windowless, connecting to the Berg's apartment on one side, a staircase on the other, and a hallway on the north wall.

Handsome, thought Laura when she looked at Beckwith, but there was much more to the man. There was an alertness about him that suggested high intelligence. He offered a professionalism, a relaxed calm that radiated trust. There was an almost swaggering quality to the way he walked. Not arrogant, confident. He had a strong jaw line, the kind that Hollywood cameras loved. The color of his eyes shifted from green to gray depending on the shadows in the room, eyes that seemed to take in everything. His hair was dark brown, not quite a crewcut, but short. Probably regulation at one time.

Something about Beckwith reminded Laura of an older Sam Mikkelson. It wasn't the physical appearance, it was the overall look of someone who was always at the top of their class, best at sports, smarter and faster than any of their classmates. Used to winning.

Of course, Admiral Noah Sackett was in the room. The one that always won. The one who personified rank, excellence, and grace.

Beckwith greeted people as they entered the room and motioned for them to sit down. Molly Berg was filling coffee pots, setting ice water in the center of the table, and setting out an assortment of pastries.

"I don't know if Beckwith wants me in on this meeting," Molly whispered to Laura as she walked through the door. "But I'm staying. I was there when Charlie and Audrey were killed. The FBI will have to bodily haul me out of here. Besides, I own the place. If he doesn't want me here, he should have said so."

"You're fine," said Laura. "Beckwith knows what he's doing."

Noah Sackett, Sam Mikkelson, Laura Kjelstad, Molly Berg, and Agent Beckwith sat around the table. Beckwith lifted the carafe and began filling cups. Laura gestured no; everyone else took the coffee, Mikkelson and Noah reaching for the donuts.

"The investigation is just beginning," said Beckwith. "I'm expecting that anything said in this room be kept strictly confidential. However, we won't be discussing the specifics of the case. That's between my investigators and me. I called this meeting so you'd know where to reach me if you hear anything." He looked at Laura and Molly and said: "Or if you two remember anything that you haven't told us."

Molly's right eyebrow rose. "I've nothing to add." Her tone was matter-of-fact. "You can bet that I want these guys found."

"I appreciate that," said Beckwith. "We all want this case to be solved quickly. I've set this room up for one specific purpose. Governor Cummings needs an office for his staff. The governor wants to keep a low profile, but he plans on visiting Birch Bay whenever he can. In the meantime, he's sending some staff members up here to keep in touch with the investigation. Mrs. Berg has graciously offered the governor and his staff accommodations when they're here and she's offered the use of this room for as long as the governor needs it. The one advantage of this room is that it has a private staircase that connects to the Berg's garage. Staff can move in and out without causing attention."

"Where are all the government units located?" asked Laura. "I've heard there are teams at the schools and hospital."

"That's correct," said Beckwith. "We have that information posted in a news release for the media. The football field and soccer fields are being used for helicopters. Parking lots are used for our vehicles; gyms in the schools are being used by all the agencies. Each unit has a special task. The high school gym is the main command center; that's where I'm located. Everything that the other agencies learn will be sent to my staff. BCA mobile units are being used to identify evidence. Anything we find that needs further inspection is immediately flown to the proper laboratory. Our prime objective is to solve this quickly. Every politician in the country is nervous. When they get nervous, they get real shitty."

Noah reached for a chocolate covered donut, took a bite, and swallowed some coffee. He was focused on Beckwith, absorbing every syllable.

"Do you have any theories?" asked Noah.

Beckwith reacted with a "Yes, sir, Admiral."

"What theories have you formed?" asked Noah.

"They're all over the board," said Beckwith. "One theory is that it might be an isolated incident of violence. We've speculated that it might be politically motivated. That's where you can all help out. You knew the Dahlbergs personally. Give me your perspective." It was clearly a command.

Laura leaned forward, her elbows spread along the edge of the table, her eyes piercing as she looked at Beckwith. "I know there was a lot of controversy because Charlie refused to get involved in Indian gaming. He vowed to leave the casinos alone and not try to get any of the money they were amassing. He was very much an advocate for the tribes. There was a lot of pressure to have him ask for a share of casino profits or threaten to start state supported gambling in Minnesota. He fiercely opposed legalized gambling for the state and supported a tribal council's right to operate and profit from casinos.

"Charlie was getting some negative reaction on his stand on wetland mitigation. He was pushing for stronger rules, faster action. Whenever a political decision is made on any topic, someone is upset. It comes with the territory."

"Or it could be some nut," said Molly. "Some deranged person who knows how to use explosives wants to blow up someone in the news. The only trouble is, how do you narrow down a bomber from that standpoint?"

"That's clearly a theory," said Beckwith. "We're not ignoring any possibility."

"Have you checked with all the other agencies?" asked Noah. "I know there's a computer link with names of suspected terrorists, offbeat political groups, all the way to people who just like the excitement of a kill."

"Staff is studying the lists," answered Beckwith. "We've set up computers in the high school with access to all the links available to us. I have a full contingent of agents working on dozens of possibilities."

"It seems like the public is handling the news in a calm manner," said Noah. "That's thanks to you and Sam. You've done a great job with the media. Keep talking to the people. They need assurances continually. The more they hear from you, the more relaxed they'll be. You don't need mass hysteria."

"That's right, sir," said Beckwith. "Sam and I have set up a series of live press conferences on a regular basis. An informed public is an orderly society. We'll keep at it."

"When's the next press conference?" asked Laura. "I'm going to be there. It's important for the community to see me actively involved."

"Great. Keep it short and direct. Are you going to be out and about in town?"

"That's my plan," she answered. "I expect to be part of the system for processing information, to get control of the day, and deal with the sheer number of issues that need my attention. As soon as we're through here, I'm hitting the streets."

"Good thinking," said Noah. "People need to see their leaders taking charge. The FBI, BCA, and everyone else looks great, but there's nothing like the local mayor reaching out."

"Political disturbances are going to erupt," said Laura. "I need to let people know they can reach me; people need to be aware of the intensity of the investigation. How many agents are in Birch Bay?"

"Two hundred," answered Beckwith.

"People need to know that," said Laura. "I didn't know how many there were until just now. It would help if you announced the number of agents and all the agencies responding to the disaster. I know you touched on it earlier, but it needs to be said over and over. Sometimes the public's not paying attention. Get the media to reinforce everything you're saying. I'll start by speaking at the press conference and then start walking the downtown area and into the neighborhoods."

"Good," said Sam. "I have a press conference scheduled in forty-five minutes and we'll lay it all out for the press. They like names and numbers."

"And I'll be there," said Laura.

"Name some of the agents," said Noah. "Personalize the investigation. Let the public know who is in town and what they're doing. Give the press background information on the men and women working to solve the case. I know you can't give details about all two hundred plus agents that are in town, but you can give bios on some of them. Give the public some faces they can associate with the investigation. Have some of those same agents go to the local coffee shop. Eat lunch at a local restaurant. Connect the dots for the public."

"You're absolutely right, sir," said Beckwith. "I'll put some of our media specialists on it at once."

"Two hundred plus?" Molly was flabbergasted. "No wonder the town is overflowing. Where are they all staying? What about meals?"

"They're staying all over the county. We're having a lot of meals brought in. The units are doing shift work so we're using the cafeteria in the high school to serve meals."

"How does that work?" asked Molly. "Who fixes the food?"

"We've contracted with different restaurants and grocery stores. It's all taken care of."

"Good grief," said Molly. "You have quite a team in place. And what do two-hundred law enforcement people do?"

"There's twenty-four hour guards at the house alone," said Beckwith. "Three agents are assigned at a time to the house and grounds, we have two people on the road, and a couple more circling the periphery. That's twenty-one people covering guard duty just at the lake house. You can imagine the team needed in investigation."

"Are you conducting an internal investigation?" asked Noah. "There's quite a staff in the state office building, the governor's office, and every state department."

"We have a team centered in St. Paul that's covering that aspect of the investigation. All state employees are in a data base and we're looking at all of them."

Bell tones interrupted the dialogue. Beckwith answered his cell phone.

"The governor has just landed," he said. "He's on his way over."

CHAPTER NINETEEN

"Laura," called Jack Cummings as he walked through the door. "It's so good to see you." He came beside her, caressing her shoulder and planting a kiss on the top of her head. "I didn't try to call because I hoped you were resting." His voice was heavy with concern. How was she? Did she or Molly need anything? He'd put every agency at their service; just let him know when and where.

Molly was next with a hug and handshake and the renewing of old memories. Since the Dahlbergs had bought their lake home, friendships had been forged that went far beyond political relationships. Jack moved through the room greeting everyone warmly.

Governor Cummings was good looking, never married, thirty-four, and one of the state's most eligible bachelors. Honey-blonde hair, a radiant smile that reporters said could replace the Kennedy smile as the most photographed, and a body that was toned and lean added to his charismatic image. He inspired confidence, a confidence that would take him through the political turmoil that awaited him.

Laura visualized Jack standing in the capitol's rotunda just a month ago giving a rousing speech on education. It had been late May when she'd driven to St. Paul to testify before the senate subcommittee on teacher licensure and stayed on to watch Jack in a dynamic speech to a crowd of state educators. His talent and drive had propelled him to the top positions in political office.

She thought about all the people whose lives had been forever changed by the murders, people reeling under the weight of an assassination, and she felt the adrenaline rising in her again.

Audrey and Charlie's family.

Sam Mikkelson. He'd left the high crime district of St. Paul to come to a peaceful resort town. Shattered images.

Molly. Resolute in finding the killer.

Jack. A new governor thrust into the center of a state's mourning.

Noah. Called out of retirement to be chief consultant to the FBI.

Minnesota's citizens.

And the people of Birch Bay.

It reaches further, thought Laura. She knew the national implications, even international repercussions. Charlie Dahlberg had been approached by the party to be a candidate for the upcoming presidential election. The personal and political ramifications of their deaths was astounding.

Governor Jack Cummings circled the room, greeting everyone, asking questions, and being brought up to date on what had been happening. He was talking to people individually, then focused on the FBI lead administrator.

"And you're the clearing house, correct?" Jack's gaze was on Beckwith. "If I want to know anything, I just ask you."

"Correct. We're operating like a team; all the information ends with me. I want to hear all the suggestions, all the arguments, and give everyone a chance to contribute. I won't know everything so I will seek advice from those who are more expert in their field than I am. But if this is going to run smoothly, there has to be one leader."

"I agree," said Jack. "I'll look to you for counsel and advice. In a case like this, the FBI will definitely take the lead."

"I'm calling in more agencies every hour," said Beckwith. "Anyone who can give us assistance is going to be part of our team. That includes the State Highway Patrol and Birch Bay's Park Department. We're putting everyone to work." He leaned in toward Laura, smacking his hand on the table. A corner of his mouth turned down. "I give orders to everyone. No political interference. Period."

Laura thought she detected a snarl. Almost imperceptibly, she raised her eyebrows. "Wouldn't think of interfering," she said.

"Keep it that way." Beckwith gave her a withering look.

Irritation swelled in Laura's throat. "I'm not expecting to be told FBI information, but I won't be blindsided either."

Beckwith turned his back.

"Settle down, Beckwith," said Mikkelson. "We don't need any theatrics. Laura's the mayor. She's the connection to the locals. We need all the help we can get."

Beckwith's eyes were smoldering, but he moved to the wall and kept quiet.

"We also called in social service agencies in case our medical facility gets overwhelmed with counseling needs."

"Good, idea," said Jack.

"The more information we give the public, the more likely that people will process the information without too much upheaval," continued Sam. "We know people are shocked and strained, but we're working to alleviate some of that pressure."

Mikkelson handed the governor a file, then passed files to everyone in the room except Molly. "Sorry, this is for the elected officials and law enforcement."

"Makes sense to me," said Molly. "Whatever gets the job done."

Jack flipped through the file, moved to the table, and spread the documents in front of him. It became apparent that the sheriff's department and FBI were on highest alert. He looked through the pages of notes, charts, staff assignments, and hourly work plan.

"One of us will update you periodically," said Beckwith.

"I'm glad I came," said Jack "You've created quite a paper trail. This is all good news, really great investigating. Thanks."

Beckwith filled him in on the meetings they'd had and the orders of the day.

Jack ran his hand over his face, rubbing his eyes in a reflective gesture. "Impressive. This investigation couldn't be in better hands. Of course, nothing beats having Admiral Sackett as a consultant."

Beckwith turned his attention back to the files. "By the time we're through, we'll have hundreds of pages. We have to find the person or persons responsible for the Dahlberg deaths, but we need evidence that will convict them."

Molly poured coffee and buttered a slice of banana bread. She turned her back on the group and whispered to Laura. "As soon as Jack Cummings walked into the room you could feel the electricity. He radiates power. And good sense. Thank goodness he was next in line for governor."

Jack turned to Laura. "Have you been interviewed by the media yet?"

"No. I'm going to be part of the next press conference with Sheriff Mikkelson and Agent Beckwith. Then I'm going to go downtown and start visiting with people and answering questions. I won't comment on the actual incident; people will understand the importance of keeping the investigation confidential."

"No matter how secure you keep the ship, there will still be rumors of leaks. If you're out and about, you'll be able to hear the rumors. Be careful that the bad guys don't see you as a threat." Jack moved in closer. "You can give me the details of the afternoon over dinner this evening. I'm flexible so you let Molly know the time and I'll meet you in the dining room."

Laura gave Molly a questioning look.

"Don't worry," said Molly. "As of this afternoon the dining room is closed. We're leaving every space in the Inn available for the task force."

Mikkelson narrowed his eyes, shifted in his chair, and watched Laura's reaction. She said dinner would be fine. But who could blame her? Besides, they needed to work on the case. He'd have to stop in around supper time himself and update Governor Cummings on the investigation.

"I have a favor to ask Noah and Laura," continued Jack. "This has all been devastating for the Dahlberg family. Laura, I'd like you to visit Charlie and Audrey's kids and give them my condolences. Anne Bradley can handle the details, give you addresses, times, and whatever else you need. Noah, I'd like you to visit the offices of Homeland Security in St. Paul and the FBI in Minneapolis. I'll inform them that you're my personal emissary to get an update on the investigation. Tomorrow or the next day if possible. Assure them that I'll be visiting with them soon."

Jack dialed Anne when Laura and Noah agreed to visit the Twin Cities the next day. Anne would call as soon as a schedule was set. Conversations continued with Jack writing notes on the file that Sam had given him.

Governor Jack Cummings stood by the window listening patiently to the conversation. He'd taken off his jacket and tie and looked more relaxed. Laura had a slight crease in her forehead, projecting a thoughtful, intelligent look. As the governor watched her, he noted again that her beauty and intelligence were extraordinary. He smiled affectionately at her when he caught her eye and gave her a subtle wink.

It was a somber group; people moving into small groups as they read through the file that Sam had passed out.

"I'll talk to Beckwith about his comments," said Sam. "He was out of line."

"And what good will that do?" asked Laura. "He's FBI."

"Exactly. They're held to a very high standard. Bullying a local mayor is not part of the operating procedure."

Sam moved across the room answering questions, filling in details.

Laura leaned over to Molly, her eyes darting from person to person: "So what kind of evil walked into town?"

Chapter Twenty

Mayor Laura Kjelstad was introduced as the last speaker at the press conference. She promised that everything would be done to find the people responsible.

"Governments work or they fail miserably," she said. "I'm here to assure you that we will not fail in our quest to bring the killers of Charlie and Audrey Dahlberg to justice before the American judicial system. Government will work here.

"We may roll up the sidewalks pretty early in Birch Bay, but we are now committed to twenty-four hour work days.

"I've heard it said that the citizens of this town feel frightened and neglected, but I have heard the words of Agent Beckwith and Sheriff Mikkelson as they walked along the beach and through the broken wreckage of the Dahlberg garage. They spoke words of promise and hope that they would not rest until the case was solved.

"People have said that the government will not respond, that they are sluggish and silent, but today the voices of our agents and politicians are united in their cries of anger toward the guilty in this heinous crime.

"Word on the street is that government is indifferent, even rude, but I have seen the dedication of the men and women working to rescue the bodies of Charlie and Audrey, working through the wreckage, fighting back tears of anguish.

"Our local rescue teams were marvelous; they were at the scene quickly and were highly professional. You should all be proud of the dedicated men and women that make up our emergency response units.

"The FBI and BCA arrived as soon as possible after the explosion. There are now two-hundred agents in our town and countless law enforcement groups across the country working together, joining forces to find the guilty and build a case for prosecution.

"We have a mobile-emergency response team in the gyms of our schools. There are dozens of computers with access to the Internet and other agencies around the world. There is a radio system in place, a satellite communications system, and fifty-two phone lines. There is a dedicated line straight to the president.

"Certainly, we are a small town. But small does not mean inept. I fully believe that the citizens of this town will help in this battle to conquer the evil that has struck our community. Listen and report anything that might help our team of agents.

"We will not hesitate to move mountains."

Laura pulled the microphone off the stand and moved closer to the crowd. "We will also kick over rocks and look into the depths of the underworld to find the killers.

"I know you will help the agents working in this community. You will be the ears and eyes of men and women who are not familiar with this area. You will also show them the heart of our small town.

"I have seen the people of Birch Bay do marvelous things. I saw it when the EMTs revived Tom Gibson during his heart attack.

"Consider the experience we all gained when we watched the firemen rescue the Johnsons when their house burned and the town helped them repair and repaint and remodel their home.

"Remember the forest fire that started at Cranberry Lake? It was under control in no time because of the dedicated work of the volunteers from Birch Bay.

"Who will ever forget the dramatic delivery of little Baby Lily when her mother was stuck in the snowstorm? Snowmobilers for miles around responded immediately and made sure mom and baby were safe in the hospital before any of them went home to the warmth of their own fires.

"It's absolutely essential now that Birch Bay uses its' collective intelligence to help the FBI solve this crime.

"How? Non-interference for one. Let them do their job. More specifically, recognize that law enforcement does have a plan.

"Sweat the small stuff. Pay attention to everything. Write it down. If you have something that may help in the investigation, turn it over to the proper authorities and let them make the judgment call. Our success will come because of the amazing diligence of the people in this town.

"Remember – I was there when Charlie and Audrey died. The ground shook and the air burned. If you don't know who else to give information to, give it to me. I'll pass it on to the FBI.

"Whoever is responsible for this reprehensible crime must realize they have a whole town to contend with. Not by vigilantes, but by vigilance. Together we will move that mountain."

Television cameras zoomed in on her face, print media snapped random pictures, and the TV reporters started doing voiceovers highlighting what Laura had said. As the press conference ended, reporters surged toward Laura, asking lots of questions, but left her when Sam Mikkelson moved to the microphone. He knew several of the reporters by name now and encouraged them to ask questions. He gave vague answers until Laura was well on her way down the street. She turned around once, smiled, and mouthed a "Thank you."

Laura walked along Portage Avenue, alone, but making sure she was fully noticed. She bustled with energy, waving to people as she passed the shops, greeting many by name, smiling assurances to the questioning looks. Questions were answered with bold candor, saying all she could on the matter of the Dahlberg's deaths.

Yes, she agreed, the explosion was a catastrophe; the administration had a state-of- the-art command center located in the high school gym. No, the public could not have access to the building where the response teams were working. Agent Beckwith was handling the dissemination on all leads.

As shocking as the deaths were, the various state and federal agencies were working together to find the people responsible. We are prepared, she said. Each governmental unit was working as one. The feds were foraging through evidence, fingerprint samples, and forensic data.

She walked through Wood Whistle Gifts, Hook's Bait Shop, and the Cold Water Fish Market talking to the workers and owners. At the Big Timber Café, she sat down to an iced tea and asked to see the owner, Ed Monroe.

Ed's in-your-face attitude was mellow, but the air around him was always charged with energy. His eyebrows furrowed when he saw her as he dodged around the tables and joined her in the booth.

"So what in the hell is happening?" Ed shook his head in disbelief.

A sudden quiet settled over the room as people strained to listen. If anyone knew what was happening, it had to be the mayor.

"You probably know as much as I do," she said. "You may have even heard stories I'm not privy to. What's the word on the street?"

"You know the talk in this town. It's everything from a terrorist attack, to the Nazis, to aliens from outer space."

"Aliens. That would be Dick Metcalfe. The Nazis would be Hank Thornberg. And the terrorists would be Helen Gabler, Leo Nelson, and Bob Risberg."

"Right on the nose. Dick believes the alien invasion has already started. Hank doesn't like the Nazi party in America and who can blame him? Helen, Leo, and Bob blame everything on terrorists."

Laura looked at him, a slight bit of humor lit up her eyes. "Last time their electric bill went up, those three blamed it on terrorists taking over the country and the money being sent to some revolutionary despot."

"At least they didn't blame it on you."

"Until they think about it. Leo has a blame-city-government topic of the day every day."

"Any motives talked about?" A voice came from a center table.

Laura glanced around the room. She wasn't saying anything that hadn't already hit lumberjack dot-com. "Nothing and everything. Charlie was a political figure. National prominence. Somebody out there always has some hatred for an elected person. The FBI is looking at everything. Weirdoes, ex-employees of their corporation, analyzing recent legislative decisions, voting by counties. Everything's being looked at, but there's no suspects. I think I'd have some inkling if there were a break in the case just because the energy level would change. It hasn't."

Laura slid out of the booth and faced Ed. "Keep me posted. I'd appreciate it if you let people know that the investigation is going well."

"Will do. Right now everybody's happy to see the FBI. Word has it the FBI is so paranoid that they're checking out each other." Ed greeted customers as he sauntered back to the kitchen.

Laura walked through the café chatting and listening to the same questions she'd heard several times already. Tension breathed through the air, then dissipated as Laura began a friendly disclosure of the investigation's process.

Laura was analyzing the city's priorities as she walked along. With any emergency, it was necessary to set up a command center. The second need was to communicate with people in town. The FBI had immediately set up the command center; a national tragedy had been handled efficiently by federal agents. As good as the agents were, she knew it was important that local leaders communicated quickly and deliberately.

She walked through October House, a local gift shop, and The Wildflower, the town's flower shop. Both places had long lines at the cash register so she'd come back later, she said.

She spent more time at Birch Ridge Grill, sitting at the counter, and Ridge View Café, sitting at a center table, waiting for people to approach her. Within minutes she had been surrounded and once again answered the same questions, routinely now, with a confidence that soothed the crowds. She wondered if that's how Agent Beckwith dealt with reporters; know the questions and formulate the answers before talking to the media.

Hiking through the campground helped settle some nervous tourists. By the time she had visited the library, bank, The Raspberry Patch, and Blueberry House, she felt that the town was returning to a vigorousness of trust and hope. Emotions weren't as raw; people saw the feds as helpers, not interlopers. How long the feeling would last, she didn't know. Tomorrow, when Laura and Noah were gone, Molly and Sam had agreed to walk around town, encouraging, explaining, making their presence felt.

Laura walked to city hall and was greeted by Ruth Steiner. Cliff Fredrickson was in a meeting with the PUC manager; Sharon Wahl, city secretary, had taken some files to the library, and PUC secretary, Alice Kaiser, was on the phone.

"Great job at the press conference," said Ruth. "I could sense a difference in people as I walked back here. More relaxed maybe. The conversations were more about what they could do to help than about what was wrong with the FBI. Mikkelson sure inspires confidence, too. The feds could learn some lessons from what we're doing here. It seems that we're doing everything right."

"I agree. Let's just hope this is solved right away. Can you imagine the turmoil if this case hangs on?"

"Or is never solved?" said Ruth.

Laura flipped through her mail and phone messages. Two calls from Leo Nelson asking what the FBI was doing. One call from the DNR regarding the boat ramp in the campground. Two calls from Helen Gabler saying she didn't feel safe in "this town" anymore.

"Would you call law enforcement and have them check on Helen Gabler?" she asked. "She really does get scared some times. Have a patrol check on her periodically. Have them stop in and see Leo Nelson, too, and tell him the investigation is going full force. A paranoid, vengeful Leo can do a lot of damage."

She went through the rest of the messages and put the notes in the mailbox of the appropriate department head.

"Nothing pressing," she told Ruth. "I'll keep walking around town. I have my cell phone. Let me know if anything comes up."

By the time she had walked up the hill and neared the high school, her adrenaline was pumping. The high school and elementary schools were located across the street from each other. Bay Boulevard was a north-south street in what had been a quiet area of schools and parks. Now the area was filled with cars, vans, mobile units, helicopters, and communications units. The media was parked along the side streets with reporters standing around outside, drinking coffee, eating pastries, and talking to each other. It was clear their energy was high.

Laura hurried through the alley before the media spotted her. Determined as she was to cover the whole town, her steps were almost a run.

Eagle Ridge Restaurant, on the palisade above town, was filled with people asking intelligent questions as a calmness settled over them. She was thankful there was no hysteria, that she could look people in the eye and give an uncorrupted assessment.

Laura continued her walk, telling people that every resource available was being utilized to solve the horrendous crime. The Dairy Queen, Laundromat, two gas stations, and the grocery store finished the circle she'd made of town. Straight ahead was the Big Timber Café. She glanced at her watch. Time for a hamburger.

Sunlight glimmered off the lake, a shimmering peacefulness rested on the water.

"Mrs. Kjelstad." A voice called to her from the beach.

Why did that voice send a chill along her spine?

CHAPTER TWENTY-ONE

Lance Hanover waved, running on the pebbled shore and to the sidewalk where she stood.

"Mrs. Kjelstad," he yelled. "I need to talk to you."

"Of course, Lance. What can I do for you?"

"Let's walk over by the water so no one can hear us."

Laura followed silently until Lance stopped.

"Good. No one close enough to hear."

"What is it?"

"I was at the courthouse when you talked to the press today. You said everyone in town had to help solve the crime."

"Yes."

"I know something." Lance put his hands in his pockets and kicked at the rocks.

"Go on."

"You have to promise not to tell anyone. You said you can keep a secret."

"I also said it would depend on the secret."

"I think this is important."

"Tell me and I will keep it private if I can. You have to know that I will tell the FBI anything I can to solve this crime."

"Could I be anonymous?"

"Yes. I can do that."

"Even if they say you have to tell."

"How about if I tell Noah Sackett and he can tell the FBI? That way I will be the anonymous person?"

"That would work. Noah's a very special person."

"Yes, he is. Now tell me what you know."

"I was at the Dahlberg's that day. There's a tree close to the beach that I like to climb. You can see way out into the lake and watch everything on the shore. You can even see through the woods, but no one can see me when I'm at the top of the tree."

His voice was strained, his words rapid. For a moment he was quiet.

"I saw a man walk through the woods and stop near the Dahlberg's garage. Then his cell phone rang and I heard him swear. He was wearing grey jogging pants with a white stripe down the side and a white T-shirt.

"The ring tone on his cell reminded me of The Dukes of Hazzard, but I couldn't remember what the song was. But it was definitely a Hazzard type song."

Silence filled the air again. A worried frown etched across his face and the pupils of his eyes focused on the shoreline like an eagle after prey, not missing a thing.

"I heard him say: 'I thought you were two-hundred miles away'. Then he said not to call him again. He seemed really angry and used the 'f' word a lot."

Laura waited for any more words, but Lance was silent.

"When did this happen?" she asked.

"Just before the explosion."

He was quiet again, tears forming in the corners of his eyes.

"I didn't know what was going to happen or I would have done something."

"Did the man see you?"

"No. He walked further into the woods and I ran for home. No one knows I spend time in that tree and I just wanted to get out of there. I didn't want him to see me. He wasn't a nice man."

Lance wiped his eyes with the back of his hand.

"I walked through the Dahlberg's yard to get to my tree. They let me cut through their driveway and walk down to the beach whenever I want to. I dropped some money and had to stop to pick it up and I didn't see anyone. It was after I'd been in the tree a while that I saw the man."

The penny that Molly had stopped to pick up must have been part of the money that Lance had dropped.

"Did you go through the Dahlberg's yard on your way home?" she asked.

"No. I was afraid the man would see me so I went through the woods and up to the road."

"I need to call Noah."

"I know."

"I'll tell him it's an anonymous tip. It's a solid lead, Lance. You've been very helpful."

"I didn't tell my mom."

"I'll leave that up to Noah. Noah needs to know where I got the information. In fact, I'll call him right now while you're here and if I make a mistake, you can correct me right away."

Noah answered on the first ring.

"This is an anonymous caller," she said.

"He'll know it's you," said Lance. "His cell phone will show your name."

Laura put her hand over the mouthpiece. "I'll explain it's information on the case and that it's confidential. I'll tell him it has to be anonymous."

"Have him erase it off his cell when he hangs up." Lance looked around and lowered his voice. "Otherwise all someone has to do is look at his call memory and they'll know you talked to him."

Lance listened to the conversation with Noah Sackett and nodded approval. When Laura was finished, he said he would go home.

"I'm scared, Mrs. Kjelstad."

"I know. I'll ask Noah to keep a watch over everyone who lives near the Dahlberg's house. The FBI has a good surveillance team in that area now. No one will know you told me anything. I promise."

Even so, a cold hand seemed to grip her bones and fear rippled across her skin.

CHAPTER TWENTY-TWO

Pine Crest Inn
Afternoon
June 26

Montana was waiting for her when she got home. Laura had skipped the hamburger at Big Timber Café. Noah and Sam were both at the high school and it was her turn to feed, water, and give Montana a potty break.

"I'm going to go out for a hamburger. Would you like to ride along?"

Montana's ears picked up like he knew what she was saying.

"What kind of vocabulary do you have?" she asked.

Montana wagged his tail and woofed. She rubbed his ears and told him she had an idea.

"We'll drive out to Pine Crest Inn and visit Cindy Snyder. A lot of locals call her Sexpot Cindy. She really is quite pretty. Besides, if anyone knows guys with Dukes of Hazzard rings on their cell phones, it'll be Cindy."

Cindy was behind the bar chatting with a gray-haired guy that looked like a leftover from the Sixties. His hair was in a long ponytail; he wore wire-rimmed glasses, and his denim jeans had holes in the knees. He didn't look like the kind of guy who would pay an obscene price for scruffy looking jeans.

Cindy smiled and waved as Laura came through the door.

"What can I get for ya, darlin'?" she asked.

"I need a menu. I didn't have lunch so I'm starved."

"Sit anywhere you like sweetheart." She looked Laura over and tapped the ponytail guy on the shoulder. "You remember Laura Kjelstad, don't you? That's the Birch Bay mayor."

"Pretty little thing. I remember her."

"I remember you, too, Matt."

"Call me Hippie," he said and gave her a toothy grin. "Everybody else does. Fits."

The Pinecrest Inn was quiet. An elderly man and woman were seated at a table by the window, a young man was in a back booth, a couple of teenagers were hunkered over the pool table in the back, and there was Hippie at the bar.

"I'll be in a booth," said Laura.

"Choose your seat, honey." Cindy smiled and gave a sweeping gesture with her arms.

"You anglin' for big tips," said Hippie.

"Hey you nasty. Did you ask if I was danglin' my big tits?"

"No need to ask that," he said. "I got eyes. Don't you ever wear a bra?"

Cindy strutted to the booth and took Laura's order.

"I'll have a cheeseburger and a vanilla shake."

"Little thing like you can handle all that fat. You work out?"

"I'm working on my black belt in Tae Kwon Do and I run every day."

"Hey Hippie. Don't mess with the mayor. She'll drop kick your ass across the county line."

"Whaddya mean?"

"She's working on her black belt in Tae Kwon do."

"Holy shit," he said and gave Laura a wide-eyed look. "You could beat me up."

Laura gave him a smile and shook her head. "I wouldn't do that."

"But you could. Cool."

Cindy turned her attention back to Laura. "You want whipped cream and a cherry on that shake?"

"Yes, please."

"Thought you might be into the whipped cream and cherry thing." She winked at Hippie. "She's into whipped cream."

"Hunh," was all he said.

Laura leaned against the table. Adolescents. They sounded like fourteen year olds sitting in the back of a school bus.

"I was wondering if you could give me a few minutes of your time," said Laura when Cindy brought the shake. "Do you have a break coming up soon?"

"Hey, Hippie," Cindy yelled. "Tell Maryanne I'm taking five. Bring over the cheeseburger when it's ready."

"I appreciate this." Laura gave her a smile. Cindy wiggled into the booth.

"Not exactly the busiest time. July and August it'll be busy all the time, but it's slow right now. Busy around nine or ten o'clock when the bar gets busy, but otherwise it's a little slow. You know that of course. You being the mayor and all."

"I just wanted to ask you to keep law enforcement aware of anything that might help with the case. You must hear a lot here."

"Sure."

"I'd appreciate that."

"Dirty business this assassination thing. The governor and his wife came out here to eat some times. Real nice people. I'll help catch the bastards that killed them. Heard you were there when they got blowed up."

"Yes."

"You're tough. I hear some of the good 'ol boys in town give you a hard time."

"I can take care of them."

"I know you can. I admire that. You don't take shit off of those guys."

"No, I don't. The good 'ol boys are what inspired me to run for mayor."

"And you kicked butt."

"I did. And I intend to do it again."

"How are you feeling?" she asked.

"Fine."

"You're a bullshitter, too."

"Right now my main focus is to catch the people that killed Charlie and Audrey."

Laura sipped her shake and nibbled on the little vanilla wafer that had been placed beside the cherry.

"You make a good shake," said Laura.

"And I shake really good."

"Have you always worked in bars and restaurants?"

"No. I went to high school once."

"Where else have you worked?"

"Besides bars?"

"Yes."

"Waitressed when I was in high school. Worked at a book store the one semester I was in college."

"What was your major?"

"Men."

"Seriously."

"I am serious, honey. College wasn't for me. I wanted to find a husband."

"Did you?"

"Oh yeah. He stayed in college. Did really well. I worked the whole time so we had money. Then he went to law school, met a pretty young law student, and I was out the door. Don't ever try to outdo a lawyer."

"Any kids?"

"No. That's a good thing, though. Divorce is tough on kids. I have fun here. Guys are falling all over me. Work long hours, but I make really good tips."

"Ever thought of going back to school?"

"No. I'm investing my money. Some day I'll own my own restaurant. With a bar. I have my eye on a little place north of Two Harbors. You know how much profit there is in booze?"

"Lots."

"You got it."

Laura reached for her cell phone. "You know how to fix the ring tones on these things. I'd like something different. Maybe something like the Dukes of Hazzard."

"Need to have it programmed in. Funny you mention the Dukes. Guy comes in here that has a wireless with a Dukes sound. His cell plays Dixie."

"Does he come in often?"

"Sort of. I noticed him because he changed the color of his hair. Not many guys into fussing with their hair. I wondered if he was dodging an ex-wife."

"How did you know it was the same guy? You must get lots of tourists in here."

"I always look at people's teeth. Can't change that. Women walk in here all the time with different hairstyles, colored contacts, change of clothes and they're always surprised that I remember their names. It's all in the teeth."

"What makes this guy's teeth so special?"

"His amalgam tattoo."

CHAPTER TWENTY-THREE

Laura pushed the ice cream aside and lifted her sleek brown eyebrows. "I'm not sure I know what an amalgam tattoo is. You're sure this guy has a cell phone that plays Dixie?"

"Sure."

"Did you say you could recognize the guy because of some kind of tattoo? On his teeth?"

"Not actually on his teeth. On his gums around his teeth. Don't you know what an amalgam tattoo is?"

"No."

"Amalgam is the stuff they use to fill your tooth after they drill out all the cavity crap."

"Okay."

"Sometimes, maybe it's rare, I don't know, but sometimes, that silver leaks through onto the gums. It leaves a bluish, purplish look to the gums around the teeth. Dentists call it an amalgam tattoo."

Laura looked puzzled. "And this guy has that around his teeth. Some of his teeth."

"Sure does. He's probably had it so long that he doesn't even notice it anymore. That happens to a lot of people, especially if the tattoo happened when they were young. It becomes part of your body just like a freckle."

"It must be toward the front in order for you to have seen it."

"Actually, it's in the upper left side of his mouth. You can only see it if he gives you a smile or if he curls his lip back. That's how I first noticed it. He was grumping about something and he sort of snarled. I spotted it right off. He has a habit of clenching his teeth, sticking out his chin, and raising his left upper lip."

"How did you know what it was?"

"Because I have an amalgam tattoo. Once you find out that the bluish, purplish thing around your teeth is permanent, you tend to notice other people's teeth."

"I never noticed it on you."

"Bet you will from now on." She gave Laura a wide smile. The tattoo, though toward the back of her mouth, was indeed noticeable.

"Interesting."

"You can bet the guys don't notice it on me," said Cindy. "They're eyes are always at chest level."

"Did this guy have a name?" asked Laura.

"Never said. I can ask him how to get that ring if he comes in again."

"No, thanks. I'll ask someone to help me get my phone set up so I can do some different ring tones. No need to bother a stranger."

"Sure, honey. Anything else?"

"Would you ask Hippie if I could talk to him for a few minutes?"

Cindy smiled. "Hippie's a nice person. He's part-time dishwasher, part-time cook, and sometimes janitor. He hears a lot, but he's tilted off center. Trouble is, there's no telling from day to day which way he's sloping. Too many chemicals got added to his diet when he was young. His choice, of course."

"I've heard."

"Hey Hippie," yelled Cindy. "Come over here to visit with the mayor."

Cindy glided from the booth, sashayed into the kitchen, and Hippie came out wiping his hands. Hippie looked at Laura as Cindy leaned in close and whispered something in his ear. He didn't move any further than the counter.

"Could you talk to me for a few minutes?" asked Laura.

He nodded. Still didn't move.

"Why don't you come over and talk to me?"

Hippie grinned, brought his beer over, and sat across from Laura in the booth.

"I didn't know if you wanted me to actually sit in the booth with you. Somehow I didn't now if it was right. Proper. You know?"

"It's cool."

"Yeah."

"Could you spend a few minutes talking to me about some people?"

"That would be nice." He paused for a moment, maybe synthesizing the brain cells. "We could talk about Rebecca down at the convenience store. Or maybe Brad over at the video place. You pick. We have to say good things though. I don't bad mouth people."

"I meant we should talk about anyone you may have seen here that might have talked about the governor. Maybe threatening him. People might not worry about saying things in here. Lots of background noise and they might not realize you can hear what they're saying."

"Sure. What did you want to tell me about them?"

"Actually, nothing. I'm interested in what you might know. I understand Charlie and Audrey Dahlberg came in here for a hamburger occasionally."

"Hey, Cindy," he yelled. "Do I know Charlie Dahlberg?"

"You do."

"What's his name?"

"Charlie Dahlberg."

He turned to Laura and grinned. "Yeah. I was right. I'm not as spacey as some people think."

Laura wasn't going to try to follow his train of thought, but she persisted. "Ever hear anyone threatening him? Behind his back, I mean. You hear a lot of things sitting in here every day."

"I'm sorry. This is one of my spacey days."

Cindy brought Laura a refill of iced tea. She handed Hippie a root beer float and took the beer away. "He's got some good days and some spacey days." She gave him a hard look. "You know what the doctor said. Absolutely no alcohol. Period."

"Yeah. I know." He looked at Laura and shrugged.

"Give him some time," said Cindy. "He mellows out a bit when he has something sweet."

Laura sipped her tea and waited while Hippie enjoyed his float. She looked out the window and saw that Montana was on guard in the front seat of the car.

"You got Mikkelson's dog with you." Hippie gave her a measuring look. "You Mikkelson's girlfriend?"

"No. I'm watching the dog because Sam's working on a case."

"Oh, yeah. Dogs don't like to walk alone. I know that."

"Have you heard anything that might help us find the Dahlberg's killers?"

"I'll listen. I won't drink any alcohol or smoke any …you know…"

Hippie ate the ice cream and ran his tongue around his lips. "Do I have any ice cream sticking on me anywhere?"

"You're fine."

"That's good. I wouldn't want to look oinkish in front of the mayor."

"And Audrey Dahlberg?"

"Oh my."

"Have you heard anyone talking about her?"

Hippie giggled. "Oh. I thought you meant that Audrey Dahlberg was oinkish."

Oh, sure, thought Laura. Give Hippie a poorly phrased question. He caught it, though, so maybe the root beer float was organizing his brain cells. She sighed. Hippie would keep her focused.

"So what do you know?" asked Laura. "Do you have anything you can tell me?"

Hippie was quiet for a moment. "Bad vibes. Bad vibes."

"Take your time," said Laura. "Would you like some more ice cream?"

"No. Not many people are nice to me. They talk about me like I'm not there. Well, like I'm too stupid to know anything. I know I fried my brain when I was in college. Well, maybe high school, too, but that doesn't mean I have to be treated like I'm a nothing."

"You're right." Laura sipped her tea and gave him a couple of minutes.

"I'm not dumb either. People figure the likes of me couldn't tell the difference between Monet and Chagall. I can. Majored in art history. Graduated, too. Probably in the lower third of my class. Not sure. Senior year was sort of a haze."

"Art history is an incredible major. Congratulations."

"I'm working on the chemical thing."

"That's a good thing."

"People think Cindy's a sexpot. Well, yeah. She is. But she's nice to me. Treats me like I'm a real person. She can cut any man down to little teeny pieces, but she only does that if they're running off at the mouth. She's been good to me. I don't want you thinking anything bad about her."

"I'm glad she's good to you. Does she call you Hippie or Matt?"

"Both. Doesn't matter what she calls me, matters how she treats people. She's a nice lady. You need anything else? I've got to catch up on the dishes before the supper crowd gets here."

"Thanks, Hippie. I'd really appreciate it if you listened to the talk here. If you hear anything that can help the investigation, call Sheriff Mikkelson. He'll come right over."

Laura stuck out her hand. "Thanks, Matt."

"Anytime." He walked back to the kitchen and yelled to no one in particular. "Holy shit. I had a root beer float with the mayor."

Montana's head was hanging out the window and his tail started thumping when Laura opened the driver's side door. He wasn't too happy about moving to the passenger side. She reached across the seat to pat him, but he jerked his head away. For a moment she was puzzled, then she saw Cindy walking toward them waving a doggie bag. Montana wagged his tail when he saw Cindy, his tongue doing slurpy twists around the drool dripping from his mouth.

"It's a hamburger, big guy." Cindy reached through the window and scratched his ears. "Mikkelson usually orders something for Montana when he comes out here." She handed the bag to Laura. "I'll let you give it to him since you're his assignment."

"I'm his assignment?"

"Of course. Montana is watching out for you."

Montana gave a discontented whine, eyeing the bag while he wiggled in the seat.

"Something captivating about those big brown eyes and slippery tongue," said Cindy. She gave a wink and went back inside.

"Sexpot Cindy strikes again." Laura gave him a pat on the head and took out the hamburger. "I guess you deserve a snack since you're working so hard."

Montana put the whole burger in his mouth, part of the bun hung from his lip, most of the meat dropped to the floor. That didn't slow him down any. He bent his head to the floor, gulped the burger, licked the carpet, then looked at Laura.

"That's all there is. Now I suppose you want some water." She poured some water into his dish. Montana slurped, dripped, and belched. She kept the windows open, then scratched behind his ears and he went into a dreamy dog haze.

"So, Montana. Hippie's a lot smarter than he lets on. Cindy's a lot nicer than anyone thinks she is. What do you suppose is happening in town right now?"

Montana focused his intelligent brown eyes on Laura's face and gave a sigh.

"My thoughts exactly. I don't like any of this one bit."

Montana sniffed the air and turned his gaze back to the parking lot.

"I'm not giving up," she said. The sibilance of her voice caused Montana to thump his tail. He surveyed her with expectant eyes, sniffing the air for another treat.

"Sorry. No more food."

Montana whimpered and swiped his tongue around his nose.

"It's going to be all right. We need to remember the Old Scottish prayer my grandmother used to say. 'From ghoulies and ghosties and long-leggety beasties, and things that go bump in the night, Good Lord deliver us'."

Montana thumped his tail and Laura drove the car over to the edge of the parking lot. No sense letting everyone in the area watch her talking to a dog. She held up her cell phone to see if there was a signal.

"I need to be a little repentant."

Montana looked at her with enormous eyes, listening to the rhythm of her voice. He twitched his tail while Laura did a slow motion replay in her head.

"Sometimes I judge people. I think I've been jealous of Cindy so I've just dismissed her as being …sexy. That's all. I never gave her credit for being a decent person trying to make a living." Laura felt the tension mount in her neck. "Cindy and Hippie are fine. I need to think about my stupid opinions."

Laura reached in her purse, but there were no treats for Montana. She saw a piece of the bun under the seat and gave it to him. He rolled it around in his mouth, then started to lick the floor. She patted his head and he took another whiff of air.

First on her list to call was Noah. She told him what Cindy had said about the amalgam tattoo. Noah would pass the information on to the FBI.

"Is this anonymous, too?" he asked.

"Yes. Above all else, I want to protect Lance. You can give anonymous tips to the FBI and they won't ask questions. You were a special agent. They trust you completely."

Next she dialed her mom.

"How are things, hon?" asked Emily.

"Montana's a good companion."

"Are you sure you're safe?"

"I don't feel I'm in any danger, Mom, but I've got my cell phone on the floor beside me."

"Maybe it should be on the seat."

"Montana's there."

"Dogs are like that. They always want the front seat and as soon as you get out of the car, they're behind the wheel."

Mrs. Hansen urged Laura to come to Duluth to see them. Like today. For supper.

"I'll drive over soon. Love you, Mom. I'll keep in touch."

Molly was next on her call list.

"I'm glad you called," she said. "You sort of disappeared."

"Cindy Snyder and I just had a conversation. I talked with Matt Wrenshall, too."

"Hippie?"

"Yes."

"What about?"

"I figured as long as I was making myself seen around town, I should come out to the Pine Crest, too. I asked Cindy and Matt to let Sam know if they heard anything that might be relevant to the case."

"That's good."

"Do you know Hippie?"

"He's a nice enough guy. A little loopy, but dependable. He's had some chemical dependency issues, but he's dealing with them. I've heard he's in counseling. The word among resort owners is that he's a hard worker."

"And is he loopy or dependable?"

"Probably both. Depends on the day. He's the kind of guy that would stick his thumb in a light socket to get a buzz."

"He says Cindy's a nice person. Good to him. That sort of thing."

"That could be true."

"I'm going to run over to Duluth to see my parents. They're worried and they'll feel better if they see me for a while. Would you tell Jack I won't make that dinner tonight? There's just no time."

That was taken care of.

Cindy was a good person, Hippie was smarter than anyone thought, Montana was licking her arm.

"When we get home, I'll get you a special treat," she said to Montana.

Montana thumped his tail and swiped his tongue around his nose.

CHAPTER TWENTY-FOUR

The Oslo House
Duluth
Late Afternoon – June 26

Tenseness was working its way through her flesh, moving through her cells and sending a feeling of agitation to her fingertips. It was such a concentrated pervasiveness that it felt like a nasty case of the flu coming on. Her life was in suspended animation, interrupted by an evil person. Laura let the thoughts coalesce, anger surging through her like a tsunami.

Laura drove some of the country roads into Duluth, less traffic and more pleasant countryside than the freeway. Anger and tenseness would not be to her advantage. Once in Duluth, she turned up the hill on Canal Street and headed for The Oslo House.

She pulled into a reserved parking spot, rolled the window down in the car, and gave Montana some water. "Watch for the bad guys. They might want to plant a bomb or something. Noah might be right. I need to be more vigilant." She cranked the window down another notch so Montana could leap out if someone came around with a lethal weapon. He thumped his tail and hung his head out the window.

Wait staff greeted her as she walked through the door and headed straight for her dad's office. As she walked into the dining room, a familiar voice gave her a "Yoo hoo."

Clara Hixson was leaning over a table, her gray hair bobbing, and her plump figure maneuvering around the chairs. "Laura," she called. "Over here."

She moved across the room and clasped Laura in her arms. "My goodness, Laura. I didn't expect to see you here. Not with all this nasty business going on. I was going to call, but then I thought better of it. Didn't want to be a nuisance. Besides, I figured your phones were tapped by the FBI. Cops listening in. Last time I saw you was in the sunroom at the Inn. Remember? I was sure you'd be a nervous wreck. Having tea at the Inn is such a relaxing thing to do. FBI all over the place, though, so I didn't want to stay and visit this morning. Well, who would? I mean. They probably have the whole place bugged. Microphones in the flower arrangements and all.

"Could you come over to my table? I'd like to introduce you to some of my friends. They decided not to stay in Birch Bay tonight and they convinced me to spend the night in Duluth, too. You don't mind, do you? Meeting my friends, I mean. Of course you wouldn't say. You're always so gracious. We were just talking about the assassinations when you walked in. I thought right away that it was meant to be. Oh my. I don't mean the bomb was meant to be. My goodness, no. You being here, I mean."

"I'd be glad to meet your friends," said Laura.

"Good. Yes." A little fluttery, but that was vintage Clara.

She led Laura across the dining room and introduced her to three women. They were Nora, Jenny, and Amanda. Laura guessed they were all in their sixties, a mixture of faces that were studying Laura intently. Out for a nice evening meal and conversation, it was unfortunate that the discussion was focused on the assassination of Charlie and Audrey Dahlberg. On the other hand, maybe their adrenaline was surging, excitement generated by the grotesque crime, yet knowing they were safe. The assassination had been on the news nonstop. Why wouldn't they want to talk with her about it?

"We were just talking about you," said Clara. "You know. Wondering if you'd be out in public. You did a wonderful job at the press conference. It was on CNN." She turned and looked around the room. "You're not alone are you?"

"As a matter of fact, I drove over here alone. I'm visiting my parents."

"Oh my. What if you get shot?"

Clara looked at the three women seated at the table, their eyes were filled with curiosity, and their mouths were set in a firm line. Nora was a petite brunette, Jenny was rather robust with a hint of an attitude, and Amanda started questioning by raising an index finger, but Clara had full control of the conversation.

"Mayor Kjelstad isn't afraid of anything. Makes us all stand taller. We're so proud of you." Clara sat up a little straighter. "You go, girl." She smiled brightly, then said in hushed tones, "Makes me think I should get involved in city business. Why the hell spend my golden years playing Mexican Train Dominoes? Kicking butt doesn't have to belong to the young."

Clara pondered that for a moment. "I don't want my gravestone to read: Jens Hixson and wife."

Everyone agreed on that point.

Amanda opened her eyes wide and gave Laura a big smile. "I admire you, Laura. Most of the time in politics the regular, working people keep losing. The guys that win are all bullshit and money and special interests. You're different." She turned to Clara. "So what office do you want to run for? We could be a formidable team of campaigners."

"No elections at first. I'll apply for one of the city boards. Not the library board," said Clara. "Everyone thinks the library board is where the older women should be. What do you think, Laura."

"Park board. Most definitely."

"Some of those people give you trouble, don't they?"

"Some do. They want to get rid of the conservation easement."

"Can they do that?" asked Clara. Her brow broke into a worried frown.

"No. It's solid, but they create a lot of negative feelings."

"The big whiners," said Clara. "I know which ones they are. Good at bitching and moaning, but won't do any real work. The park board should be happy about saving the land."

"Most are, but there's a group of people that want big time development."

Clara's foot struck a purse on the floor and something large slid from inside.

"I'll get it," said Laura as she leaned over to pick it up.

"Don't bother," said Clara. "Really."

"That's a Glock." Laura spoke in a hushed tone as she turned around to see if anyone saw the gun.

"What?"

"You've got a gun at your feet."

"Of course I do. You don't think I'm driving around without some sort of protection. Someone assassinated our governor. We all have to be prepared. You said so yourself, Laura. At the press conference. You said we all had to help."

"Not by carrying a weapon. You could hurt someone. Or get arrested."

"Or both. I know. But we have to think of the greater good."

"That's a lot of gun."

"I know that. Quit fussing. I've been using guns all my life. I'm a very good shot."

"Is it loaded?"

"Of course it is. The safety is on and if you've noticed, it's not pointing at anyone."

She was right. It had landed with the barrel pointing toward the wall. Laura could see the purse had been positioned so Clara could pick it up in one swift movement.

"Are you telling me you don't have a gun in your car?" asked Clara.

"I didn't say that."

"What kind?"

"Small caliber, twenty-two. But I'm an excellent shot. I don't need anything bigger. Besides, I have a permit. Do you have a permit, Clara?"

"I do."

Laura grabbed a tray, knelt to the floor, and covered the gun with a napkin. "You can pick the gun up on your way out," whispered Laura. "I'll put it in a take-out box."

"I don't need a bigger gun either," said Clara, her teeth clenched and her voice an exasperated whisper. "But there's something about a Glock that's rather comforting."

Laura couldn't argue with that.

"Let me take this to the office and I'll see that you get it back on your way out."

Clara continued chatting with her friends, ignoring the questioning looks about the gun, and explaining what a conservation easement was. She was good. They continued a hot and heavy discussion on Birch Bay politics while Laura smuggled the gun through the crowded dining room.

Some of the regular customers waved and gave a concerned greeting. Laura stopped momentarily, assuring everyone she was safe and that her parents were doing fine, too.

Knut had come in to check on the restaurant during the rush hour. Emily said she'd prefer to stay at home, but Knut wanted her close. Didn't work. Emily was home making supper, waiting for whenever Laura could make it. Knut took Laura in his arms, then questioned the tray.

"Clara had a gun on the floor?" Knut was tired. Maybe he'd heard wrong. He lifted the napkin. "A Glock? Good grief. I wonder how many other people are sitting around with guns hidden on their body some place."

"I know. The media has mentioned citizens with guns in their reporting. Maybe they've been talking to Clara."

"That wouldn't surprise me," said Knut. "I'll follow you home. Your mom has supper waiting."

Wariness ran through Laura as she looked around the parking lot. Montana was asleep on the front seat, so she figured there weren't any bombs planted anywhere on the vehicle.

CHAPTER TWENTY-FIVE

Emily and Knut Hansen's house was a country style home on 160 acres on Mill Pond River just outside Duluth. A law enforcement vehicle was parked at the side of the driveway as Laura drove toward the house.

Emily greeted Laura with hugs, a few tears, and lots of questions. Laura filled her parents in on the investigation. "But there's not a break in the case," she said. "Sam told me he'd let me know if there was any news."

Montana did a thorough inspection of the yard, marking territory, and sniffing everything in sight. Knut brought out a dish of water and some doggie treats.

"I ran downtown and bought some food for Montana," explained Knut. "The store isn't far from the restaurant. Figured we needed to take care of our visiting canine."

Montana thumped his tail and sniffed Knut's pockets.

"When we have our supper, you can have something else to eat," he told Montana. Montana pranced expectantly, a rumble in his throat, and his tail wagging.

"Let's sit on the deck," said Emily. "It's such a glorious evening. We don't get that many warm days in Duluth and another half-hour or so and the mosquitoes will be out in force. We may as well take advantage of the good weather. I have a chicken in the oven that should be ready about the time we need to go inside."

Exquisite views of Lake Superior, an open field, majestic old growth forest, and Mill Pond River were all visible from the large deck. The deck wrapped around the south and east of the house, away from the road and facing the field and woods. Colorful perennial gardens and a multitude of flower boxes filled with annuals were scattered throughout the yard.

"It's wonderful sitting here," said Laura. "Relaxing. Everything that has happened seems so disorienting when I sit here and look at this beautiful land. This whole place insulates a person from the realities of the rest of the world."

Laura spent the next few minutes recounting the events, from the minute of the explosion to the press conference and the visit with Cindy and Hippie.

"That's all I can tell you," she said. "Mikkelson, the FBI, BCA, and all the other agencies are absolutely incredible. Very professional. They're all working together as a real team. Other than that, I'm not privy to any information on the investigation."

"You did a wonderful job at the press conference," said Knut. "It was on CNN and they gave you most of the air time. Very well done."

"Absolutely," said Emily. "We're so proud of you. You've always done well under pressure."

Laura shrugged. "It's all surreal."

"I know," said Emily. "It may always have that effect."

"Why is there a deputy still parked on the road?" asked Laura. "It's obvious the targets were Charlie and Audrey Dahlberg. Why are they protecting you? I was at the scene of the crime so I understand a patrol around my house. Noah was at my house because he's a friend and I'd just witnessed an assassination."

"We've been wondering the same thing," said Knut. "I think it's our connection to Lisa and Mark. Mark was an explosives expert. Lisa worked for us. Mark came to the restaurant a lot. He brought different people with him. Word on the street is that Mark may have supplied the bomb that killed the Dahlbergs."

"Makes sense," said Laura. "I heard that Mark's dad made his living handling explosives for the construction businesses. Lots of talk about Mark and Lisa in Birch Bay, too. When they were first killed, people talked about the drugs found in the car, but then some of the locals started talking about Mark's work with explosives. No one ever expected the Dahlbergs would be a target for assassination."

"I'm sure the FBI is following every lead," said Emily. "From what I heard on CNN, there's an excellent task force at work on this case."

"It's a hardworking team. They're trying very hard not to make any mistakes. Everything is extremely well organized. Still," Laura took in a deep breath and exhaled slowly. "I'm sure they have leads and tips coming in. Have you heard anything from Chief Gunderson?"

"He's making no comments." Knut's accent became heavier, a sign that Laura knew was from agitation. "I'm sure the FBI is working on every angle possible to tie the murders of Lisa and Mark to the assassination. Gunderson has lunch at the restaurant almost every day and I'm sure the men he's with are FBI or BCA or some other law enforcement unit. You can tell Gunderson's under a lot of pressure because his arthritis is flaring up. He's been massaging his hands a lot lately."

"Overheard anything about the case?" asked Laura.

"No. They're perfect professionals. Closed mouth philosophy."

"That's a good thing." Laura took in the peaceful quiet of the land, the place she would always associate with good memories. Somewhere in the distance she heard a dog barking and Montana raised his head, ears alert, sniffing the air. "Have you heard anything from Lisa's family?"

"They're not talking to anyone. Keeping quiet," said Knut. "It's all been a shock."

"Heartbroken," Emily said slowly. "Overwhelmed. The media is persistent in the search for a story." She got up from her chair. "Let's go inside. Supper should be ready."

They walked up the wide timber steps that led to the kitchen door. Smells of spices and chicken and coffee mingled in the air. The kitchen was spacious, exactly the kind of room that guests expected of a family that owned one of the finest restaurants in northern Minnesota.

Familiarity had a comforting feeling. Laura moved to the windows in the living room on the southern part of the house and looked out over the yard and forest beyond. A huge, natural stone fireplace dominated the north wall, flanked by bookcases that held leather-bound classics and knickknacks that reflected the north woods. Carvings of moose and bear, birch bark baskets, and wildflower bouquets were artistically placed among the books.

Leather chairs were mixed with large couches covered in a textured burgundy leaf material. The room was sunny and tastefully decorated. Big wooden planters filled with bright red geraniums were set by the windows.

Paintings by local artists covered the walls. Oils, watercolors, and ink sketches were part of a collection gathered over a number of years. Framed art that the Hansen children had done in elementary school covered one wall.

They ate at the dining room table with a wonderful view of the lake. Emily had prepared a wondrous meal. Despite the burger she'd had earlier, Laura found she was famished. She started with a cup of cheese tomato soup with a brioche and butter. The main course consisted of roast chicken breast baked in a delicate pastry, roasted potatoes sprinkled with chives, thinly sliced green beans with slivered almonds, and portabella gravy. Knut had prepared a side order of mushroom toast that was a specialty of The Oslo House.

It didn't surprise Laura that her mom had spent the afternoon cooking. After Eric died, Emily spent a lot of time at Laura's house in Birch Bay cooking, cleaning, and campaigning. It was a way for Emily to deal with her grief and help Laura at the same time.

"I wish you'd spend the night," said Emily as she served a chocolate torte covered with chocolate ganache and a scoop of ice cream. Coffee was hot with a side of rich cream.

"Can't," said Laura. "I'm leaving early in the morning for St. Paul. Governor Cummings asked me to visit the Dahlberg children and Anne Bradley set up appointments for most of the day tomorrow. It's important that I go right away. Besides, I want people to see me in town tomorrow morning. I can make contact with the early morning crowd at the restaurants and convenience stores. People need to see me around town."

"You certainly finished your walk to the businesses quickly this afternoon," said Knut.

"It doesn't take much time to cover a town that's only a few blocks long. After the press conference, I sort of did a walk through, answered some questions, went out to the Pine Crest Inn and came here. I did skip dinner with the governor, though."

"So how does Sam feel about the attention you're getting from Governor Cummings?" asked Emily. "And I don't mean politics. It seems like Sam is taking an interest in you. Is he a bit jealous?"

"He is totally involved in the case. Right now, that's all I'm interested in, too. I can't imagine the bad guys getting away with this. Law enforcement is focused on catching them very quickly."

Laura's cell phone rang. It was Governor Cummings.

"I'm sorry I didn't make it to dinner," she said. "My mom and dad wanted me to come to Duluth for the evening."

"Of course. I just wanted to make sure you're okay."

"I'm doing fine. Nothing like my mom's cooking to set me at ease."

"Are you staying there overnight?"

"No. I'll be home in Birch Bay tonight."

"Jeez, Laura. It's late. Are you sure you'll be all right?" Jack's voice was husky and there was a slight emotional edge to it.

"I've done this lots of times. You know the drill. Meetings at all sorts of places and then there's the drive home in the dark. I'm used to it."

"Give me a call when you get home so I know you're safe."

"I will."

Laura hung up. "I was going to tell him I had Montana with me, but thought better of it."

Emily smiled. "Probably a good idea. He's probably well aware that Mikkelson finds you attractive and available. Having Mikkelson's dog with you might stir up questions that aren't even worth discussing. Are you sure you won't stay the night?"

Knut agreed. Of course Laura should stay. Rule number one for his kids: Be Safe.

"Sorry."

"It is getting late," said Knut.

Knut's rule number two: We'd love having you home for as long as possible.

"They're expecting me back in Birch Bay tonight. I'll keep in touch."

Knut nodded. Rule number three: Don't get pushy with the kids. They're adults.

Laura honked good-bye as she drove out the long driveway and gave Montana a pat on the head.

Knut picked up the phone and dialed a number. "She just left. You'll check on her when she gets home?"

"Absolutely," said Mikkelson. "I'll be waiting for her. Noah's going to stop by, too."

"Thanks."

Rule number four for Knut: If the kids don't follow your requests, always have a back-up plan.

CHAPTER TWENTY-SIX

The Pine Crest Inn
June 26 - 11:00 p.m.
Birch Bay

Cindy Snyder was busy. The late night crowd was getting drunker, tips were getting bigger, and the noise level was out of sight. Must be nervous tension, she thought. With all the FBI, BCA, and every other federal agency in town, people were downright hyper. She couldn't tell for sure, but she guessed a lot of the bar hoppers were media types. Nothing going on and what else did you do in a small town once it was after eight o'clock at night? Besides, she couldn't imagine the FBI here. They were all straight arrows, on a case, seeking justice. Never mind. Whoever was here, they were good tippers.

She and Hippie were playing a little game; see which one would predict the cigar smokers. Guys that would never light up a cigar on their home turf would haul one out in an out-of-town bar. So far, Hippie was ahead two to nothing.

"Not many cigar puffers in this crowd," said Hippie. "Must be the health conscious group."

"Reporters," said Cindy. "Maybe they pay attention to their own columnists."

Hippie wasn't noticed in the chaos of the drinkers. Cindy was in the limelight. Guys were grabbing and panting and being drunkenly silly. She talked to the bartender about taking some car keys away and then got on the phone to the sheriff's office. Couldn't let these guys drive drunk.

Wally sat at the bar and pulled out his cell phone. Always on vibrate now, it was a damned irritation. Another call from an unknown person was showing on the display. Private name. Private number. Hell if he'd answer it. Had to be that damned Kjelstad woman.

Anne Bradley hadn't tried calling the mysterious number a lot. No one had answered since she'd first tried, but it wouldn't hurt to push a few buttons. Maybe she'd eventually hear a voice. After all, Charlie and Audrey had been assassinated. Evil was lurking somewhere.

The women in the bar looked bored. One of them asked Cindy to turn the damn game off and put on CNN. "At least we can see what's happening in town."

"The big reporters aren't here." One of the women was talking to Cindy, but she hadn't been listening. "They all got invited to some rich guys house over on the lake. They're having steak and very good wine and we're having beer and hamburgers."

"Maybe we're being watched by the FBI," said a young woman with short blonde hair and big blue eyes. "Could be interesting. See anyone that looks like a federal agent?"

No one could tell.

Cindy kept making the rounds. Some nights she got tired of the noise and the mess, but tonight it was a diversion from the tragedy. People needed to work off some of their excess energy. She felt good, useful. In her own small way, she was helping the town.

At first she walked right past him. Then he asked for another beer and she noticed the amalgam tattoo.

"I remember you," she said. "Richard Jamison. Changed your hair color. New clothes, too. Lookin' good." She gave him a wink. "I'll be right back with your drink, sweetheart."

Remembered? How in the hell did she recognize him? Wally's anger seethed. If he were going to give voice to his wrath right now, he would say, "it runneth over". He watched her closely, took the beer when she came back, and handed her a big tip.

"So how do you remember me?" he asked. "And if you're so good, when did you see me last?"

"I never forget a face or a name. Special talent." One thing she never did was tell people how she remembered them. It could make them uncomfortable knowing she was spotting their flaws. For this guy it was the amalgam tattoo. "You've been in here a couple of times before. You like our cheeseburgers, with onions fried 'til they're practically burned. Your exact words. Right?"

"Right. I'll see that you are properly compensated for such an outstanding memory."

"And you like your fries really crisp."

"Right again. Is there anything you don't remember?"

"Not likely. Keep coming in here and I'll probably know your social security number, too. Anything else?"

"That's it for now. I'd like to see you later, though. Special order. Later."

Cindy worked her way through the crowd, making small talk, smiling, generally being the perfect waitress. Hippie watched her with admiration. She got all the attention. The other waitresses were low key, but not Cindy. She'd make triple the tips. Nice thing about Cindy, she always shared her tips with him. Said without his help getting the dishes done, there'd be no work for her. Besides, he brought out the food when it was hot. Customers wanted their burgers and fries steaming.

Half an hour later, the crowd was still raucous. Wally watched Cindy. He needed to talk to her while there were people around; he didn't want to be noticed. He gave a subtle wave when she passed by.

"What can I get for ya, darlin'?"

"I was wondering if you'd take a picture of me outside by the large carving of the moose. I have an excellent camera. I won't be back here again and I want to send the picture to my nephew. He's eight." Wally smiled through the lie. "Every time I find something interesting, I send him a picture. He lives in Idaho and I don't get to see him often so the pictures are a good way to keep in touch. He's a computer whiz so I send him the little mini disk from my camera."

"I'd be glad to. You're sure it will turn out? The outdoor lights aren't very bright."

"My camera will handle it just fine."

"Can you give me a few minutes?"

"No. I need to get back to my motel room and make a phone call. If it gets much later, my friend will have a fit that I've called so late."

"Let's go. We need to make it fast so the boss doesn't see I'm gone too long."

Wally handed her the camera as they walked out the door. The moose carving was at the side of the building, just at the edge of the parking lot. A car was pulling out the driveway, headed toward town. Wally slowed and began limping. Let them see the limp, not the man. Wally waited.

"Ready?" asked Cindy.

"Yes. Let me show you how to work the camera."

He was at her side in an instant; he lunged forward, grabbed her hair and pulled her to the shadows at the side of the building. She started to scream, but he punched her hard in the mouth. A gut-wrenching wail rose from her throat, but Wally's fist smashed into her stomach with such force she staggered backward. She was flailing like a wounded bird, pain rippling through her body, fear rising like fire.

With a sudden burst of fear-driven power, Cindy recovered, thrusting into him with her entire body. Her right fist connected with his face with such strength that he let out a primal scream; she continued the attack with a front snap kick to the chest. He stumbled, floundering to keep his balance, pain sinking into his bones. Cindy clasped his nose, twisting fingers deep into his flesh.

Wally smoldered with venom; his breathing came in ragged puffs. His adrenaline had kicked into madness mode. He broke free, grasped her by the throat and crushed her larynx as his thumb pressed into her flesh.

He shuddered with rage. Grabbing her blouse, he threw her against the side of the building with an intensity that caused her body to stiffen, then crumble as she rolled to the ground. Skull striking concrete made a clunking sound and her head wobbled to the side.

"I would have liked to make this slow," he told her, not sure if she was still conscious. "But you're too damn strong."

It only took seconds to slit her throat. Even in the dark he knew the job was done. The blood was spurting; he could feel the warmth of it covering his hand and he knew it was on his clothes. Another thrust of the knife was too tempting to pass up and another, just for the feel of it. He swung the knife across her face and felt her teeth shatter. He hadn't planned the night to end like this. Of course, there was no way anyone could link him to the murder. Richard Jamison hadn't been in Birch Bay.

Actually, this killing would add to the confusion facing the FBI and all the other fool agencies staying in town. He'd have to report to the boss, but the boss wasn't here and he was. When you were a soldier in the field you got to pick your battles.

He dragged her behind the building, across the service entrance, and dumped her body in the brush behind the Dumpster. The Dumpster was surrounded with red ozier dogwood, hazel brush, and a grove of poplar and birch. Very discreetly hidden from public view.

A squad car was in the parking lot watching for drunks trying to drive home. No matter. He had left his car a couple of blocks away, parked in a row of cars near the house of a man having a party. He'd put his bloody clothes in a garbage bag and dump them in the outdoor bin of a fast food restaurant in Duluth.

Cindy's body would probably be picked over by birds and vermin by the time morning came around.

"Stupid woman." He gave her one more kick and walked through the darkness to his car.

Chapter Twenty-seven

The Pine Crest Inn
Morning
June 27

Coffee was the first thing on Hippie's mind when he walked into work in the morning. The place would be a mess after last night's crowd. Usually there weren't nearly that many people, but Cindy was probably right. They were all media types.

It was never easy cleaning after a large, rowdy crowd had been in the bar. There was a hungover smell in the air, garbage on the floor, and the tables hadn't been completely cleaned. The bathrooms were always the worst, sour and squalid. Drunks were never careful about where they vomited or relieved themselves. He decided to fix some breakfast before he tackled the bathrooms. Grills and coffee pots were turned on first, then he'd start emptying the kitchen garbage while he waited for the grills to heat up.

Aside from the crowd, everything else seemed normal last night. That's why he couldn't figure out where Cindy went. He'd told the boss that someone should check on her, but the boss just laughed. Said she was probably earning some extra cash in the back of a van somewhere.

"She isn't like that," Hippie had told him. "You know she wouldn't do that."

"I know she's one hell of a sex kitten," said Ernie and he pumped his hips back and forth.

"Sex goddess," said the cook. "I'd worship at her temple any time."

"She could make a lot of money offering her services," said Ernie. "Hell, I'd pay her big time myself to get her into bed. There were guys throwing around lots of money last night."

"Acting sexy is how she gets big tips," Hippie had said. "You know that. She's a lot more straight arrow than people give her credit for."

"Whatever." Ernie had sneered, then he turned to one of the waitresses and said: "Hippie's losing a few more links in the chain."

Hippie had hurried outside to see where Cindy had gone, but the parking lot was empty. He had circled the building and found it remarkably quiet. First thing he saw her today, he was going to ask for an explanation. Cindy wasn't the kind to walk away from the big tips.

While the coffee was brewing, Hippie fried some bacon and potatoes, then threw in a couple of eggs. He never drained off the fat. Hell, if all the chemicals in his body didn't finish him off, why should he worry about a little bacon grease? He buttered his toast, slid everything onto a white ceramic dish, and carried it into the dining room.

He sat at the counter, reading the morning newspaper, and ate his breakfast. The front page was still covered with the assassination. Other than that, it didn't say much. Everything was no comment and we cannot give out any information at this time and all the other noncommittal crap. They were all trying to save their asses. Hell, he'd do the same thing.

Still, he considered the involvement of some of the media. It seemed like they were hungry for blood, that they reveled in the tragedy, searching for a way to rise higher in the eyes of the corporate moguls. Some of the reporters stood out. They were the ones who offered a passionate look at the horror that engulfed Birch Bay, examining the effects of the crime on real people.

His mind kept coming back to Cindy. Maybe he should call her. On the other hand, what if she had gone home sick or something and was sleeping in. By the time he cleaned out the place, she'd probably be in for work. She liked to come in early and have Hippie fix her breakfast so they could sit around and talk before the rest of the work crew came in. Their conversations covered everything from world politics to the Vikings football games to women's history. She was a Civil War buff, too, and because of that, he'd started checking out a lot of books and videos about the war.

He brushed his toast over the plate catching the last of the egg yolk, enjoyed the tasty morsel, and finished off his coffee. A few dishes were still in the sink from last night. He had decided to finish up this morning; get an early start and the place would be spotless by the time the rest of the crew came in. Garbage was piled high in all the receptacles and he wanted to empty it before it started smelling. As he expected, the bathrooms were sickening. Pigs.

He slid the plastic garbage bags onto a cart and headed for the Dumpster. It was a beautiful morning and as he walked out the service entrance in the back of the building, he caught a fleeting glimpse of robins in the large birch overhanging the parking lot. His footsteps crunched on some loose gravel and the cart wobbled in front of him.

Red osier dogwood, wild roses, hazel brush, and a grove of birch and poplar trees surrounded the Dumpster. Crows were picking at something on the ground, creating a scene with their boisterous chatter. He caught a fleeting glimpse of a figure behind the Dumpster and wondered if one of the drunks from last night had passed out, left by his buddies. Flanked by wildflowers and bushes, the person was enveloped in shadow.

"Oh, God, no," he cried. It was a Cindy. He screamed and ran toward her, chasing the crows away. Her legs were splayed out in front like a rag doll. She could have been taking a nap, except for the bugs drilling into her body. The branches of a large pine sent lacy shadows across her face, but it didn't hide the fact that birds and vermin had been pecking at her.

Cindy was lying in a broken heap, puddles of blood had coagulated around her; she had been slashed so brutally that bits of teeth were hanging like broken shards of glass. She was like a crushed marionette, pieces of flesh clinging to her hair, gelatinous masses of tissue splashed across the blooming wildflowers. Blood like a dried riverbed had streamed across the parking lot.

He kept screaming, but no one came. His cries were like a howling across the edge of the wilderness.

When the police came, he was holding Cindy in his arms, tears streaming down his face; he was still screaming for help.

CHAPTER TWENTY-EIGHT

Kenmark Neighborhood
St. Paul
June 27

It was early morning when Laura took Highway 169 south, following the route of countless lumbermen of the late nineteenth century. Those first settlers had come by water and rugged trail, working for forty dollars a month. The railroad had reached Grand Rapids in 1890.

Highway 169 moves through a sparsely populated area, wooded, picturesque, and historically important to the growth of the state. Hundreds of lakes of all shapes and sizes dot the area; the whole Lake Park region is famous for it's beauty; the rugged morainic topography had been sculpted by post glacial erosion.

As she neared St. Paul, she took the Selkirk exit off the freeway, finding Kenmark Square and the Kenmark Hotel well marked. The neighborhood smoothly transformed from freeway clutter to well-manicured, exclusive homes, giving the distinct impression that the very rich lived and worked here.

Laura did a quick survey of the affluent neighborhood: flowering shrubs, lovely ponds, and well-designed office buildings stretched to the west. Sunny skies seemed to be the harbinger of the coming day. The radio said the high was expected to be in the low eighties with sunshine lasting through the afternoon, a typical Twin Cities June day. Chance of a possible thunderstorm toward evening.

The Kenmark Hotel was St. Paul's most exclusive hotel. It had a definite upscale feel to it - elegant, impressive, catering to the ultra-rich. Well-dressed, high energy guests slipped in and out discreetly. It was one of many hotels and restaurants owned by Charlie and Audrey Dahlberg.

Laura parked the car and checked her make-up in the visor mirror. Her cheeks and lips needed a hint of color and her eyes required some delicate accents. She had decided to wear her comfortable flax colored slacks of pebbled linen and a dressy white blouse. Simple gold earrings and a gold chain gave just the right touch.

The chemicals in her body were joining forces, energy rising with the adrenaline rush. Emotions were close to the surface and a tenseness was moving through her shoulders and neck putting her on edge, the brain on high alert.

Anne Bradley was already drinking coffee when Laura walked in. Laura extended her hand and Anne reached forward projecting an image of composure and self-confidence. She had strong hands and long luminous nails painted a very pale shade of pink.

"I hope I'm not late," said Laura. "Sorry to keep you waiting."

"I'm early. Habit." Anne's voice was throaty and mellow, with precise diction that would be perfect on radio or in the theater. "I always like to be prompt. Whenever I scheduled things for Charlie, I made sure to get him there five minutes early. It impressed the hell out of everybody. Usually, you have to wait for the big shots to show up. Not Charlie. He and I were on the same wavelength when it came to meetings. Never keep anyone waiting. They'd get testy or talky or lose track of why they were there. Charlie would be early and greet people as they came in the door."

Anne's face was smooth, skin as creamy as any model. She had a well-defined chin and large eyes that were a glorious shade of blue. Her light brown hair, with just a few strands of gray, was cut in a soft wave framing her face, falling pageboy style at the nape of her neck.

She exuded sophistication and wealth, giving the appearance of a high-paid CEO in any number of Minnesota's companies. Her makeup was expertly applied, her brows feathered, and her lips glossy with just a hint of color. She wore a knee length, tweed tulip skirt, with six panels of lightweight material. Her short sleeved white sweater was airy cotton, embroidered and beaded giving it a soft shimmer.

Anne rubbed shoulders with CEOs, heads of government, movie stars, and national celebrities. Charlie had friends across the board and had gained a national following. Several Hollywood types had given their support if he wanted to make a run for the presidency. Anne was at the center of all the fundraising, conversations, and conventions. Charlie hadn't given any indication that he'd seek a higher office, but he was a great campaigner and fundraiser. He was a hit on the speaking circuit for the party.

"You probably have a multitude of questions for me," said Anne. "I have the schedule for the day in this file with maps showing you exactly where to go. You've probably noticed this neighborhood has lots of trees and gardens and the streets circle and meander to give a secluded look to the houses."

Laura looked briefly at the file. "Thanks. Tell me how you're doing. I know this has all been dreadful for you."

"I've been keeping busy." Anne paused for a moment. Her face was calm and when she spoke, her voice was controlled, no stress visible. "I'm cleaning out my office. I told Governor Cummings that I'd have Charlie's things out as soon as the FBI lets me in the office. Jack can't get in yet, either. That's probably one of the reasons he's in Birch Bay. At least he can be near the investigation. Government is sort of at a standstill here right now anyway."

"I only know what I've been watching on network news."

"They've been fairly accurate. You're the one we've been concerned about. You and Molly. I can't imagine being witness to such a horrific crime."

"We're keeping busy."

"Good. I don't know if you know all the details yet, but Charlie and Audrey's family is planning a memorial service tomorrow in Birch Bay. They've been talking to Molly and there will be a gathering at Raspberry Point Inn. Molly's going to serve food outside on long tables for anyone who wants to join in. No one can get near the Dahlberg property yet, but the family is going out in some boats and they'll get a look at the house from the water. The FBI won't let anyone too close, but it's important for the family that they get up there."

"I understand," said Laura. "It'll be good for them to talk to people in the area. Is the community invited?"

"Absolutely. Molly said the Inn could handle the numbers. They've hosted lots of big parties."

Laura studied Anne's face. It didn't show the strain of the last couple of days, but her voice was hoarse and strained.

"What are your plans for the future?" asked Laura. "Has Jack made arrangements for staff?"

"He asked me to stay on, but I declined. I couldn't think of being in the office after what's happened. Too many memories. I'll help Jack make the transition and help interview candidates for the top jobs. Then I'm going back into the antique business. That's what I was doing before I joined Charlie's campaign. After my husband died I needed something to keep me occupied so I opened Tin Tub Antiques on Market Lane. My sister has been running it for me since I've been working in the governor's office. She's thinking we should open an antique shop over in Hastings. Sounds like a great idea to me. It's something we both enjoy and having a second shop will help us stay busy without either of us getting annoyed. We love each other dearly, but sometimes, it's best to keep a little separation."

A waitress brought more coffee. Laura commented that the atmosphere was exquisite and Anne agreed. Orbed, silk-screened light fixtures cast a delicate glow over the Tuscany-style tiled tables; exposed brick walls were imaginatively decorated with abstract wrought iron figures. A collection of very old picnic baskets was arranged on one wall with a short informative paragraph detailing the age and origin of each. An outdoor garden jutted playfully along the edges of the hotel ending with a waterfall that cascaded toward a pool.

Anne reached in her purse and took out a small notebook. She tore off a page and handed it to Laura. "I don't know if this might be important or not," she said. "I don't understand the workings of the FBI. Charlie gave this phone number to me before he went up to Birch Bay. He said we needed to talk about it when he got back. That's all he said."

"Do you think it might have something to do with his death?"

"I don't know."

"I'll call Noah right away and give him the number. Noah is my feed to the FBI."

"Isn't he wonderful?" said Anne.

"He is a gem."

Anne stood and shook Laura's hand. "I'll see you tomorrow at the memorial for Charlie and Audrey."

Laura went to her car, called Noah with a report, and studied the map.

Anne drove home, but not knowing the owner of the phone number bothered her. What would it hurt just to call? If it was a business, she could let Laura know that tomorrow. She parked in the alley behind her house and called the number.

Wally looked at the number on the incoming call. "Who is this?" he asked.

Anne hung up. She hadn't recognized the voice. At least no one could trace the cell phone number to her. It would just say 'private name, private number'. She was anonymous as far as the person on the other end of the line was concerned.

She would try again later, just in case she could glean some information.

Wally held the phone and wondered how anyone had gotten his number. Only the boss had this number. Someone was meddling where they didn't belong. Just like the damn mayor, walking up

NORTHERN EXPLOSION

and down the streets being chatty and all ears. Not that anyone knew anything. Still, the mayor had been out to see Cindy. Then Cindy recognized him.

Mayor Kjelstad was starting to make him seethe. Eliminating Cindy had been quite satisfying. He hadn't contemplated killing again so soon, but the thought energized him. Killing Kjelstad would be pleasurable. Wally was sinking into his pool of evil.

167

CHAPTER TWENTY-NINE

Laura pulled out of the parking lot, turned right on Kenmark Boulevard, and drove through Kenmark Square. She noted the distinct subdivision of the Kenmark community, the comparative hierarchy that shouted ultra rich. Personal real estate had to be assessed in the millions of dollars. Flowers, shrubs, and ponds dotted the area; size and number of gardens were another measure of wealth. Driveways were long, lined with trees probably planted after the house was built; they were too perfectly arranged to be natural. Besides, this had been farm country and forty-foot Norway pine would not have been native to this area. Some of the trees would have been delivered by helicopter, the only way to deliver massive sized conifers so the homeowners could live in a forested area without waiting twenty years for the tree to reach a pleasing height.

Most houses were on lots the size of a square block, professionally landscaped, and right off the cover of an architectural magazine. Many of the homes had guesthouses, large garden sheds, and four-stall garages. Storage was necessary for every motorized, mechanized vehicle possible. Something for every season.

Rose and Bill Haugen lived on Elm Creek Lane on a lot larger than any other in the neighborhood. The house was spectacular, stone and glass dominated the front. Berms throughout the front entrance added visual interest and defined boundaries between driveway, walking paths, and gardens. A sloping path of red brick led to the double-glass doors and a dramatic garden of colorful annuals was set off to the right, accenting an exceptionally large weeping willow that majestically ruled the yard.

Off to the west, a berm about three feet high and forty feet in diameter was filled with Scotch pine, loblolly pine, and white cedar. Flowering shrubs and prairie grasses filled in the outer sections giving added privacy to the already secluded house.

Before Laura was out of the car, a very attractive young woman opened the doors of the house.

Rose Haugen was Charlie and Audrey's daughter. Raised in wealth, she nevertheless had a down to earth sensibility about her.

Rose hugged Laura warmly, then brushed back tears.

"Sorry." Rose wiped her eyes with a tissue and drew in a shallow breath. "I really should be all cried out by now. Bill had to go into the office to pick up some sympathy cards that were sent there. Everything's piling up."

Laura put an arm around her, holding her, a silence engulfed them and a shudder went through Rose's body.

"You've never been here," said Rose. "Let me show you around."

The house was stunning. The living room literally flowed into the dining area, an early nineteenth century hutch the only division between the two rooms. The hutch was filled with antique blue willow dishes, a collection of rosemalled boxes, and blue stoneware.

"I think I need a couple of minutes to get the tears under control," said Rose. "It'll help to talk about something else."

Laura didn't need to ask what the 'something else' was. Charlie and Audrey's deaths had permeated the whole country. Since Eric's death, she'd come to understand clearly the horror of a sudden loss.

"I'll show you around and then we can sit down and be comfortable while we talk."

"I'd be delighted," said Laura. "It's a lovely home." Understatement, but words failed her at the moment.

"We designed the house to be a place where family and friends could feel welcome," said Rose as she led the way into the kitchen. She wiped her eyes and blew her nose. "Cynthia Varese designed the glazed stoneware in the hutch especially for me. The yellow-ware belonged to my mother. She thought it looked better displayed here with all the wood walls and cabinets."

Rose began crying again. "I'll be right back. Maybe if I splash some cold water on my face. Please, look around."

Usually, Rose was a bubbly, vibrant woman. She had wide-set brown eyes that seemed to be perpetually smiling, like she had just heard an amusing story. Rose's hair was a soft pile of brown curls, parted on the side, and she wore just the faintest amount of make-up that was so artfully done it seemed like her natural skin tones. She was about Laura's height, but slightly heavier, a becoming plumpness that gave her the look of a 1950s model. Flawless skin gave a healthy glow to her appearance and when Laura had first met Rose, she thought of the smiling women on the old Coke ads.

"Your kitchen is absolutely marvelous," called Laura, looking around at the clerestory windows on the west, floor to ceiling windows on the south, and a twelve-foot butcher-block center island. A six burner stove, indoor grill, two ovens, and a large refrigerator fit nicely in the architecturally designed kitchen.

A walk-in pantry was near the refrigerator and a half wall of built-in bookcases running floor to ceiling added texture and dimension to the room. Fluted pilasters, crowns, and arches presented a visual counterpoint to the fireplace in the adjoining room. Decorative redware, framed photos, and a collection of antique school lunch pails was artfully arranged among shelves of cookbooks. A walnut side chair, patterned in a balloon-back, was placed near the floor to ceiling window, allowing one to sit and view the backyard gardens.

Stunning, old black and white photographs of the Twin Cities area hung in the family room.

"Framed by Miranda Estes. A master, don't you think?" asked Rose as she returned, wiping her eyes with her fingertips. "These are all photos from before the mid 1950s."

"Your kitchen is just right for a gathering of cooks. Do you do some of your cookbook writing here?"

"I do. Sometimes I have lots of people in to test recipes for me so I need the big kitchen. Before I approve a cookbook for publication, I try all the recipes. People like to cook; there's an atavistic need to prepare food and the cookbook industry is strong."

"Did I hear that you might do a show for The Food Channel?"

"They've been talking to me. Right now, that's the farthest thing from my mind. My brain seems scattered in all directions. Listen. Let me get you some iced tea or soda. And some cookies."

Rose pointed to a worn nineteenth century French farmhouse table in front of the windows. "Please sit down and make yourself comfortable. Tea or soda?"

"Tea, please."

Laura watched as Rose took large antique glasses from one side of the cupboards, dropped in some ice cubes, and poured the tea. She handed out napkins decorated with plump blueberries and a gold swirl and set the cookies in front of them.

"You never expect something like this to happen," said Rose. "Mom and Dad were in excellent health, exercising, eating right. Did you know they wouldn't have anything with caffeine? They hardly ever touched alcohol." Rose dabbed at her eyes.

Laura reached across and took hands.

"The grandkids have had a tough time," said Rose. How do you explain it?"

"You can't. Assassination is incomprehensible. All we can do is find out who did it." Laura tried not to think of the smell of smoke, the ground shaking, and watching Charlie and Audrey become human torches. It was a memory that she would not share with the family, a memory that needed to be tucked into the shadows of her brain. Right now, keeping that shadowed door shut was impossible. She felt the adrenaline pumping.

Laura gave Rose a quick recap of the investigation in Birch Bay, from the 911 call she'd made to the press conference and conversations she'd had with people in town. "How are plans coming for the memorial service in Birch Bay tomorrow?"

Rose looked pensive. "Fine. Molly is handling everything. It's going to be simple. No big speeches. Pastor Wallsten from Concordia Lutheran will share a few thoughts and that's basically it. We don't want a big fuss. Mom and Dad wouldn't want that. There have been offers from across the country for senators and governors to give testimonials, but we've declined. They're all welcome to come to the memorial in Birch Bay, but we've scheduled a funeral in St. Paul as soon as the FBI gives us the okay to bury the bodies. That might be a more appropriate place for everyone to gather. Even there, it's going to be strictly a religious occasion. We will celebrate their lives and their faith. No political speeches. Period."

"It's what Charlie and Audrey would have wanted."

Rose relaxed a bit and took another bite of a sugar cookie. "I'm glad you're here, Laura." She brushed a crumb from her mouth with the napkin. "Did you see any FBI agents when you drove down the street?"

"No. Have they been around?"

"They've questioned all of us. Even my kids. They've got the governor's mansion all taped off and they have Mom and Dad's house surrounded with agents. Dad's office is unavailable for any business. All the state offices are under twenty-four hour security now. It's worked out great that Molly has let Jack use Raspberry Point Inn."

"But no FBI around now?"

"I'm sure they're in the neighborhood. Did you see a Cable Repair Service truck on the street?"

"No. I saw a lawn service truck."

"Probably the FBI. A couple of hours ago it was the cable truck. I think we're under surveillance. Not sure what they'll find out. I don't know if they're trying to protect us or watching to see who stops by. There have been a lot more joggers and bikers in the neighborhood than usual."

Rose walked to the bookshelf and took down a large box painted in a scroll and leaf pattern. She raised the lid and took out some pictures, letters, and a notebook.

"Mom gave this box to me quite a while ago. She was always worried about someone getting her private writings when she was living in the governor's mansion. Both my parents were journal writers and they kept copies of letters they wrote. They thought it would be part of history some day. Mom enjoyed visiting the archives at the Minnesota Historical Society. She was fascinated with letters and diaries that the early pioneer women had written. It wasn't conceit or ego. It was a sense of history. She said a hundred years from now, maybe someone would want to read what a woman of our time had to say about current affairs.

"I'm not up to reading through them now. It could be a very long time before any of us wants to look at them. Maybe they will give a clue into what happened. We'd like you to read them."

"May I take them with me?" asked Laura.

"Please, do. Take the whole box. Read them whenever you like. Julia has Mother's laptop that we've decided you should take. Ken and Carl and I trust you implicitly."

"Have you looked through the documents on the laptop?"

"No. I know Mom has a separate e-mail address that she only accessed from this computer. She kept the computer here. We've wondered if Mom or Dad had any inkling of danger."

Danger, thought Laura. Like murder.

CHAPTER THIRTY

Laura drove west along Elm Creek Lane circling the Dahlberg properties, all very exclusive and private. She hadn't taken time to look through the box that Rose had given her. She'd have plenty of time when she got back to Birch Bay.

Dahlberg Park was on the south side of the lane. The family had put eighty acres of land in a residential park. It was great for the neighborhood and sent land values up even more. The family had influenced the design of the houses in the area; they wanted to control the type of residences being built. They had worked with architects and buyers to keep the type of neighborhood everyone wanted.

The Dahlbergs had a real golden touch. They also had a sense of responsibility attached to their wealth. The Dahlberg Family Foundation gave away huge amounts of money. Julia Dahlberg, Ken's wife, was the head of the foundation. Julia studied the proposals, became knowledgeable about the details of every request, and did the research and follow-up with the people involved in the implementation of the work.

Julia met Laura at the door. She was petite, slender, with short brown hair and flawless skin. She had a well-defined chin, small nose, and full lips with carefully applied lipstick. Her hands were small, fingers bare except for a simple gold band on her left hand. She wore loose khaki slacks and a boxy ribbed tee in light blue denim, a simple gold chain hung around her neck. Julia had a poise that was unforced, nothing about her was affected.

Laura smiled, going through the greetings that had become part of her day. Julia closed the door, pushed buttons on the touch pad for the security system, and led the way into the kitchen.

"Coffee's hot. There's iced tea in the fridge. Cookies are on the counter. What would you like?"

"Coffee, please," said Laura.

Julia and Ken's house, wondrously designed, was another tribute to wealth. The flow throughout the house was comfortable.

"The ceiling beams are recycled from an old farmhouse near Ortonville," said Julia. "Let me show you around. The guys are on the way. Michelle, Carl's wife is already in Birch Bay getting things ready for the memorial service tomorrow."

Laura found the house fascinating. Stained glass windows from an 1890s church that was demolished. Kitchen cabinets made from old lumber from a one-room school that was being torn down. An intimate living room, anchored by a double-sided fireplace, had bookshelves jutting toward the back wall.

Several old butter churns, antique teapots, and an assortment of aged rolling pins were displayed throughout the cupboards. Julia noted that artist Ian Riley designed the Redware. "The watercolors were done by Marcia Scott Winthrop. She had a show in Birch Bay a couple of years ago."

"She's coming back to do a show in the fall," said Laura.

Julia went to a grand expanse of window and pointed out a large guesthouse, studio, garage, and garden house. A large patio and lush gardens were centered among the buildings. The architecture was strong and simple.

"Let me show you outside until Ken and Carl get here," said Julia. "I'm sure they'd like to be part of any conversation about Charlie and Audrey."

"Those metal bird sculptures are striking," said Laura as they sat down on brightly painted Adirondack chairs under a towering oak tree.

The gardens were exceptional, including a water garden complete with a gently flowing waterfall. Julia remarked about the birdhouses, twenty of them, all individualized by artist Maura Hayes.

"Rose said you might have Audrey's laptop for me," said Laura. "She gave me one box, but said you may have more for me to take back to Birch Bay."

"I do. We've all agreed not to look at anything right now. It's things from both Charlie and Audrey. They wanted to keep some things private and worried about keeping things in the governor's mansion. It was way too open and public. They enjoyed living there and hosting events, but they felt a keen sense of history and wrote down some very strong opinions. As you know, they were quite critical of the current president. They thought their writing would add to the state's history a hundred years from now, but right now none of us can handle going through them. There are postcards and pictures and journal entries. None of us has the heart to look at anything for a while. Our emotions are quite raw. Ken and Carl are getting edgy; they want to find the guy that did this and they're not too patient."

"The FBI is doing all they can."

"They know that…" Julia rubbed her hands across her face. "I don't know how we're going to handle the memorial service and funeral. It's all so public and we really need private family time."

Laura saw how vulnerable Julia looked, showing signs of shrinking from within. How did someone cope with the assassination of their in-laws? Parents? It was a place that very few people had ever been.

"I'm having trouble accepting the fact that Charlie and Audrey are dead," said Julia. "Assassinated. I can't seem to synthesize the fact that they're gone."

Ken and Carl, the Dahlberg sons, walked across the lawn. They went through the introductory rituals, hugging Laura, thanking her for coming.

Ken was the older brother, lithe and agile, moving with athletic ease. His hair was the color of honey, shaded with blonde streaks that were natural, probably from being in the sun playing tennis and golf. Prominent cheekbones were nature's gift, giving him a model's good looks and adding to the prosperous upper-class style that was intrinsic to everything around him. His dark blue eyes conveyed a sadness, a melancholy over the death of his parents.

Carl had smooth skin, with just a few wrinkles in the corners of his blue eyes, genuine laugh lines that added charm to his good looks. He had always been irrepressibly good-humored, smiling brightly, charming his guests. Not today. His look was grim, shadows hugged his eyes, and his mouth was set in a hard line. He brushed the golden hair from his forehead and shook his head wearily.

Carl and Ken were dressed in business casual. Carl had on a pair of tailored twills the color of wheat and a short-sleeved classic oxford white shirt. Ken's outfit consisted of khaki chinos and a three-button polo, also in white.

"We always enjoyed going to Raspberry Point Inn," began Carl. "Birch Bay was special to us. We all loved fishing at Cranberry Lake. We had fun together. What in the hell is going on?"

Laura regarded them all as friends. She crossed her arms and said: "I have no idea."

"Sorry," said Carl. "It must have been terrible being there. Witnessing the brutality. I don't know how to deal with this. That's one of the reasons I won't give a public statement. Keep my mouth shut so I don't embarrass the memory of my parents. At first I was so overwhelmed I cried and cried. Then the anger set in and it's still there. If I ever get my hands on the damn..." He lowered his head, rubbed his eyes, and held onto the bridge of his nose.

"We all feel that way," said Ken. "We're sad, angry, hopeless. You name it. We've run the gamut of emotions. Then we sit here. Empty. Our kids are with my dad's brother. We're trying to keep them out of sight."

"And safe," said Julia. "We don't know if someone has the intention of harming another family member."

"How are you keeping the kids safe?" asked Laura. She was incredulous and it showed. "They're all in one place. Doesn't that make them more vulnerable? What kind of protection can you give them? If another bomb is detonated, you lose your whole family."

"The bomb squad went through the house, all the out buildings, and surrounding property. We've hired some retired cops to keep an eye on the place to give round the clock security," said Carl. "The FBI has some agents watching us and the local police are checking the house. We figured it would be easier to have law enforcement watch the family if they were all in one spot. They may not be worried about us, but we have used all the political clout we could muster to make sure our kids are protected."

"Plus there's Uncle Harold and the men cousins," said Ken. "I wouldn't want to mess with any of the Harold Dahlberg family."

Laura knew what they meant. Harold's sons were big, strong, excellent marksmen and highly intelligent. They also were black belts in Tae Kwon Do.

"Rose said you had some information for me," said Laura.

"Just the laptop and a few files," said Julia. "Unless Ken or Carl have anything they want to share."

"That's the frustrating part," said Carl. "We don't have a clue. There was the usual political back stabbing, but that's par for politics. Assassination doesn't fit. Our parents were nice people."

"Doesn't it seem strange that they didn't want to keep personal papers in the governor's residence?" asked Laura. "Were they afraid of somebody?"

"They never said that," said Ken. "Never gave any indication that anything was wrong. You have to remember that they were two very public people that had kept their family affairs quiet."

"Have you told the FBI about the boxes?"

"No." Carl cut her off before she could ask another question. "They asked so many questions that my mind was numb. I never thought about the letters and papers that Mom mailed to us. Now I'm not sure I want the FBI to see them."

"Mailed?"

"Sometimes Mom would write something and drop it in the mailbox to be sure it got to one of us."

"And you think it was just for history?" asked Laura. "It sounds like she may have been worried about something or someone. Why wouldn't you want to give them to the FBI? They're trying to find out who killed your parents."

"We're not sure we can trust them. Our dad was governor of the state. The party wanted him to run for the presidency. Doesn't it seem possible that someone didn't want that to happen? We want someone to read everything before it goes to the FBI. Once it's in their hands, it's public. Sure, they'll keep it under wraps for a while, but eventually the media will demand disclosure. Someone will scream cover up if the FBI doesn't show everything. They can't disclose what they've never seen. You're someone we can trust."

Laura studied their faces. They were a loving family. She had witnessed that. Church members. Civic leaders. Ken was president of his church's congregation and Carl had been the church treasurer. Rose was a Sunday School teacher. They were good corporate citizens, had their own philanthropic foundation, and supported several charities.

Something evil was lurking in the shadows. A prince of darkness had moved in on the family; the picket fence traded for a cast of demons.

Chapter Thirty-one

Birch Bay
Evening – June 27

News of Cindy Snyder's murder spread to all the households of Nordland County and flashed throughout the community with a flood of inaccuracies. Telephones rang, people chatted on street corners, and merchants and customers gave commentary to every media person that had camera or pen. The crowd gathered outside the Big Timber Cafe was in animated conversation.

"So what did Cindy Snyder ever do wrong? She was sexy, but that's no need to kill her."

"Could be some jealous wife."

"Hit with a hammer, she was. Blood all over everything. They'll never get those blood stains out of the car."

"She wasn't in a car. I heard they found her in the bathroom at Pine Crest Inn."

"The way I heard it there wasn't much blood at all. A clean blow to the back of the neck."

"She was shot right between the eyes. Gang style. Done by a pro."

"I heard she was hit by a car when she was leaving for home. Deliberate of course."

Laura and Noah walked into the cafe to have a late supper. As they were seated, Sam Mikkelson moved across the room and joined them. A couple of tables away, the conversation was centered on Cindy's murder.

"Yeah, but that means there's a killer running around loose. Does sort of send goose bumps up and down the old bod, don't it."

"I'm mostly worried about walking the streets. It would be easy for some crazy nut to open fire. He could kill a street full of people before anyone even knew what was happening."

"He? It could be a she."

"Someone could walk in here and start shooting. Are we really safe anywhere? I mean. If they kill the governor and his wife, none of us are safe."

Mikkelson waved to a young man walking by, smiled, and said," Hey, Ryan. Next time you wave, use all your fingers."

"Oh no man, was that you? I thought it was the new deputy. Don't even know his name, but he gave me a speeding ticket."

"For speeding?"

"Well, yeah. He seen I was a local, but kept on writing out the ticket. That's who I thought it was. Honest. I'd never give you the finger, Sam. You know that."

"I do. I expect you to give all the deputies the same respect you show me."

"Right."

"Make sure you follow the speed limit."

"Sure." Ryan stuck out his chest and winked. "Be on my best behavior."

Laura moved to the side as the waitress set the food in front of them. Sam moved toward her and put his arm across the back of her chair. Something about the gesture was so comforting that Laura let out a breath. "It's so good to be home," she said. "I missed all of you today. Thanks for calling about Cindy's murder." She reached across and took Sam's hand. "Hearing the news about Cindy was so overwhelmingly sad that I just needed to see a friendly face. Thanks, you two."

"Are you going to the Inn after this?" asked Sam. "I know you wanted people to see you out and about, but Molly has some dessert ready for you later on. I need to get back to headquarters."

"I'm going over there as soon as I'm finished eating," she said. "Molly told me that she's given Hippie a room there for a few nights. He's quite distraught and Molly didn't want him to spend a night alone. There's lots of activity at the Inn." She paused reflectively. The boxes and laptop in her car were going to her house, but no one needed to know that. Not until she'd had a chance to read through the journals and letters that the Dahlbergs had entrusted to her.

Forty-five minutes later, Noah and Laura were in Molly's apartment. Governor Jack Cumming's temporary office was down the hall, his accommodations were one floor below, right next to Hippie. Hal Marshall was serving refreshments.

"Chocolate torte for everybody?" he asked.

"Of course," said Molly, not waiting for anyone to answer. "There's coffee, tea -hot or iced, milk, soda. Everybody just help yourself. I need some hot tea to soothe my nerves. Not iced. Good, hot tea always settles the nerves. Too bad there's not a shot of brandy in here. Oh well. I'll have some chocolate torte, too, with a scoop of ice cream. Eating tends to ease the stress, especially chocolate." She absentmindedly pulled at the waistband of her slacks and ran her hand over her stomach. "That's a scientific fact. It's better to be a little overweight than to let your nerves send the blood pressure up."

"I'm on my third aspirin," said Hal, not sure where the conversation was headed.

Laura walked to the window; the moon moved to the west, sending shadows across the lawn and touched the lake with shimmering flecks of gold.

She moved across the room and looked out on the lane where she'd parked her car under a bright security light. Whatever was in the papers she had been given, they were important to Charlie and Audrey. The journals needed to be kept somewhere safe and there was lots of security at the Inn. She couldn't take a chance on anyone seeing her take the boxes inside. Besides, Molly would be too full of questions. Even if there were nothing important in what she found, just day to day writings, other people wouldn't know that. If word got out that she had some papers of the Dahlbergs, someone might try to steal them just to sell them to the tabloids.

"I hope the media leaves everyone alone during the memorial service," said Laura.

Molly considered that for a moment. "I know what you mean. The Dahlbergs are grief stricken, but they'll put on their public faces. You know how the tabloids do it. Cut and paste and make up a sentence out of paragraphs worth of words. It's happened all too often."

"I don't suppose there's any way of keeping the media away during the memorial tomorrow."

"Maybe," said Molly. "There's lots of law enforcement around this place. Gary's coming home early tomorrow. He'll make sure the Dahlbergs are left alone. After all, this is private property."

"How is Gary's mother doing?" asked Laura.

"His mother's the one that insisted that he come home. Said he should be with me. One of the grandkids is staying with her for a few days and then will drive her up here."

"Her knee still doing okay?" asked Noah.

"Remarkably so. She's quite a woman." Molly sighed. "It'll be good to have Gary home. There are lots of people here, but I'm still very lonely. I need him."

"What time is the memorial service tomorrow? Asked Laura.

"Three o'clock. The Dahlberg family is going out on the water first and then they'll be coming to the Inn. It's going to be a very informal gathering on the beach."

"I think I'll make some visits first thing tomorrow," said Laura. "Maybe talk to Gloria Minot. I might go over to the art gallery, too, and see what they have to say about the Dahlbergs. Charlie and Audrey recently bought some paintings."

"What would they tell you that they didn't tell the FBI?" asked Molly.

"Maybe nothing. It gives me something to do."

Molly wasn't surprised. Working kept her mind off things, too. "Good plan."

Noah recapped his day at Homeland Security and the Minneapolis FBI office.

"There's not a thing they know that we don't already have on all our computers here. I didn't think there would be any information, but it doesn't hurt to have someone checking in with them. I didn't apply pressure, but the very fact that I was there sent a strong message that screw-ups won't be tolerated."

"What about your day with the Dahlberg kids?" asked Molly. "How are they doing?"

"As expected, they're overwhelmed." Laura explained the plans for keeping Charlie and Audrey's grandkids safe. "The whole Dahlberg family will come in a car caravan tomorrow with the FBI and Homeland Security providing a safety net."

"Which means they'll fake the car trip and fly up," said Molly. "Or maybe they'll pretend to fake it and really drive. Well. Whatever."

There was a knock on the door and Hippie came into the room looking as forlorn as Laura had ever seen him. His eyes were bloodshot and his clothes were disheveled.

"I was lonely downstairs," he said. "You said I could come up for dessert."

Molly and Hal both rushed to get him some coffee and torte.

"Unless you'd prefer soda," said Molly.

"Or milk," said Hal.

"Coffee's fine," said Hippie. "Thanks for letting me stay here, Mrs. Berg. I couldn't have stood being home alone tonight. It was terrible. I can't forget the way she looked. Someone has to be insane. They brutalized her."

Laura watched the group, grateful for friends who cared. Hippie was clearly devastated.

It was one o'clock in the morning before she went home. There was a lot of fussing about her staying alone. Noah and Sam followed her, but didn't ask questions when she carried the boxes and laptop inside.

"I have some work to do," she said. "Part of the mayor's job. Lots of homework." Noah and Sam never asked about city council business; she wasn't about to give them any other information. She had promised the Dahlberg family to keep the files confidential.

She argued when Sam and Noah wouldn't leave. She insisted. She finally left them at her dining room table, took Montana with her into the bedroom and shut the door. Let them stay up all night talking Navy SEAL business if that's what they wanted. She needed her sleep.

Still, there was something rather special about having Sam and Noah worried about her.

She fell asleep wondering if anyone else was on the killer's hit list.

CHAPTER THIRTY-TWO

Hollingsworth Galleries
Duluth
June 28

The Hollingsworth Gallery was on Mitchell Street high on the hill overlooking Lake Superior. Hippie had asked to ride along; he said he was too nervous to stay in Birch Bay and he'd help watch Montana. He stayed in the car reading the newspaper; Montana moved into the driver's seat as soon as Laura got out of the car.

Bonnie Hollingsworth opened her office door looking as if she'd just walked off the pages of Vogue. She wore a high collared gold silk blouse, long white skirt, and stiletto heels that would have been too high for most runway models.

"You are such a darling little thing," she said. "How tall are you?"

"Five four," said Laura.

"I'm six feet. Then I add a few inches with my heels."

Ms. Hollingsworth motioned Laura to sit down at a group of chairs in front of a small glass table. She took a chair opposite Laura and crossed her legs. The skirt had a long slit at both sides, showing beautiful legs. Stylish, yet seductive. Her thick golden hair was glowing, the sun coming from the window highlighted her hair as if an artist had designed it. She knew exactly where to sit to have the advantage.

"Thanks for seeing me," said Laura. "I wondered if you had any clues about what happened to Charlie and Audrey."

"They were wonderful people. I'm as shocked as anybody."

"I imagine law enforcement has talked to you."

"Of course. And the media. I keep giving a no comment, but they don't take the hint."

"Did you help Charlie and Audrey select the paintings for their house?"

"I was their designer. When it came time to hang the paintings, I went out to their lake house and helped Audrey decide where they should go. You know, Audrey was there alone sometimes. She liked the quiet and solitude, but she could hardly wait until Charlie could come up to the house. They tried not to be away from each other overnight."

"She was a busy person, active in lots of organizations. But you're right. Nights they were together as often as possible."

Bonnie considered her next words carefully. Assassination didn't fit the picture of Charlie and Audrey at all. Had she been wrong? "She was a nice woman. Good mother, great wife. Those two were deeply in love. You could see it when they were around each other. Did you ever see the way they touched each other? They held hands, they liked to sit by each other on the couch. She'd lean into him and he would put his arm around her. You don't see that between husband and wife often. Especially after they've been married a few decades."

"Were you invited to the lake house often?"

"An occasional party. I think Charlie and Audrey just enjoyed being together in Birch Bay. Just family. They enjoyed entertaining, but family time was important to them. Their kids were always busy with work in the Cities so when they came up here, they kept the time private."

"Did you ever see anyone hanging around the place when you were there?"

"You mean like somebody walking on the beach or something?"

"Anybody at all that didn't seem to belong?"

"No. Kids walked on the beach. A boy down the road cut through the driveway sometimes. That was it."

"Do you know the name of the boy?"

"Lance. I don't remember his last name, but he skipped through the yard frequently. Nice kid."

Laura thought about the very bright child who right now needed FBI protection. If Bonnie Hollingsworth knew his name, there was a good chance that the assassin would eventually learn about Lance. How long would law enforcement watch out for him? No one had protected Cindy.

"Did you know Cindy Snyder?" asked Laura.

"Sure. I went out to the Pine Crest to eat on occasion. She was a great entertainer. All that sexiness radiating from her. Quite a show. I guess it's going to take a while for me to grasp that Charlie and Audrey and Cindy have been murdered."

"You mentioned how much Charlie and Audrey loved each other. Did you ever see anything to the contrary? Was there any reason for you to doubt that they weren't what they appeared to be?"

"Never. That's what made him such a favorite with the bigwigs in the party. I'm a conservative myself, but I would have voted for him just like that." She snapped her fingers. "He was just what this country needed and now he's dead. Seems that someone didn't want him in office. Not in Minnesota. Certainly not in Washington."

"Did you ever meet any of the people that worked at the lake house?"

"Just cursory. You know, the 'hi' as you walk in the door. There weren't too many people working there. The interior painting was all done when the Dahlbergs were away. I came through a couple of times to check on the paint colors to make sure they were matched up with the art work we would be hanging."

"Did you know the contractor?"

"No. He was from out of town. Actually, north of Duluth somewhere. Near Cotton I think. Someone will know who it was. Unless you think they were a cover-up for getting on the inside. You know, that would be a great way to find out about every aspect of the house. Every nook and cranny of the house was completely redone."

The sun had moved across the horizon, sending shafts of light against the glass tabletop, reflected light touching her arms. The room was heating up. "Did you notice anyone who seemed out of place?" asked Laura.

"When you mention it. Yes. There was one guy who wasn't careful. Didn't pay attention to detail on the window frames and light switches. It seemed odd to me because every house painter I've ever known removes the switch plates before they paint. This guy didn't. The boss really chewed him out a couple of times about it. That is such a simple concept that anyone who works on houses should know."

"Did you notice anything special about him?"

"No. It may sound a little snobbish, but he was a laborer and I just never associate with them when I'm on a job. I talk to the contractor." She pursed her lips. "I know that sounds shameful, but it's the way it is."

"Except you noticed that he wasn't attentive to detail. Was he young? Maybe this was his first job."

"Not young. More middle aged. I remember that because he was a Dukes of Hazzard fan. Always humming Dixie or the theme song from the TV series. I thought it was a little weird for someone his age to be all hung up on Daisy Duke. But then, what do I know?"

"Did he have a cell phone?"

"Of course. The cell's ring tone reminded me of the Dukes theme song. The TV series, not the movie. I have no idea what songs were in the movie. Never did know how he got that ring tone hooked up. Like I said, he didn't quite fit in with the rest of the crew."

"Do you know his name?"

Bonnie replayed the scene in her mind. "Sorry."

Laura took out a small notebook and began writing.

"There were those two murders over in Duluth, too," said Bonnie. "That young woman worked for your parents. Is this all connected some how?"

"I don't know."

"Of course not. It just seems peculiar that in the course of a few weeks we have a whole string of murders. Do you know that I bought a dog? One that's already a year old so I didn't have to do all that potty training stuff. Sometimes my husband works late and, frankly, I was afraid to be home alone. I never knew how attached you could get to a dog. Anyway. How is the investigation going in Birch Bay?"

"Unreal. Helicopters, evidence bags, a couple of hundred FBI agents. The media is everywhere. I understand why the media is there, but they just add to the crowd on the streets. Sam Mikkelson and Noah Sackett have been wonderful. They're both keeping an eye on everything."

"What about Governor Cummings?"

"He's set up an office in Raspberry Point Inn. The governor's office in St. Paul is sealed off."

"Gives me the creeps. Fear is palpable in Duluth. Drive up the streets at night and everybody has their outside lights on. Several of my neighbors have had security lights installed. Until this is solved, the big question is still there. Was this a political assassination or is it a nut that kills randomly?"

Laura shrugged. No one had answers. "That question is haunting the Birch Bay community, too," she said.

"No answers keeps the citizenry spooked."

"You're right. Keeps me a little spooked, too."

"Sorry. I wasn't thinking. It must have been horrible seeing the explosion. Molly, too. How's she doing?"

"Okay. She's keeping busy at the Inn. It's not just Governor Cummings. Lots of state office staff there. Some legislators have come to Birch Bay to meet with the new governor. Lots of political maneuverings. Molly's husband has been out of town, but he's coming home tomorrow."

"Would you like a soda or something?" asked Bonnie. "There's coffee. Rolls in the freezer that I can pop in the microwave."

"No, thanks. Are you going to the memorial service this afternoon?"

"I am. I'm closing the gallery. My husband is taking the afternoon off work. He's shutting down the law office."

"Did either Charlie or Audrey talk to you about how they felt living in the governor's mansion?"

"Audrey did. She really enjoyed it, but she said things weren't private. When they were at the lake house she could write and e-mail without fear of someone seeing what she was doing. I thought that seemed strange. I mean, don't they have private quarters at the mansion?"

"They do. Audrey did her own housework in the mansion apartment and I think there was a separate key for the apartment. It is a state building, though, so there was always someone who had access."

"Someone who Audrey didn't trust," said Bonnie.

"Did she ever mention any one in particular?"

Bonnie furrowed her brow and took on a faraway look. "She did say something one time. When I was helping her hang the paintings, she received a phone call and didn't sound too happy. I didn't pay much attention, eavesdropping is not something that designers are supposed to do, not good for the image of the business. When she hung up, though, I remember her saying something that was so uncharacteristic of Audrey."

Laura waited, but Bonnie was quiet.

"What did she say? You're not giving away private information now. There's a criminal investigation going on."

"Of course."

Bonnie walked across the room and poured herself a drink.

"Would you like something?" she asked.

Laura declined, moved forward in her chair, and waited for Bonnie to look at her again. "Do you remember what Audrey said after the phone call?"

Bonnie let the feel of the wine spin through her body before she answered. "She looked unhappy. I remember her shaking her head and then she said: 'If someone named Mary Wallace ever comes into the gallery asking questions, please don't talk to her. Send her on her way, but give me a call and let me know.' She was quite agitated."

"Did she say why?"

"Just that sometimes people aren't what they pretend to be."

"Mary Wallace." Laura took out a small notebook and wrote down the name. "Someone that Audrey didn't trust."

CHAPTER THIRTY-THREE

Office of Minot's Catering
Highway 34
June 28

It took less than an hour to reach Minot's catering. Laura pulled onto a curved driveway with large trees on each side. A nicely manicured lawn with an abundance of flowers flanked the small parking area. An old-fashioned porch added a touch of down home charm to the business.

Hippie took Montana for a walk and said he'd read the paper to Montana when they were done. "Dogs like the sound and smell of the news," he said. "I always read the newspaper to my grandma's dog when I visit her. Some day dog psychologists are going to figure that out."

"Maybe they like the special treatment," said Laura. "Have you tried reading books to a dog?"

"They like poetry. I think that's all."

Hippie walked to the back of the building with Montana tugging on the leash. "He wants to go for a walk. See, he's smiling."

Laura had to admit that Montana did have a happy look. "Right."

It was close to lunchtime and the office was quite. Gloria was sitting behind a desk, her blonde curls bouncing as she clicked the computer keyboard. She was wearing beige pants and a white blouse; her only jewelry was a single gold band on her ring finger.

"Thanks for seeing me," said Laura as they went through the greeting rituals, shaking hands, and agreeing on the importance of doing anything possible to find Charlie and Audrey's killers.

"Did many of your employees help you when you catered for the Dahlbergs?" asked Laura.

"I only have a couple of people working for me on a regular basis. They're the only ones I allowed to go to the Dahlberg's house. I have some temps that I call in for big weddings and such, but I only sent the regulars to Dahlbergs. After all, he was the governor. I wanted to make sure that they had people there who knew exactly what they were doing and how to prepare any food on the spot."

"Is there any way I can talk to those two regular employees?"

Gloria looked at her watch. "I have a late afternoon reception scheduled. The two employees will be here in a little while. I wanted to go the memorial service so my staff will do all the work for me this afternoon. I do most of the cooking and my husband helps me with prep. My two servers put everything in the food containers, load it in the van, and deliver it. And of course, they're invaluable for serving the guests. They put everything on the serving platters, check the beverages, you name it. I always plan for plenty of lead time, so they could each give you a few minutes."

"Tell me about your employees."

"Well, it's just the two, actually. I haven't had any temp servers for quite a while. Kari Parker and Mike Sullivan. Kari's thirty and has two young children. Mike is a senior in college. They're both excellent workers. I don't think either of them know anything more about Governor and Mrs. Dahlberg than I do."

"I'll probably be very brief with them."

"They'll be used to it by now. They've been interviewed by the sheriff's department, FBI, a couple of newspapers. I was very proud of them when they talked to the newspapers. They were professional, refused to comment on the Dahlbergs at all. I don't think the reporters were very happy, but we're a business. What do they expect? A scandal?"

"You can never figure out the media. They have an agenda that's unlike regular people. I've come to deeply respect the really good reporters."

Gloria drew a shallow breath; her hands were shaking. "It's amazing how speedily one comes adept at saying no comment. I guess I'm on the reporter's list because I had delivered food to the Dahlbergs that afternoon. It seems so unreal."

Laura looked straight into Gloria's eyes and gave a reassuring nod. Give her time; let her talk.

"You can use the outer office when Kari and Mike get here," said Gloria. "Come into the kitchen if you'd like. Have a sample or two. I'd be interested in what you think, especially since your parents own one of the finest dining establishments in northern Minnesota. You must have a discriminating palate."

"I guess so. Growing up with exceptional food has become second nature to me. There are a couple of restaurants I don't visit a second time."

"I could probably tell you which ones they are," said Gloria.

"Your kitchen is absolutely marvelous." Laura looked at the gleaming stainless steel counters, the large refrigerators, three ovens, and lots of cupboards.

"My husband decided to add the extra glass," said Gloria pointing to the clerestory windows. I get the entire range of light without the afternoon heat. Helen and James Ingersoll helped design the kitchen. They analyzed the business and cooking needs and this is the result. I couldn't be more pleased."

"You have a wonderful piece of property, too."

"It's an area that people have overlooked. People forget how much land is available between Duluth and Birch Bay. They drive along the Mall corridor or hit the North Shore and miss the whole lakes area here. We're a short driving distance of several communities."

Out of the corner of her eye, Laura caught a flash of movement that she presumed to be Kari and Mike. Gloria moved quickly across the room and talked briefly to the two people. She pointed in Laura's direction.

"I told Mayor Kjelstad that we had plenty of time to meet with her." Gloria made the introductions. "Which one would you prefer to interview first?"

"Mike," said Laura. "No preference really, but I'll start with Mike."

Mike was young and athletic, moving with the grace of a figure skater. His hair was light brown, streaked by the sun. He had dark brown eyes and the smooth skin of a twenty-something college student.

He had been devastated by the assassinations. "Heard about it right away. Gloria had been there earlier in the day and someone called her as soon as they heard it on the scanner."

"I thought they had scrambled the messages," said Laura.

"Really? Well, it must have been the lumberjack telegraph, then. Anyway, as soon as Gloria heard about it, she called me. Called Kari, too. It was really bizarre. This is Minnesota. What's up with assassinating our governor? Must be a nut. Dahlbergs let people use their beach, didn't really worry about security. When they were gone, they had someone watching their place. Had an alarm system, too. Otherwise, it didn't seem necessary to worry about anything. Maybe some drunk kids that want to mess up the yard or something, but who would ever think that someone would kill them?"

"Did you know the Dahlbergs well?"

Mike was sitting very straight, almost rigid, and Laura wondered if he thought she brought bad karma with her.

"They were really nice people. Don't get me wrong. But, he was the governor. He was always busy talking, being the host. Same with Mrs. Dahlberg. She always thanked us, made sure we had food to eat. She let us use her kitchen to actually sit down and eat. That doesn't happen often. We were servers, though, and Mrs. Minot had strict rules for our jobs. Be professionals. Period."

"And you were all right with that?"

"We worked receptions, parties, you name it. I didn't get a chance to talk to any of the guests nor did I want to. My job was to tell when we needed more mushroom caps on the platter, not to stand around and visit with guests. We're a business."

"And a couple of bad receptions can sink the business."

"Right. Gloria's reputation depends a lot on us," he said. "She can make the best food in the world, but if we screw up, the food can be ruined. Not to mention that the service has to be impeccable."

"Do you have any idea who might have wanted to do such a thing to the Dahlbergs?"

"Not a clue. I don't spend much time here after we're through cleaning up. Neither does Kari. She's got a couple of kids. She tries to get home as soon as she can."

"You're at the University?"

"Majoring in business management. This job is perfect experience. I'm looking for a job in a restaurant. I hope to own my own café some day."

"A café. Not a restaurant."

"I like the ambience in a café. You're sort of investigating on your own, huh?"

"Seeing two people killed by a bomb does kick the motivation up a notch."

"Yeah. Sorry. Had to be awful."

Laura thanked him and shook hands again. He kept looking out the window and paused at the door of the kitchen. "You're sure you weren't followed?"

"I'm sure. I have a dog and an associate with me. They're keeping an eye on things."

"Like watching your car so no one can plant a bomb?"

"Something like that."

Kari came into the office quietly. She was petite, with curly brown hair and lovely blue eyes. She wore the uniform of the day, tan slacks, white blouse, no jewelry except a wedding ring.

"Gloria told me you think I might know something about the Dahlbergs assassination. I don't."

"Not the assassination. Just anything that you might know that could give some understanding to what happened. Something you saw or overheard perhaps."

"It's all so bizarre. Why would anyone want to kill the governor? In Birch Bay?"

Well, that took care of a couple of my questions, thought Laura. "How well did you know the Dahlbergs?" she asked.

"They were strictly acquaintances from work. I never saw them any other time. But then I never see Gloria or Mike anywhere but work either. I've got a three-year-old and a five-year-old at home. That sort of takes care of my social calendar."

"Did anyone ever come here trying to get information about the Dahlbergs? Or stop by at any of the places you were catering?"

"Gosh. I don't know. Minot's Catering does a good business. Mrs. Minot charms everyone. She always made people comfortable, sort of like an old school chum." Kari chewed her lower lip a little and scrunched her eyebrows together. "Do you think the person that committed the murders might have come to one of the places we were serving?"

"I don't know. It's just a thought."

"A real scary thought."

"Anyone come to mind?" Laura persisted.

"Do you think they might be watching us? Maybe they think we know them. I've got to call my husband." She rose to leave.

"Could you give me a couple of minutes?"

"I suppose. I don't think I want to drive home alone tonight. Aren't you afraid to be alone?"

"No, but..."

"Maybe none of us are safe."

"I think you're fine." Laura gave her a reassuring look. "The Dahlbergs were involved in government."

"But so are you, and you're here. We could all be in danger."

"I won't stay long. I promise."

"Good. Did you check to see if you were followed?" Kari shifted in her chair, her eyes darted toward the door then back to Laura.

"I'm sure I wasn't followed." *She's not tracking*, thought Laura. *Too nervous, I must have spooked her somehow.*

"Did you know anyone that asked questions about when Minot's would be catering at the Dahlbergs?"

"No."

"If you think of anything that might help the case, will you give me a call?"

"Would that be safe?"

"Yes."

Kari stood to leave. "Aren't you afraid?"

"I feel I'm safe."

Kari crossed herself. "I can't believe this is happening to me. This should have been a nice, stable job. Now there's assassination and mayhem."

"You'll be fine." Laura gave her a convincing smile. "Please. If you think of anything at all, will you let me know? Or tell Gloria and she can call the FBI."

Kari turned thoughtful for a moment. Laura let the quiet settle on her.

"Has anyone been around that's a Dukes of Hazzard fan?" asked Laura.

"No."

Laura told her she appreciated the help. Kari crossed herself again and left the office.

Gloria was stirring something on the stove when Laura walked back through the kitchen. "Thanks for giving me some time. If you hear anything that might be helpful, give me a call."

"We'll all rest easier when this is over," said Gloria. "I'll keep an eye open."

Kari was loading containers to be transported to the reception that afternoon. "I don't know why you're asking about the Dukes when there's been two murders." She raised her shoulders; her head moved turtle-like into her body. "Who cares about the Dukes of Hazzard?"

Before Laura could respond, Gloria turned pale. "Ohmigod," she yelled. "Dixie. I just remembered. When I left the Dahlbergs that day there was a rattle in the back of the van. I didn't want to break anything so I stopped to adjust the boxes. That's when I heard it. It sounded like a cell phone playing Dixie. It was only an instant and I didn't think of it again until just now. Do you think it means anything?"

CHAPTER THIRTY-FOUR

Raspberry Point Inn
Dahlberg Memorial Service
Afternoon – June 28

The memorial service for the Dahlbergs was held on the beach at Raspberry Point Inn. Politically and financially powerful people from around the country mingled with Birch Bay's residents. Most of the group were friends, relatives, and politicos, but Laura thought a few were probably there out of morbid curiosity.

The Dahlberg family followed Pastor Wallsten to the edge of the water; as they walked they exchanged whispered words with the gathered crowd. Pastor Wallsten's face conveyed sympathy and strength and hope, all in the span of a couple of minutes.

Ken and Carl Dahlberg were dressed casually. No suits. Instead, it was chinos and polo shirts. Rose wore a silky blue blouse and light-gray designer jeans, her incredible tan showing off luminous brown eyes and white teeth. Anne Bradley stayed near the family, clearly keeping the schedule moving along while enabling the family to visit briefly with the mourners.

Julia was stunning in a short-sleeved black sheath with flowers of pink and purple embroidered across the hem. A purple scramble-stitched cardigan was draped over her shoulders. She greeted members of the state legislature, members of the county board, the city council, and Sam Mikkelson. Ken Dahlberg grabbed Sam by the shoulders and whispered something in his ear. Sam lifted his hand as if to stop the conversation, took out a notebook, and began writing.

Leo Nelson moved across the yard to greet Michelle Dahlberg, Carl's wife. Helen Gabler was at his side. Michelle greeted them warmly, nodding graciously, looking wonderful in a respectable navy linen dress. Leo was gesturing, locked in a diatribe of some sort. Noah skillfully moved to Michelle's side and maneuvered Leo to the sidelines.

The Dahlberg grandchildren were with Rose's husband, Bill Haugen. Clutched into a self-protective circle, they stood by Mark Lundquist, the church youth pastor. He murmured something to the children that was inaudible to the surrounding crowd. His face was lit up with the blazing confidence that comes from a positive attitude and a faith that is unshakable. His energy was contagious. It was obvious that he had the full attention of the grandkids. The littlest child, Emma, held tight to Mark's hand.

Laura watched as Governor Cummings greeted the Dahlberg family. Jack was relaxed as he leaned down and talked to the Dahlberg grandchildren. Several state legislators joined the small group gathered by the pastor. Jack stood, looked out on the crowd, and waved to Laura. He gestured for her to join him, but she held her hands up, palms pointed outward.

Laura continued down the path, noting the familiar faces: Milly Sylvester, mid-seventies, but claiming sixty-three, was looking extraordinarily lovely in one of her characteristic hats. It was amazing how Milly managed to find a hat that was not only suitable for the occasion, but attractive as well. Jennifer Ehlers and Katherine Chaffey, both on the Birch Bay City Council, greeted Laura, then moved away. Three council members together would break the open meeting law. Memorial service or not, it was best to keep everything proper. Leo was watching her every move.

Knut and Emily Hansen were near the front, joined by Governor Cummings and the Dahlberg family. Jack Cummings hugged Emily warmly and grabbed Knut by the shoulder and shook his hand.

"I guess Laura wants to stay in the background," said Jack, searching the crowd for her face.

Voices, snatches of conversation, continued as Laura made her way to the beach.

"...the FBI don't have a clue. Sitting on their overextended back sides."

"...sitting on our taxes is what I'd say. An assassin on the loose and they have no comment."

"...not much to go on."

"...shh. The pastor's ready to begin."

Guitarist Lenny Mahlberg began the service by playing Amazing Grace. Pastor Wallsten invited people to sing along. In his customary control of the situation, the pastor kept his message brief and offered prayers for those gathered to honor Charlie and Audrey. He talked about the promise of heaven and that everyone needed to support the family as they faced the desolation of these horrific deaths. Proper. Conventional. Then he departed from the norm and urged everyone to help the agents solve the crime. "Remember the words Mayor Kjelstad said in the press conference, 'You will be the ears and eyes of men and women who are not familiar with this area. You will show them the heart of our small town'." He gave out phone numbers for the FBI and paused so people could write them down.

Prayers were said, songs were sung, and Pastor Wallsten closed the service with an invitation for everyone to partake of the lunch set up on the deck.

It wasn't a slick memorial; it was a touching example of the way Charlie and Audrey lived. Despite their power and wealth, they had never abandoned their beliefs and their concern for people.

The deck at the Inn was a three-level affair with plenty of room for serving tables and chairs. Tables laden with food were set outside as well as in the sunroom. The gardens outdoors were in glorious color.

Molly had a flair for flowers as shown by the profusion of blooms on the geraniums, petunias, marigolds, and a host of other annuals. Perennials were ablaze with varying intensities of colors.

Across the garden, the Dahlberg family was busy greeting people, avoiding any discussion of the assassinations. They had encouraged everyone to focus on the life of their parents and talk about the good times.

As the reception continued, people drifted in at various intervals. Sam Mikkelson worked through the crowd shaking hands, touching a shoulder, sharing an occasional hug. Governor Cummings was surrounded by state legislators, county board members and Birch Bay citizens.

Children were running along the beach tossing pebbles into the water and some were trying the age-old custom of skipping rocks. Young women in flowing skirts and espadrilles mingled with intense looking young men in jeans and T-shirts. A festive feeling hummed through the resort despite the heaviness of the occasion. Clara Hixson ensconced herself in a lounge chair and was slightly out of breath from the stimulation of the crowded atmosphere. Hippie pulled a chair alongside and started a quiet chatter about the weather.

Noah waved to Laura and continued shaking hands as he walked toward her, watching the movements of the crowd. Navy Admiral at the alert, she thought.

Hal Marshall, serving coffee with one hand and carrying a tray of pastries in the other, stopped momentarily to chat with Clara, commented on the current state of affairs, and proceeded to back clumsily into Helen Gabler. Helen's face went as stiff as if she'd been flash frozen. She set her seething gaze on the perpetrator and moved toward Leo. In the midst of the small group, Hal's uneasiness was palpable.

"Don't worry about it," said Clara. "It's bound to happen with such a large crowd. You didn't even spill a drop." She dropped her voice to a whisper. "I've know Helen since she was a teenager. She's always been like that. Snobbish hypocrite." Clara paused. "Well, okay. So I've been known to call her a bitch."

The beach was noisy with the vocal contributions of assembled tourists and locals all moving about with plates of food, beverages, and napkins blowing in the breeze. Their voices spread a miasma of sound over the area, a sound that gave a completeness to the time of mourning.

Noah looked handsome in a white shirt and light blue pants. He took his food and sat in the shade of an ancient pine, it's patriarchal roots surfacing on the path that led to the lake. Huge, gnarled limbs formed a canopy of protection from the sun's glare. There, in a rustic wicker chair, amidst the flowers, the lawn, the lake, and the trees, he was the personification of a military officer.

A canoe was coming near the shore as two men paddled easily and smoothly in the direction of the Inn. There was a relaxing fascination to the dip, push, and swing of the rhythmic paddling, to the unity of body, paddle, and canoe. They paddled in leisurely cadence along the ancient, primeval shore with its twisted trees leaning over the water and large, gray boulders dotting the edge. A breath of wind was touched with the scent of forest, of tall pines and wildflowers mingling together splendidly. A haze of campfire smoke hung over the western edge of the lake.

Sheltered within a crowd, people spoke in hushed tones, delaying their trip home or to their motels and cabins. Fear had become a powerful reality; the dread of the unknown deeply affecting the people gathered to honor the Governor of Minnesota and his lovely wife.

Clara Hixson was drinking a glass of cranberry juice and chewing on some mixed nuts as Laura walked past her. She said something that Laura didn't understand.

"I'm sorry, Clara, I didn't hear you."

"Just as well," said Clara. "I saw Leo and Helen and I uttered an improper word that caught in my throat. Well maybe it was a peanut, but nevertheless, I need to watch my language."

She had turned a noticeable shade of red.

"I am just so upset over Charlie and Audrey's deaths," she continued. "Nothing like this has ever happened where I've been; I guess it has me under a strain. I don't like the feeling of fear, never been scared like this ever."

Clara waved to a woman standing near the refreshment table.

"Do you know Sylvia?"

"No. I don't."

"She's my third cousin once removed. Or is she my second cousin twice removed? Well, never mind. We share some ancestors somewhere along the way. I was getting too nervous staying alone so she came to stay with me a few days. Then I'm going to go to her place near Eveleth. It's spooky staying alone after something like this has happened. I've talked to lots of people in town who are terrified. It's not just the Dahlbergs getting assassinated. It's Cindy's murder, too. What did she see that got her killed? Or what did the killer think she saw? Any one of us might see something that the killer thinks could incriminate him and then…" She made a knife motion across her throat. "I'm not ashamed to say I'm scared."

For a long moment, Laura was quiet. "I understand," she said.

"And then there's those two murders in Duluth. There's a connection to your parent's restaurant there. Everything is too interrelated to be a coincidence."

"Are you still carrying the Glock?" asked Laura.

Clara tapped her purse and smiled. "Now I wouldn't tell you. You'd take it away." She put the bag between her feet. "You'd look really bad taking an old lady's purse."

"You got a gun. Cool." Hippie looked admiringly at Clara. "Really cool. Clara's carrying."

"Oh my. I didn't see you," said Clara. "Of course I don't have a gun."

Hippie looked around at the crowd. "Sure. Okay." He winked at her and whispered, "Want to go inside and show me how it works?"

Two deputies had loaded their plates with food, took some lemonade, and sat down near Clara. Clara nudged her purse under her chair.

"Nothing like a good clock," said Hippie. "Clocks give a certain feeling of security. Telling time's important."

Clara gave him a roll of the eyes, but Hippie just smiled.

Hippie turned toward the deputies. "Just a little joke between Clara and me. We both have a liking for clocks."

The Dahlbergs walked across the lawn to chat with Laura. They were pleased with the memorial service.

"We're just grateful that you and Molly are all right," said Julia. "It all seems so bizarre. Right now we are in total chaos, but when things settle down we plan on coming up for a few days and we'll take you out to dinner. We'd like to have some time to talk to you. Charlie and Audrey thought so highly of you and all you did for the lakes country and Birch Bay. Not to mention your great teaching style."

"Forgive us for leaving right away today," said Ken. "We're deluged with letters and memorial gifts and cards and plans for the funeral in the Cities. We don't think the church will hold everybody so we're trying to figure out where to hold the service."

"Maybe one of the colleges," said Rose. "We'd like you to be one of the speakers at the service when we decide on a date."

"I'd be honored," said Laura. "Just let me know when and where."

Pastor Wallsten interrupted. "There are some people who want to see you before you go back to St. Paul. Friends of your parents."

"Thank you again for what you did for our family," said Michelle. "We'll stay in touch."

Molly was by the beverage carts, lifting the lid of the coffeepot to see if it need refilling.

"Let me give you a hand with that," said Sam. "Is it empty?" Mikkelson was maneuvering to the dessert table.

"Almost. You can carry it into the kitchen. I still have one full pot. Just set the empty one on the table inside. One of the assistants will take care of it."

Laura helped herself to some raspberry pie and coffee and started back to join Clara.

"Laura," called Sam. "Grab me a raspberry pie, too, will you? Join me inside. It's getting too hot out here."

Laura and Sam settled in a corner of the sunroom.

"This is the first time in hours that I haven't had a phone to my ear with one hand and the computer keyboard in the other." Sam sighed with relief. "How are you holding up?"

"I've been too busy to let things worry me. My visit to Hollingsworth Galleries and Minot's Catering was interesting. Have you found out anything about this Mary Wallace that Bonnie mentioned?"

"Nothing. FBI is handling everything. I just feed them the information."

"Did you tell them that Gloria Minot has confirmed Lance's story about a cell phone with "Dixie" as its' ring tone?"

"I did. They're on top of it."

"Good." Laura relaxed a little. "It's good to know that there may be some clues. Agent Beckwith doesn't know who told you?"

"As far as he knows, it was an anonymous tip. He'd go ballistic if he knew you were asking questions."

"Especially after he told me that he was handling everything. No interference, he said." She sighed. "I'm not interfering. I was just visiting and asking some questions."

"Just be careful."

"I am being very careful. Stupidity isn't at the top of my list."

"Good." Sam reached across, caressing her hand. "Laura. Right now I don't have much time to devote to a social life. Not even a meal. Give me a few days and I'll fix that meal I had planned. Salmon, asparagus, baby red potatoes. If you like, I'll even make some popovers."

Laura smiled at him. "I'd …"

"Mayor Kjelstad." Agent Beckwith was striding across the room with a scowl clearly intended for Laura. "I just talked to Bonnie Hollingsworth. What in the hell do you think you're doing? She said you'd been out talking to her this morning. Asking questions that are strictly FBI business. Seems like you've forgotten about political interference. I'll meet you back here in two hours. We need to talk."

Laura's back went rigid. "I have a right to talk to whomever I please. The questions I asked are everybody's business. Everything I do is transparent. I haven't tried to hide my discussions."

"Could be you're hampering our investigation. I could take you in for questioning." Beckwith's eyes were hard and probing.

"Bullshit," said Sam. "What's up? Don't take your damn frustration out on Laura. You know better than that. We need all the information we can get."

"Damn, fool politicians." Beckwith's eyes were venomous.

"I darn well better know what's happening in the investigation." Laura returned the fiery look.

Beckwith gave her a belligerent grimace. "Like hell."

Irritation swelled in her throat. Beckwith didn't get it. "I want to know every step along the way. I'm not expecting to know inside information that would jeopardize the investigation, but I don't want to be blindsided either."

"Watch CNN if you want to know what's happening." Beckwith was flaming.

"I'm out of here," said Laura. "You want to arrest me for something, do it. Otherwise, keep away from me. I'll keep Noah informed."

"Like hell. I'll see you later," Beckwith thundered. Tension crackled around him. "Don't make any plans for this evening. Like it or not, we will talk."

CHAPTER THIRTY-FIVE

Bay Loop
Late Afternoon
June 28

Agent Beckwith irritated Laura. She'd gleaned information that the FBI hadn't because she had talked to people and listened. Mikkelson had told Beckwith about the cell phone ring, but law enforcement didn't seem to be following that lead.

She mulled that over.

Of course she didn't know what all the agents were doing. They wouldn't involve her in anything. She clearly would not be included in any discussions. Political interference was considered an aberration by the FBI.

Beckwith was a damn blister.

Beckwith was also FBI. Chief investigator.

Twenty minutes after her encounter with Beckwith, she had changed into her running clothes and was driving down Portage Street toward the highway. Driving south on Cant Hook Road, she made the circle of town and turned left on Raspberry Drive. The Bay Loop followed the contours of the lake with the expensive homes clustered along the lakeshore. The wealthy have a penchant for water, whether it is lakeshore, river frontage, or ocean views. Money buys the homes that are windows and marble and space like a hotel lobby.

As she parked on the edge of the road, a young couple walked past, holding hands and laughing. Behind her, a gold-colored Chrysler Intrepid was maneuvering as far off the pavement as possible.

A couple of quick stretches and she was on her way, avoiding the man from the Intrepid who started moving in her direction. The Duluth Dukes baseball cap covered her head, partly to keep the sun out of her eyes, but mainly to keep the mosquitoes out of her hair. A gentle breeze was moving across the lake, keeping the bugs under control.

The daylight was shifting as the sun continued it's afternoon descent, sending shadows across the pavement. The sound of waves gently lapping the shore, the cry of seagulls, and the canopy of trees was rejuvenating.

The man from the Intrepid was wearing blue Oakleys, a Bass Master baseball cap, moss colored polo, and khaki pants. When he lit a cigarette, she wondered how serious he was about exercising. Maybe he was meeting someone here, biding his time until they came. He made her uncomfortable, causing a feeling of uneasiness that she couldn't explain. Even though she couldn't see his eyes, she knew from his body position that he was watching her.

Arms pumping, she began pulling away from the man, a purposeful swiftness in her running. She wondered if the man worked out often, if he'd be able to keep up with her. Don't look back again, she thought. He doesn't need to know I'm wary of him. Don't show any sign of weakness.

A middle-aged woman with a golden retriever rounded the curve ahead, nodded in Laura's direction, and continued her quick pace. Laura smelled cigarette smoke and wondered if the man was close. She increased her speed. As she neared the curve, she crossed the road to catch a glimpse behind her. The man was returning to his car and she decided he wasn't interested in the cardiovascular rewards of exercise.

The lake was transforming as the sun drifted west. Subtle changes in color glistened and the light played with the delicately swaying trees, creating a scene of enchantment. The road swung to the left, away from the lake, allowing space for the homes that were overtaking the shoreline.

At the sound of the approaching car, she moved to the shoulder of the road, allowing plenty of room for the vehicle to pass. She turned around to make sure the car was passing safely. The hair on the back of her neck tingled when she saw the gold-colored Intrepid following, making no effort to pass. The license plate was unreadable, covered with mud, purposely, she noted, since the rest of the car was spotless.

Reflexes kicked in; all the stories she'd heard about women being attacked on lonely country roads set her in survival mode. She felt her heartbeat quicken, fright surging through wildly and unexpectedly. Just because she'd been lucky when the Dahlbergs were murdered didn't mean she'd be lucky again. Laura didn't frighten easily, but the guy was definitely following her and that could only mean some kind of trouble.

She made a quick decision, cutting through the brush alongside the road and running toward a house near the shoreline. Tree branches slapped her face and arms as she increased her speed. The man stopped the car, saw the direction she was headed and pulled into the driveway. Laura scrambled across a rocky ledge and flung herself behind the safety of the detached garage, bent double, moving faster than she'd ever moved before.

The sound of gunfire, glass shattering, and shards of broken glass exploding across her body sent waves of horror washing over her. A second shot hit the garage and sprayed her face with splintering wood. At first she couldn't see the man, but then she caught sight of him at the corner of the garage, holding the gun with both hands as he centered on her head. He appeared confused, probably wondering why he'd missed. He had been careless, cocky, sure that he could finish her off quickly and easily.

It had been a surprise that he had missed, though she could taste blood in her mouth, feel it running down her face. Maybe he thought he'd wounded her, that she was so terrified that she'd stand still like a deer caught in the headlights. Her decision was simple. Escape. Run. Do whatever necessary to reach safety.

She skimmed over the driveway running toward the lake. The boulders and cliffs could offer some protection, a place to hide. She wondered if anyone had heard the shots, wondered if there was anyone in the house, but she didn't dare look back. Tumbling on the rocks, she lost her balance and gasped from the pain of flesh striking stone. She caught sight of the man taking aim; this time when he fired she felt a sharp hotness strike her arm. When she reached an outcrop of rock, she pushed off with all her strength, lifting through the air, and landing on gravel below. Her footsteps crunched across the loose beach gravel, changing to a hollow thudding when she hit the ledge rock. Trees and boulders dotted the shore and she rushed on, the firmness of the solid rock allowed her to increase her speed.

The sound of gunfire exploded across the water. Different guns, more lethal and powerful than the first shots he'd fired. She wondered if there were others after her now. Town was a couple of miles away, but she couldn't risk working her way back to the road. She'd be too visible. Who else had joined the attack? she wondered.

Laura turned once to see if anyone was following her, but there was no sign of the man or anyone else. It would make sense for him to go back to his car, head toward town, and wait for her at a secluded stretch of land where Raspberry Drive curved to the north. She knew this area well, knew where he would likely be waiting, but that section of beach was also a popular swimming area and this was a hot day. She repeated the first verse of the Twenty-third Psalm and it helped sustain the rhythm of her run. It also gave her courage to go on.

Ahead, the gravel beach ended as a narrow cliff, about four feet high, jutted out into the water. If she climbed the cliff, it would slow her down, make her an easy target. She chose the water, slipping on the moss that covered the rock, and felt the flesh on her knee tear as she went down hard against cutting stone. She lay there for a minute, catching her breath, letting the water wash over her.

Laura stayed prone as she worked her way around the cliff, not wanting to chance another crushing fall. A half-mile ahead was the isolated stretch of beach where the man or his accomplices would surely be waiting. She stopped, catching her breath, saying a quiet prayer.

Approaching the area where she thought the man would be expecting her, she cautiously peered over boulders, moving slowly now, keeping low to avoid detection. The scene sent a wave of gratitude over her. A large group of young people was gathered on the road, which was about a block from the water's edge. They were unloading their cars, carrying picnic baskets, and working their way to the beach.

A man stood next to his car, but it wasn't the man who had shot at her. Maybe an accomplice. He could also be one of the many tourists in the area. One of the kids approached him, started a conversation, and pointed toward town. Good. The commotion of the kids was a great distraction.

Moving into the lake, Laura swam underwater, surfacing only to get a quick breath of air, then moved to the bottom of the lake again. The water was about three feet deep at this point, enough to cover her, to keep her hidden. With the commotion of the kids on the beach, she was praying he wouldn't notice the slight ripple she was making.

As she reached town, there were people on the beach, a welcome safety net providing a haven if she reached them in time. It was hot and the heat amplified the terror, accelerated the pain. She had run from the ridge of trees bordering Big Canoe Lake onto the rocks at the water's edge. She stared at a family group assembled about thirty feet from where she stood, catching her breath, inhaling deeply, then letting the air out slowly, trying to stop the explosion in her chest.

She'd been convinced that she was going to die, then hopeful that she could outwit and outrun the man who wanted to see her body lying twisted and lifeless on the road. She knew she was bleeding. Her mouth was full of blood and it kept sliding down her throat stimulating the gag reflex. She swallowed hard and felt the blood stream into her stomach. She tried to hold back the sickening stench gathering inside, but it erupted onto the rocks. She kept moving toward the people, to the safety of witnesses, with blood staining the front of her blouse and running from her mouth and nostrils.

She dropped to a crouch, too exhausted to keep upright any longer. She started crawling toward the lake, shouting frantically while looking with dread over her shoulder to make sure the man was nowhere near. The rocks tore at her hands and knees, but she propelled herself forward, the fear contained, the adrenaline driving her flight.

To her right, the family moved closer, but the sound of waves blunted her cries for help. They were throwing rocks into the water, laughing and playing, vacationing in the heart of the North Country. The littlest child, a boy, caught sight of her. His eyes took in every segment of her body. He stood motionless, but a scream, loud and shrill, welled from his throat.

Was he shouting for his mother? Laura's head was aching so intensely that she couldn't make out what he was saying. Her mouth was foul tasting and her eyes stung. Blood was flowing from her right arm and her whole body screamed in agony.

She surveyed her raw, bleeding hands and arms, checked her legs, and plunged into the water. Moving was tortuous, but she had reached safety. There were witnesses here, lots of people who could form a barricade between her and the gunman. The coolness of the lake water began clearing her head. She stayed submerged in the water, making a poor target if he was still intent on shooting her.

The little boy persisted in his screaming until his parents rushed toward her, putting out gentle hands to help her to a nearby lawn chair.

"What's happened?" asked the woman who Laura believed to be the Mom. "Was there an accident?"

An accident seemed to be the most plausible story, a natural response to her appearance, but she shook her head.

"Someone tried to kill me."

Right over there on Raspberry Drive. The scenic road that attracts bikers and walkers and runners. Roller bladers and parents with strollers. The road that had always been the place she walked to find peace and enjoy the beauty of Big Canoe Lake and the encircling forest.

"What?" The Mom seemed confused.

"Someone shot me. Call the sheriff."

"Call the police," instructed the woman, handing a cell phone to the man Laura presumed to be the husband. "And an ambulance."

"I need the sheriff," Laura insisted, but no one was listening. There was too much noise. Too much confusion. "His name's Sam Mikkelson."

"Mrs. Kjelstad. Are you all right?"

It was Kyle Nielsen, one of Laura's third grade students from the previous year.

"What happened?" he asked, focusing on the crowd gathered around her. "She was my teacher last year," he said with the authority of a local amidst a group of tourists. "She's the mayor of the town, too. Usually she looks better than this."

Considering how dreadful she must look, Laura couldn't argue. She gave him the best smile she could muster. Her right arm, throbbing with pain, was sticky with blood. Every part of her ached terribly and she thought about all the movies where the hero gets up and walks away from an act of brutality looking completely nonplussed. They lie, those films and television stories.

Laura turned and looked at the ridge of trees from which she had emerged. No one there. He wasn't visible in the parking lot either or in the gathering crowd. She heard sirens in the distance. She also heard Kyle call out: "Mrs. Kjelstad. Did someone try to assassinate you?"

CHAPTER THIRTY-SIX

Flight. There was no outrage, no moral indignation, no pleading with a murderer. It was a simple choice. Run. She made it to safety. People were gathering on the beach, the crowd growing large as talk of a gunshot victim fueled their curiosity. Kyle Nielsen took Laura's hand and squeezed it gently.

"There's an ambulance coming," he said. "The police are here, too. And I'll stay until you're safe." He was holding a Popsicle stick in the other hand, drops of red liquid running down his white T-shirt; both hands sticky from the Popsicle juice. His blonde hair was wet, either from sweat or from dunking his head in water, and his blue eyes kept a watchful look on the crowd.

"You need to keep back," he told the people, gesturing with the Popsicle stick. "She needs to get some air, you know."

Laura tried her best to smile at him, grateful for the familiar face, for the genuine offer of protection. Time passed in a jumble of confusion. She closed her eyes, avoiding the scene overlaid with staring faces, worried expressions, and children running playfully along the beach kicking rocks into the lake. Questions were being hurled at her and she couldn't respond.

Wally stood toward the back of the crowd. The boss wasn't going to be happy with this scenario, but he didn't give a damn. Mr. Big

Boss wanted to create chaos, well then, damn it, he was creating some chaos. As law enforcement grew closer, Wally melted into the crowd and disappeared down the street.

The sound of sirens ceased. Kyle didn't let go of Laura's hand until a policeman arrived and two EMTs crouched beside her, examining her wounds, then lifting her onto a stretcher. Wayne Simmons, the deputy, asked where the incident had taken place. Incident? She wanted to shout that someone had tried to kill her, more than an incident from her perspective, but she described the location and told him she appreciated his help. Wayne was a nice man and he was being so helpful that she decided he didn't need a cranky woman harping over the use of a word. Cranky? Well, she had a right. Somebody had tried to kill her.

"Bay Loop," said Wayne in response to a question on the other end of the radio.

They took her away quickly. Thankfully, they kept the sirens off on the trip to the hospital; the noise would have been intolerable. Voices were comforting as the ambulance driver and attendant wheeled her into the emergency room.

"We didn't know what we would find," said Ken Mattson, the driver. "We were told there had been a shooting. We didn't know who it was. How are you doing?"

"I'm doing O.K.," she said. "That doesn't mean I don't hurt all over. I was so glad to see you."

A female nurse named Amber helped her undress, pulling off soggy clothes and towel drying her body. The nurse placed a blue hospital gown around her, tying it at the neck, which didn't offer much covering of the backside.

Amber was an R.N. with two children in the local elementary school. Laura had been their teacher. Amber's blonde hair was cut short, with brown showing at the roots. Her green eyes conveyed a feeling of warmth which meant a lot to Laura; small town familiarity wrapped up in one comforting nurse.

"I'm going to cover you with a couple of blankets. They'll help maintain your body temperature until we can check all your vital signs. I need to ask you a few questions."

"Go ahead."

The nurse asked for her height. "Five feet four inches," said Laura. Weight? "One hundred ten." Insurance card? "I don't have it, but all the information is in the computer here at the hospital."

As the nurse entered Laura's name and birth date, the computer gave off a low humming sound, then a series of clicks as she entered the print command and documents flowed forth from the Hewlett Packard.

Amber took Laura's blood pressure, checked her pulse, and pushed a thermometer in her mouth; none of it making her feel any better. Dr. Hess, white hair as haphazard as ever, came in and began speaking words of encouragement. He flashed a light in her eyes, probed her scalp with gentle fingers, and pressed the soft, squishy wound in her arm.

"We need to clean all the wounds," he said. "How's the knee?"

"Hurts like the dickens," she said, wincing as she tried to straighten it. "It's stiffening up on me."

"The knee needs stitches, but I want to get x-rays done first. Does your nose hurt much?"

"Nose?" Laura felt her nose, a look of bewilderment clouding her face.

"That's where all the blood on your face came from," said Hess. "Something clipped you across the nose. Nothing broken. How's the head?"

"Aches. And I'm really thirsty."

"We'll get you some water after I've seen the pictures."

He wrote an order for x-rays and they took her across the hall. In the x-ray room she closed her eyes and followed directions, not moving, then turning over, not moving again. She concentrated on the technician's voice as various body parts were attended to, relieved she was able to respond, no matter how slowly she found herself moving. When they wheeled her back into the examining room, she closed her eyes and waited.

"Nothing broken," said Dr. Hess when the x-rays arrived. "Lots of bruising, contusions, abrasions. I'm going to put some stitches in the knee; it'll heal faster, but we need to get you cleaned up first. Your arm has a superficial wound, nothing serious. You are one very blessed young woman."

The nurse came with a large pitcher of water, poured a glass, and watched as Laura drank in gulps, dribbling down her chin and onto the gown.

Dr. Hess worked to clean the wounds, explaining the procedure as he went along. The nurse was busy washing blood off Laura's face, arms, and legs. Weariness flooded over her and she inhaled sharply. The scene of bedpans, urinals, and needles did nothing to bolster her flagging spirits.

"Let us know if you're feeling too much pain," said Dr. Hess. "Some discomfort can be expected when we're cleaning wounds, but we want you to tell us if it's too much."

Laura reflected on the words. When the pain reaches a fifteen on a scale of one to ten the doctor says: "You may feel some discomfort during the procedure." Laura didn't want to sound like a wimp so all she could think of to say was: "No bed pan. I draw the line." Well, not the height of brilliance, but it kept her mind occupied.

"Noted," he said. He patted her shoulder and she felt like a third grader again, arm broken from a fall off the jungle gym at school.

The examining room door was thrown open and Agent Beckwith burst into the room. "What the hell? Son of a bitch if someone didn't try to kill you. You really got yourself in trouble this time, Kjelstad. With all the snooping you've been doing it was just a scene waiting to happen. I'm going to have to question you."

Laura's surprise was evident, then the surprise turned to anger that was palpable. Dr. Hess reacted immediately. "You need to leave the examining room. I'm attending a female patient and you are clearly violating hospital regulations. You need to leave now."

"The hell I will. She's the victim of a crime. On my watch. In my jurisdiction. She has valuable information locked in her brain."

"She's in the emergency room," said Dr. Hess. "And, you're right, she's the victim. I'm committed to treating my patient. You can have your witness only when I say so."

"I'm FBI."

"And you're out of here. I'm sure your boss won't be happy if I tell him you were harassing a witness."

Dr. Hess is an imposing figure, muscular, and sure of himself. Laura wasn't sure if Beckwith was leaving because his training kicked in or because he was afraid of the doctor. Whatever the reason, Beckwith was gone as quickly as he had come in.

"He's such a jerk," said Laura.

"I was thinking of a part of the anatomy," said Hess. "Still, the man is under enormous pressure."

"I know. The strain is monumental. The whole town is getting tense."

"Lots of sleep deprivation happening."

Dr. Hess stitched her wounds, scratched notes on a chart, and leaned against the wall. "I'm keeping you in the hospital overnight. Mikkelson says it's important to keep you in a safe environment. Law enforcement is all over this hospital and I've arranged for you to be just across the hall from BCA headquarters. It's a little removed from the rest of the patients and BCA is equipped to give you protection. Mikkelson wants to question you later."

"Beckwith will probably join him."

"Probably."

"Tell Sam I'm ready to talk whenever he wants to see me. Will you be giving me anything for the headache?"

"I've written orders for pain medication, antibiotics, and regular meals. I'm on call, sleeping in the doctor's lounge tonight. I'll be here whenever you need me."

"What about visitors?"

"None. With BCA and FBI using the facilities, we're limiting any access to the building. The wing you're staying in is completely closed to anyone but law enforcement."

"You can't keep me here forever."

"No. But we have a plan for tonight at least."

"These gowns aren't patient friendly."

"Would you like a someone to bring some things from your house?"

Someone going through her underwear drawer. Not a good scene in her mind. "I'll be fine with some hospital pajamas and an extra gown to use as a robe."

"Sam Mikkelson is here," said the nurse walking through the door. "He wants to know if he can come in to see Laura."

"Feel like seeing the sheriff?" asked Hess.

"Sure."

When Sam walked through the door, warm memories swept over her. His movements were controlled, there was a look of urgency in his eyes, and his mouth was set in a grim line, on guard, ready for anything. Lack of sleep was evident in the shadows beneath his eyes, but nothing else betrayed his weariness.

"Is she ready to be discharged?" asked Sam. "There's a change in plans. I've arranged for her to stay in the Berg's guestroom at Raspberry Point Inn. I cleared it with Agent Beckwith. He agreed it might be an easier place to keep her safe. With the governor at the Inn, there's already a contingent of agents surrounding the place. She'll be more comfortable and she'll have Molly to keep her company."

Dr. Hess raised his eyebrows. "Laura? It's up to you. He's right about the safety at the Inn."

"Sounds great," said Laura. "The Berg's guest room is first class. Could I stop by the house and pick up some clothes? I need some files and a laptop. I probably won't sleep tonight and I can catch up on a project I'm doing."

"I'll take you," said Sam. "Noah's at your house now checking it out. Your parents are on their way over here. They were almost to Duluth. I called their cell phone and told them to meet us at your place. They'll stay at your house while you're at the Inn. Your dad thought if they were there, the bad guys would think you were staying at home and they wouldn't even think of the Inn. Molly borrowed one of your sweatshirts and your Duluth Dukes baseball cap. You're recognized by that cap. I'll take Molly over there a little later and she'll walk in the house. It'll be dusk and we'll make sure she's under heavy security so it looks like it's you we're taking in."

"And why won't someone notice when I go home now and get a suitcase?"

"Because I have Molly's car and we'll go in and out your attached garage. Your parents said you're to stay put at the house until they have a chance to see you. I have some of Noah's cinnamon rolls in the car so you can have tea with your parents and then we'll leave. Sometime later, Molly will walk in."

"Looking like me."

"Yes."

"She has red hair."

"She won't when she walks into your house. You underestimate Agent Beckwith's resolve."

Sam saw how tired Laura was; her eyes registered the uncertainty that they were all feeling. "I'll be in the hall whenever you're ready."

Dr. Hess turned to leave. "I'll get your discharge papers ready immediately."

Laura gave Sam an inquiring look. "Have you found the man who did the shooting? All I saw was the one man, but then I heard another gun firing."

"We have nothing, but like everything else, we're investigating. You'll probably hear some report when you get to the Inn."

"Why?"

"There was a jogger coming around the curve in the road, heard the gunfire, and said he saw Clara Hixson and Matt Wrenshall driving away from the scene. Matt was driving and Clara was waving something out the window. The witness was positive that Clara had a gun in her hand."

"Hippie and Clara. Good grief. They could have been killed."

"I agree."

"Haven't they given you any information?"

"They're not admitting anything. Matt's at the Inn. He may talk to you."

"And then I report to you."

"Governor Cummings is meeting with Clara. I'm sure she'll cooperate."

Sam smiled and put his hands on her shoulders, massaging gently. "As long as you remember to report to me, we'll be fine. Matt has been checked out. We don't see him as a danger to you, but we've told him he has to stay in his room until we're satisfied that you're safe. When and if you want to talk to him, someone will escort him to your room and stay in view. Hippie may not want anyone else to hear what he has to say, but he can whisper. Your safety is my top concern. How do you feel?"

"I hurt in every part of my body and I'm hungry. How do I look?"

"A little more purple and scabby than usual."

"Thanks." She laughed, but contained herself because moving hurt. "More flattery like that and I'll be looking in all the mirrors I can find."

"Doc says you'll be fine in a couple of days. The good Lord was looking out for you. The guy shot up the garage, took out a couple of windows, and blew a hole in the door. Thankfully he was a lousy shot. Or you were good at ducking and dodging. I will need your statement, but I'll stop by the Inn after you've had some supper."

"This guy doesn't sound like a professional."

"We'll find out. It could be that the arrival of Matt and Clara threw off his concentration. That happens when someone is shooting at you. Those two may have saved your life. For that I will be eternally grateful."

"I don't know how much information I can give you. I was in survival mode."

"We'll see what you remember. If you can get Matt or Clara to admit they were there, we might get an eyewitness account from them."

"Eyewitnesses are vulnerable."

"They're being taken care of. We won't let anything happen to them, but we need a description of the guy."

Laura felt a flood of relief washing over her.

Overhead she heard the deep motor and the thubthubthub of a helicopter. "Life Flight or law enforcement?" she asked.

"Law enforcement. Senator Winthrop is going to be here a few days."

"Checking up?"

"So he can report first hand to the President," said Sam.

CHAPTER THIRTY-SEVEN

Birch Bay
Evening – June 28

Eagle Ridge Restaurant is at the top of a morainic belt that is prominent in the area around Birch Bay. Nordland County has a morainic system running the length of the county that is composed of glacial drift deposited as part of the Patrician ice sheet. The long, sinuous ridge rises sixty to seventy feet above the surrounding area. It's covered with a beautiful stand of pine that was untouched when the loggers went through the area a hundred years ago.

Leo Nelson and Helen Gabler were seated at a window overlooking Birch Bay. They were having drinks with Eddie Paxton, the owner of Eagle Ridge Restaurant. They did not see the beauty of the wilderness, or the small town, or the lovely lake shimmering in the moonlight. They only thought of the money that could be made by clearing the land, removing the small houses along the shore, and building large, expensive condominiums.

"Kjelstad needs to suffer a crushing defeat in this next election," said Leo. "We need to give her a political thrashing on the November ballot. Make her an example to anyone else that ever wants to oppose the condo and marina development. There's lots of money in the Twin Cities that would love to own a condo on Big Canoe Lake. And think of all the money the boaters will bring in. Get rid of that damn campground. We need to make it happen."

"What about the conservation easement? That protects the campground property." Eddie looked worried.

"Shit. The DNR can ignore that. They know how to manipulate words and text."

"We can tie her into this assassination business," said Leo with a malicious sneer. "Let people think she's connected. Spread the rumor that she's part of the assassination team."

"And how do we do that?" asked Eddie. "That's slander."

"No. That's gossip. We only need to tell one person to get the buzz started."

"And? Who would that be?"

Leo looked at Helen. Suddenly her eyes lit up. "Sounds like fun," she said. "Leave it to me."

Eddie ordered another round of drinks.

They all smiled. Kjelstad was in deep shit.

Laura looked out the window of the dining room of Raspberry Point Inn watching the darkness overtake the earth. The moon was scattering golden notes on the dark lake, an enchanting, flawless scene that seemed unaware of the horror that had invaded it. Silence underlined the beauty of the moment. It should have caused a sense of great peace, but the circumstances of the day sent an ominous shivering through her body.

"Jeez, Mayor, you look like hell." Hippie sat down and stared at her face. "You going to be all right?"

"Doc says I'll be fine. It seems like somebody took some shots at the guy that was shooting at me. Probably saved my life."

"Well, yeah. That's good." Hippie shifted his weight. "Clara and I already gave statements to the FBI if that's what you're wondering." He looked out the window. "Duluth TV says we're getting more rain."

"Probably, but I want to hear about you and Clara. What happened?" asked Laura.

"Clara and I were the ones shooting at the guy. I drove and Clara had the gun. We were out for a ride. Something to do, you know. Neither one of us wanted to be alone. I really like Clara's car and she said I could drive it. Then we spotted the guy shooting at you. Clara rolled down the window and started firing. We figured we needed to tell someone so we talked to Noah Sackett."

"Not Sam?"

"He was at the hospital waiting to see how you were."

Hippie leaned against the table and covered his face with his hands. "I was never sure what evil was. Now I know. It was evil that killed Cindy. Pure evil."

"You're right."

Hippie tented his fingers against his lips, elbows on the table. "Noah Sackett had a good talk with me about my chemical dependency issues. I'm going into treatment. Serious treatment. For Cindy. This time it'll work. I'll be Matt Wrenshall again."

Laura leaned forward. "Governor Cummings is here."

Jack came quickly to Laura's side and took her in his arms. He kissed her cheek, keeping one arm around her shoulders.

"You don't have any idea how I've prayed that you were all right. Everybody assured me you were fine, but I needed to see for myself. I feel much better knowing you'll be staying here tonight. Makes good sense. How was your supper?"

"Fine. One of the deputies brought it over from the Big Timber Café. Timber's been doing some of the catering for law enforcement. Molly sent her staff home. Loose lips, that kind of thing. The only ones here now are your staff, law enforcement, Hippie, Hal, and me."

"I have a meeting with my staff this evening; it might go late into the night. If you need me for anything, don't hesitate to call. I'll leave word that you're to be put directly through."

"Thanks, Jack. I appreciate it."

"Sorry to rush off, but we need to keep state government organized. Now is not the time to make mistakes." He bent down, brushing the top of her head with his lips.

Sheriff Mikkelson had waited in the hall until he saw Governor Cummings leave. "What's with all the work you brought with you? Laptop, boxes of material. City hall can't be that desperate for things to get done."

"Just something I have to do. I won't sleep that well tonight anyway, so why not go over some papers, study projects, that sort of thing?"

"If it has anything to do with this case, law enforcement needs to have it. You're not holding out information, are you?"

"Why don't we talk about this in the morning?"

"First thing. I'll be here at eight o'clock. Laura, if there's anything at all, I need to know."

"I've given you every tip I've received. I fully intend to continue doing that."

Hal Marshall stopped at the table. "I'm supposed to take Mayor Kjelstad to her room when she's ready."

"Keep Laura safe," said Sam. "Lots of law enforcement here, but I don't want anyone wandering around alone. You on duty for a while?"

"Yes, sir. Until midnight."

"I'll let the deputies know. Communication is a priority." He brushed Laura's cheek with his fingertips. "Try to sleep tonight. And be sure to take the meds the doc gave you."

Sam walked with Laura and Hal as far as the stairway. "I'll call later."

Laura thanked Hal, assuring him she was fine and went into her room; anxious to look through the materials she'd acquired from the Dahlberg family.

Close the shades. Don't go out alone. Call if you leave the room. Sam's words had been full of warnings. A good brisk walk was not possible, but it was what she needed to clear her mind. Standing at the window, she stood in the shadows and watched cars on the street below. Usually the shops were closed by six or seven o'clock, but with all the media and law enforcement in town, they were open until ten or eleven. Vans and cars from various media outlets were parked along the streets.

Close the shades. Done. Flip on the lights. Done. She did a few stretches, some deep knee bends, a series of push-ups and sit-ups, and a round of Tae Kwon Do kicks. The pain level was all right, probably the meds kicking in. Her body still felt like it was on the verge of overload.

The phone rang. It was Sam wanting to know how she was doing. "One of the deputies is bringing Montana over. Montana's missed you. He's fed, watered, and had his potty break. Don't hesitate to call tonight if you need anything. Even if you just want to talk. I'll be at the high school a while longer, then I'm heading home to sleep a few hours."

Five minutes later, Montana was on the couch beside her, head in her lap. She spent the next forty-five minutes on the phone with her parents, Noah, and Molly. Molly had decided to stay at Laura's house overnight. "If I leave now, someone may suspect you're not here," she said. "I'll come home in the morning." Noah had stayed for supper, she said, so now everyone was playing Mexican Train Dominoes.

Well, fine. Laura's face clouded as Molly hung up. "We're here alone and they're all playing games." She gave Montana a hug, clicked on the TV, and surfed through the news channels.

"The governor's staff have been arriving throughout the day," said Barb Terry of Channel Twelve. "Governor Cummings has personally greeted each staff member with a hug and a thank you. He said the whole team is now in place. His senior advisors are staying with him at Raspberry Point Inn. Others are scattered throughout the town so they can hear first hand how the investigation is going and keep an ear to the public concerns. The governor wants the people to know that his office is totally involved with every aspect of operations here."

Channel Five was showing pictures of Birch Bay from the air, flying in low over the Dahlberg's lake house. The blackened and burned Chevy Malibu was still in place. She clicked to national news and watched as interviews were done with Birch Bay residents. All were horrified, but there was nothing new to any of the stories. Governor Cummings was getting outstanding coverage and support from leaders throughout the world.

"Fate has dealt Jack Cummings a cruel blow," said television anchor Tony Nelson. "And yet, he has taken on a dozen critical roles and has handled each one with adeptness, thoughtfulness, and incredible calm. His response has been extraordinary. He has been gutsy, bringing together a state and nation that is in shock. He is a strong leader, one who doesn't hold back his own pain, but fills his voice with compassion. He made it clear that the Dahlbergs were not just political partners, but good friends as well."

Laura put the television on mute and opened the laptop. A piece of paper had been taped to the keyboard with the e-mail address and the password. She switched the computer on, waited patiently for it to boot up, and briefly scanned the messages. Anecdotal records, nothing that sounded ominous.

She laid the boxes of postcards, letters, and photographs on the table. Sitting down at the small table in the kitchen, she started with the photographs. Audrey had labeled the pictures with a brief description, date, and numbers. Laura skimmed through some of the photos to glimpse Audrey and Charlie as a young couple.

Charlie Dahlberg was in several photos that were marked 'high school'. Charlie was shown with classmates in various school activities. It was the kind of pictures that would be great for a presidential candidate. The students all looked the same; the girls wore the class uniform of fluffy hair, straight white teeth, and designer sweaters. The guys had medium length hair, straight white teeth, and shirts that were designer perfect. The pictures were family, friends, and school. Nothing that would indicate any worries.

The letters had a historical note to them. They were copies of letters they'd sent to senators, representatives, and the President of the United States. Letters from various political groups were in a different file.

Another file folder had letters Audrey had sent to her children and grandchildren. Lots of attention to detail of everyday life in the governor's mansion. A large brown envelope was tucked at the bottom of the box, labeled "important", Laura laid the contents on the table. A letter and two photographs were inside.

The letter began: "These are photographs of Mary Wallace and her brother. I can't explain why, but Mary is someone I have grown wary of. She has been in our private residence in the mansion on more than one occasion. I told her that the residence was not open to anyone other than the regular cleaning lady. I came home early the next day and she was there again. I talked to Jack Cummings about it and he had her transferred to a cleaning detail in the state office building. When I asked about her a few weeks later, he said she had quit. He didn't know where she had gone. She hadn't asked for a letter of reference. He had instructed staff to let him know if anyone called asking for her."

What had Bonnie Hollingsworth said? Audrey had told her that if someone named Mary Wallace ever came to the gallery asking questions to send her on her way, but Audrey had wanted to know about the visit. According to Bonnie, Audrey had been quite agitated.

The rest of the letter talked about Mary's brother. "I had told Mary that the governor's mansion was for the governor's business, but Mary had invited her brother in twice. Once I found them in the mansion's kitchen having coffee; another time, they were in the large, official dining room. All of this bothered Jack Cummings a great deal.

"I was able to take a couple of pictures without Mary and her brother knowing that I was doing so. Photos from cell phones can be quite good if you have the right person copying them. Perhaps my worries are all in vain, but nevertheless – here are the pictures."

Laura called Sam immediately. "Two deputies will be right there," he said. "Be careful. I'll be over tomorrow morning to find out what else you have in those boxes. And the laptop."

"Look. I was following instructions from the family. I called you, didn't I?"

Laura was too tired to finish reading everything. After the deputies had left, she clicked off the television and computer and went to bed. Just as she was falling asleep, she heard thunder in the distance and then the rhythmic sound of raindrops on the roof.

About midnight, Laura woke with a start. She'd been dreaming of a body floating in the water; coming closer to shore with each pulse of the waves. The body seemed to be reaching out to her, pleading, begging for help. She saw eyes –dull, vacant eyes, eyes turning to searing flames of torment – then the face, white and lifeless. The mouth opened to speak, first haltingly, accusingly, and then the wind gave rise to a voice that screamed at her until there was no place to hide from the wrenching agony of that cry.

She clutched her pillow for assurance and looked out the window wondering what horror awaited her outside. Nonsense. She needed to get up and move around. Make some tea. She heard voices in the hall. Montana sniffed the air and raised his ears.

"Will you shut off that confounded flashlight?" an angry voice shouted. "You're going to wake everybody in the Inn. The governor's downstairs. You want the deputies to report us to Mikkelson?"

Laura opened the door a crack and saw Hal Marshall and another young man in animated conversation.

"Didn't you hear it? It sounded like someone screamed. Maybe someone needs help." Hal kept the light on and put a hushing finger to his lips. "Listen. There it is again."

"That's the squeal of tires out on the street. Some kids are probably out joyriding."

"With all the law enforcement around town? Doesn't seem likely." Hal shut the light off, letting the dim light of the security lamps illumine the hall. In a moment, he fumbled with the flashlight, pressed his thumb on the switch and pointed the beam out the window.

"Now what are you doing?"

"Did you hear that?" whispered Hal. "It sounded like someone is outside scratching on the wall."

"It's that tree branch that Mrs. Berg told me to trim. I was too busy today to get that job done."

"Well there's a chill running from my toes up to my forehead," said Hal. "My hair is tingling."

Hal breathed deeply, exhaled, and started chanting: "Aaa-uuhh-mmmm", his tongue vibrating, giving an extra zip to his ah-umming.

"Explain that to me," said his companion.

"It's a Buddhist chant; it helps me relax, get in touch with my inner self."

"Yeah? Well it doesn't do anything for the rest of us."

"Assassination, murders, and an attempt on Mrs. Kjelstad have to be taken seriously. Bombs and knives and lots of bullets suggests that the killer has a certain...a peculiar...."

"Zeal?"

"Exactly," said Hal as he continued the rhythmic breathing, alternating with his intense chanting. He flicked on his flashlight and pointed it toward the window. His excitement did nothing to improve his audibility.

Laura shut her door. It was going to be a long night.

Chapter Thirty-eight

Morning
June 29

Anne Bradley hadn't slept well. The trip to Birch Bay and back to St. Paul had been tense and hurried. Her nerves were on edge and she wondered if she had made a mistake calling the number that Charlie had given her. Charlie had said they would talk about the phone number when he returned from Birch Bay. At the time, it hadn't seemed immediate, but now she knew she should have asked some questions.

Maybe she'd dialed the number too many times. No one ever answered even though she'd tried at different times during the day. The voice messaging had been disabled, not that she would have left her number for anyone to call. Still, it seemed strange. She was done calling. Let the FBI handle it.

Wally had been up most of the night. The same damn person had called him. Again and again. Who the hell was it? Only his boss had his cell number. Had the person in charge of the whole operation given out information about his cell phone? That hadn't been part of the deal. Betrayal. That's what it was. Still, the chief honcho was paying him big money. Besides, the cell was in a fictitious name with a phony address. Damn, it was easy to do business with the knuckleheads.

Leave Kjelstad alone had been the last order. Wally had complained about the number of phone calls he'd been getting. He had seen Kjelstad dial her phone at the same time his had rung. It had to be her. He'd been watching.

When his cell phone rang, Wally was in a foul mood. He spit a "Who is it?" into the phone.

"I agree that we need to get rid of Kjelstad," said the voice. "Have Barry and Ross pick her up. Discreetly, of course. You stay put and keep an eye on things in town. I need to get the job done and it sounds like she's in the way. Kill her parents if you have to. The deputies are sitting in their cars getting bored. If they get in your way, eliminate them. Take Kjelstad to that abandoned cabin on Coyote Ridge. Find out what she knows and then dump her in the lake."

Downtown Birch Bay was bustling. The rain continued in a sporadic drizzle, thunder rumbling in the west, but it didn't keep anyone inside. Sam had arrived at the Inn early and took all the material that the Dahlberg family had given Laura. Matt Wrenshall and Laura had decided to walk down to Big Timber Café for breakfast. Montana was with them, sniffing his way along Main Street.

Sam could not dissuade Laura from leaving the Inn. "I can't stay hidden forever," she said. "Besides, once I'm in my rain poncho, no one will recognize me from everyone else in their rain gear. Same with Matt."

"Montana is identifiable," said Sam.

Laura shrugged her shoulders. "Do you know how many people there are on the streets and in the shops around town? I was alone yesterday. Today I'm surrounded by people."

Molly left Laura's house and was walking to the Inn. Sam had said Laura and Matt were going to Big Timber for breakfast. Knut and Emily would join them. They didn't think Laura should be in a vulnerable position, but if she were out, they would be with her. After a quick shower, Molly would join them and find out the latest news. Knut Hansen had offered to drive her downtown, but he was in the shower and she wanted to be on her way. She waved to the deputy in the patrol car as she passed.

Halfway down the hill the rain started again; she pulled Laura's Duluth Dukes baseball cap out of her backpack. In broad daylight, no one would mistake her for Laura.

Ross and Barry had been watching the house. The patrol cars were damn obvious. Almost like they wanted to be seen. Show of force mentality. Tiresome.

"Gives us the advantage," said Ross. "We know exactly where they are."

"Maybe they're decoys," said Barry. "Could be a setup."

"Whatever. We'll just shoot anyone who gets in our way. Killing a cop never bothered you before."

"Never been involved with something this big before. Killing a cop doesn't bother me. It's them shooting me that I have to think about."

"Lose your nerve and you're a dead man. Stupid."

One thing about Kjelstad, she always wore that Dukes cap when she went for her walk. Everyone knew that. The woman who came out the door of the Kjelstad house wasn't quite what they remembered, but as soon as the baseball cap went on her head, they knew they had her.

It was quick. One fluid motion and the car was alongside her, Barry was out of the car, and the woman was inside. Fast, that's what it was. The woman didn't even have a chance to scream.

Molly's breath had left her. Her brain was exploding, fragments going in all directions. She started flailing at the man beside her in the back seat, but he punched her face so hard that she began quivering from the onslaught of pain. She lay back against the seat and closed her eyes.

Think.

Give the impression that she was unconscious.

She had nothing with which to defend herself. She opened her eyes slowly. Both men were looking out the windows, watching the traffic.

Windows.

She pressed against the window, maybe someone would see her bloody face. A powerful slap on the back of the head sent her to the floor. The man put his foot on her back and pushed down hard.

"You're a slow learner, aren't you?" The man twisted his foot into her flesh.

She should have phoned the Inn and told them to expect her. But why? No one had any reason to kidnap her. And where was law enforcement? Watching Laura.

Fear paraded through her brain. Flags waving, terror like fireworks marching through her cells.

"If you let me sit up again, I won't try anything," she said quietly. "Really. I don't want to get hit any more."

Rough hands pulled her up and pressed her firmly against the seat.

"Listen Kjelstad, try one more time and I swear I'll shoot you where you sit."

Kjelstad. How could they think she was Laura? That didn't compute. Then Molly looked at the Dukes baseball cap in her hand. Of course. Laura's familiar cap. Laura wore it enough that the cap had become the way for people to identify her from a distance.

"That wouldn't be wise," said Molly. "Shoot me and DNA would splatter all over you."

"Rental car," said the guy up front.

"Doesn't matter," said Molly. "The blood would spurt like a geyser." DNA. That was all she could think of. Her mind was searching for a plan. Blank. Nothing.

Silence.

Her cell phone, clipped to her belt, was poking into her stomach, her jacket and blouse keeping it from view. A minute alone and she could press speed dial.

Town was behind them now, fading quickly as they drove up the hill. Where were they taking her? And why?

"I think I'm about to vomit."

"Shit. Don't puke in the car. Dammit." The driver was not happy. "Cover your damn mouth."

"Let me out for an instant. We're out of town now. Maybe some fresh air would help." Retching noises rumbled through the car.

"Stop the fuckin' car," said Barry. "I don't want puke all over me. Let her run into the woods. I can watch her."

"If she tries to run, shoot her," said Ross. He pulled to the side of the road.

Molly leaped from the car, stumbled, and ran toward the cover of woods.

"Stop there," shouted Barry. He leaned against the car. Damn if he'd go close to a woman spitting puke.

Molly stopped, turned her back, and bent over as if to vomit. Her mind was in top speed. Don't let them see the phone. Ease her hand under the blouse. Feel the key pad. Laura was speed dial two. She felt it, pressed the key, and prayed.

"Hello."

Molly could barely hear Laura, but she recognized the voice.

"I've been kidnapped," shouted Molly. "We're heading toward Coyote Ridge."

"What are you babbling about?" Barry was moving toward her. "Get in the car." Molly brushed her blouse down and walked toward the men. She kept the phone on.

"Molly?" Laura stopped to listen.

"Where are you taking me?" She heard Molly's voice.

"Just get in the fuckin' car." A man's voice.

"Kidnapping is serious." Molly's voice was loud.

Laura grabbed Hippie's arm. "Molly's been kidnapped."

Laura ran into the street, hands raised, stopping the first car that came along. Other cars screeched to a stop. She spotted Clara two cars back and raced toward her. Clara opened the window.

"I need your car. Now." Laura was grabbing the handle of the door.

"Unlock your car, Clara. I need it."

Clara was bewildered, but snapped the lock open.

"Get out," shouted Laura. "I'm taking your car."

Hippie grabbed Clara as she tumbled out of the car, a look of fear on her face. Montana jumped into the front seat trembling with expectancy.

"Do you have your Glock?" shouted Laura. She was behind the wheel.

Clara nodded.

"I need it."

"It's under the passenger seat." Clara was shaking. "What's going on?"

"Where are the bullets?" Laura was shouting. She pulled the Glock out and positioned it on the floor where she could grab it quickly.

"In the glove compartment."

Laura grabbed the bullets, shoved them on the floor beside the Glock, and shouted out the window. "Get me some help. Now. I'm headed toward Coyote Ridge. Molly's been kidnapped." She pulled around cars and drove along Portage Street.

Molly's voice was clear again. Loud. "We're heading east on Birch Drive. Why?"

"Keep your fuckin' mouth closed." A man's voice. Then Laura heard a smack and moan.

"You don't have to hit me again." It was Molly's voice, quiet and pained. "I'll keep quiet."

Okay. They were on Birch Drive. Laura reached for the OnStar button. She hoped Clara was a subscriber. The digital voice came on. "Dial," said Laura.

Laura gave Noah's number. "Pardon?" said the recording. Laura gave the number again. On the third try, Noah answered. She filled him in on Molly's capture.

"Can you track me?" asked Laura. "I thought OnStar could be tracked."

"I'll see that it happens," said Noah. "I'll drive out there, too. I have my cell. Keep me posted."

"I have to keep my cell on so I can hear Molly. I'll use OnStar. I don't know Clara's OnStar number, though."

"No problem. I'll have it quickly."

Noah's office was like visiting NASA. Or Star Trek. SEAL training and Navy Intelligence left its mark on Noah. He had state of the art computer equipment that would set Bill Gates into overload.

"I'll see that Coyote Ridge is covered with every law enforcement agency around." Noah hung up.

Montana wiggled with excitement as they drove up Cranberry Lake Road and turned right on Birch Drive.

"We're not going fishing today, big guy," said Laura. "We need to rescue Molly."

CHAPTER THIRTY-NINE

Laura was on the move, rushing along the top of Coyote ridge, rain pouring down, and the wind picking up, blasting the side of the car. Darkness was hovering along the edges of the sky, the storm like some malevolent hand ready to seize her.

She waited for Molly's voice again, but it was several minutes before she heard anything. "Lot number 3871," said Molly. "I don't know where we are."

Laura covered the mouthpiece of her cell and called Noah on OnStar. Noah's voice was disintegrating as it came over the airwaves.

"I have the number of the lot where they're taking Molly," she said.

There was no response. Noah must have entered a no service zone. Laura looked at her cell; the phone was dead.

"I'll try later," she told Montana. "We're going to be fine. So is Molly."

It took another five minutes to find the property where Molly had been taken. A car was parked in the driveway. Laura edged slowly down the road, doubled back, and parked a block away. Coyote Ridge was filled with a mix of homes; some were vacation spots with spectacular views, others were single family homes owned by year-rounders. Located between Birch Bay and Duluth, the property offered country living in close proximity to job opportunities. If the guys holding Molly did come out on the road, a car parked along the edge was not out of the ordinary.

She tried Noah again and left a message on his voice mail.

"Time to go to work, Montana. Sorry about the rain, but you're a tough guy. It'll be fine."

Laura kept the poncho on, trying to keep somewhat dry. It would have to come off if she needed to use the gun. It would be too cumbersome to take careful aim. Just before the driveway, she moved into the trees and brush, cutting through the dense forest toward the cabin. Montana followed right behind, his nose twitching, catching the scents in the air, ears up, and his eyes scanning the woods.

When she reached the edge of the lawn, Laura hesitated for a moment, taking time to get the layout of the property. The cabin was made of logs, sitting in the center of the lawn, trees surrounding the building. A two-car garage was thirty feet up the driveway, it was logs, too, with windows on the sides facing her. The interior of the garage was dark; light shone through the windows of the cabin.

Time to take off the poncho; she needed freedom of movement. She broke from the protection of the trees in a full run, raced across the open ground, and moved to the edge of the cabin. Avoiding the door seemed logical, but looking through the windows could be difficult. Montana sensed the gravity of the situation and hugged the wall of the cabin just as she was doing.

A low roll of thunder echoed over the ridge, the rain had become a steady onslaught. Laura eased the Glock out of the poncho pocket and put it in the waistband of her jeans pulling her sweater down to cover it. The rain poured down the roof and into the gutters; the wind was blowing in strong gusts and she thought no one could possibly hear them. The grayness of the day might make it difficult to see them, too. She was careful as she inched her way to the nearest window, keeping her back to the wall, and giving a sideways look into the living room.

Molly was sitting on a chair near the fireplace. Her face looked grim, her mouth was in a hard line. No one else was visible. Laura moved to another window, the kitchen, and saw a man making a pot of coffee. She moved to another window, an empty bedroom. Another small window had the shades drawn, probably the bathroom.

Laura went back to watching Molly. Molly's eyes were open and she was talking. Laura looked more closely and saw that her right hand was shackled to the fireplace.

What were the odds of the man being there without backup? Not very good. Laura had thought she had heard two men speaking to Molly. Still, no one else seemed to be around. Laura took Montana by the collar and kept him beside her while she crept to the front door.

"We're going in," she said to Montana.

Laura flew through the front door and raced to the living room. The man was pouring himself a cup of coffee. She pointed the gun at the man's head.

"Where's the key to the handcuffs?" she yelled.

The man dropped the coffeepot and lunged for his gun, but he wasn't close enough to get it. Laura snatched it from the table and put it at Molly's feet.

"Give me the key to the handcuffs," shouted Laura. "Or I'll shoot the cuffs off."

"His name's Barry," said Molly, her voice shrill and hurried. "There's another guy. Ross. He went to make a phone call, but has to walk to the top of a ridge to make a connection. I'm afraid he'll be back soon."

Barry's look was arrogant; his eyes like cesspools to the very depth of his soul.

"Whatever you're involved in, you've flunked the big test," said Laura. Her voice was crisp and clear, anger zipping through her brain.

"You're one dead bitch," hissed Barry. "Always in the way, always thinking you're in control. Well, you're not. The boss is tired of your shit. You're the one that's going to wind up in the lake. We'll take you to Quady's Inlet and drop you over the edge. You won't last long, especially today with the wind and waves. The current will suck you under in seconds. Dark water will drag you down. Suicide. We'll see that word gets around. You couldn't stand the pressure."

Laura listened to his taunting words, realizing he was waiting for Ross to return. His mocking words burned to the center of her brain, alerting her reflexes. She glared at him, eyes firing an insolent message.

"Lean as far away from the fireplace as you can," she said to Molly. "I'll shoot the chain."

Gunfire exploded through the house as she fired two shots to free Molly's hand. She turned the gun on Barry. He was in an emotional vortex, his eyes lost their focus, and his mouth quivered slightly.

"Behind you," shouted Molly.

The outside door was flung open. A big man in a red flannel shirt aimed a gun at Laura. She whirled and fired. For an instant, the man seemed confused; then he sank to his knees as blood gushed from the wound in his shoulder, the gun tumbling from his hand. He grabbed at his injured arm, pain etched across his face. Laura kicked the gun away.

Those precious seconds gave Barry time to attack Laura. His fist came at her with a violent swing. A rush of strength surged through her body, and she moved enough that he caught her arm instead of her face, but her gun twirled across the floor. Tae Kwon Do reflexes kicked in. Barry lost his balance and stumbled. Laura kicked him behind the knees, increasing the momentum of his body so that he slammed face first into the log wall. He clutched his face, blood gushing from his nose.

Mr. Red Flannel Shirt guy came at Laura, but Montana lunged at him, knocking him to the floor. Molly grabbed the gun at her feet.

Laura's eyes settled on Barry's chest and she gave a powerful front snap kick that doubled him over. She followed through with a crunching kick to his knee, followed by a quick pulling twist to his arm and a downward strike to the elbow.

Barry couldn't move. The kick had shattered his kneecap and the punch was designed to break the elbow. That's what they were supposed to do. "Kick the knees," her Tae Kwon Do instructor had said. "A kick to the groin and they can eventually come after you. Break the kneecaps and they're down for good."

A third guy burst through the doorway shooting randomly. Molly and Laura fired at the same time. Blood gushed from the man's leg and shoulder. A lamp and knick-knacks smashed to the floor as he fell onto an end table. Martin Gardner was shuddering in pain.

"Molly. Watch these guys," said Laura. "I'm just going to check the kitchen." She backed across the room, gun pointed at the men.

At the kitchen door, Laura turned slightly and checked the Glock. She hadn't counted the number of shots she'd fired. One bullet left. She took bullets from her pocket, loaded the Glock, and joined Molly in the living room.

"Fuckin' maniac," said Ross, the guy in the red flannel shirt. Desperation was evident in his face; there was a hoarseness in this voice that caused him to croak out the words. "Who the hell are you?"

Montana gave a low growl, lips curled back, as he stood beside the guy on the floor.

"Good boy, Montana. Guard," said Laura.

"A car's pulling into the driveway," said Molly.

A bolt of lightning flashed across the sky, the clap of thunder was alarmingly close. Rain lashed against the cabin.

"I hope it's Noah," said Laura, but she couldn't see anyone.

"Probably being careful," said Molly. "He doesn't know what the situation is."

Laura shut the lights off. Molly and Laura put their backs against the fireplace, guns pointing toward the door. Just in case, they reasoned.

It was Noah who came through the door, Noah who surveyed the wounded men around the room.

"I've called in the troops," said Noah. "They're right behind me."

They stayed together around the fireplace until the FBI, CIA, sheriff, and ambulances arrived.

Beckwith and Mikkelson shook their heads.

"Who dropped these guys?" asked Beckwith. "You do this yourself?" he asked Noah.

"They were like that when I came in," said Noah.

"Shit," said Beckwith. "Don't tell me these two women did it."

"No," said Molly. "Just one. Laura."

Beckwith shook his head. "Remind me never to tick you off. How do I write this one up? A kidnapping, two guys with bullets in them, and another guy with broken body parts. Captured by the local mayor. A woman. Jeez."

Chapter Forty

"Meet me on the beach by Raspberry Point." The voice was quiet, but the words were clipped as if coming through clenched teeth. "Your guys fouled up big time."

"The FBI knows nothing," said Wally. He had been careful, real tricky, fake names, clever disguises. The boss had relied on him and he'd delivered.

"Fifteen minutes."

"Yes, sir." Wally was skittish. Ross and Barry didn't know who he really was so there was no way the FBI could find him. Gardener didn't know what was happening either. It was time the boss gave him a plane ticket to some European destination.

Wally was at the beach within ten minutes. He waited in the shadows until he saw the figure approaching.

"Boss?"

"It's me. What the hell happened out at the cabin?"

"Big time screw up. I'll be the first to admit that. Those guys don't know shit. They don't even know my real name. Give me my plane ticket and the cash and I'm out of the country. I can stay hidden 'til you need me again."

"That would be good."

"I got the job done. As far as the law is concerned, they're at a dead end."

"And it will stay that way."

Wally tried to read the man's face, but it was too dark. "I'll be out of town in five minutes if that's what you want. You know I follow orders."

"You've been real tricky. No way to trace your various identities. I thought your disguises were quite professional. It's all gone well."

Wally sighed. "So, do you want me to leave tonight?"

"That's my plan." The man turned and started walking away.

"Where you going? I need the money and tickets."

"Can't stand too close," said the man. He fired two shots into Wally's chest. "I don't want blood and tissue on my clothes." He was speaking to a dead man.

CHAPTER FORTY-ONE

Birch Bay
June 30
Early Afternoon

Once the dominoes began to collapse, they took on a volcanic effect. Wally's body had been found by an early morning hiker. The beach was overtaken by FBI and the whole town was under tight security.

Media coverage was in overload.

Pictures of the men involved in the assassination were on the front pages of newspapers and shown repeatedly on television.

And there it ended.

Frustrating.

Infuriating.

Everyone agreed that something had to break, but as yet, there was no more information.

News conferences were held regularly. Furry boom microphones and television cameras were being pointed in all directions. Newspaper reporters and photographers were everywhere, getting statements from anyone willing to talk. It was noted by law enforcement that most citizens were anxious to be interviewed and then dismayed when the story came out and they're misquoted or not quoted.

Agent Beckwith and Sam Mikkelson were buried in tangles of red tape, media interviews, and political wrangling. Noah Sackett stayed in the background, professional and helpful, but out of the spotlight. Hippie and Clara were inundated with phone calls and conversations. Molly was enjoying the company of her husband and mother-in-law. Nothing was back to normal. People wondered what the long term effects of the assassinations would have on Birch Bay.

Laura was home waiting along with everyone else. Her parents had driven to Duluth and would be back in time for supper. The day was warm and sunny and relaxed. Laura went to the kitchen window and stood for a while breathing in the tranquility of the day. She hadn't slept much, her mind in high gear racing through the deaths that had enveloped the town. The microwave shrilled that her cinnamon roll was ready. She walked onto the deck with the roll, an iced tea, and her mail.

A box of eight by ten photographs was in a package sent by Rose Haugen.

"Here's a box I overlooked," she wrote. "I know you'll send them along to the FBI, but I wanted you to look at them first. None of the family has looked at them yet. Thanks for all your help."

The first picture in the box was of two elegantly dressed women, young, smiling, and looking giddily into the camera. In the background, Laura could see a room full of people in what looked like the living room of someone's house, a very expensive house.

The second print showed a young woman holding a baby, standing by the fireplace in the same house. There were photographs on the mantle, but Laura couldn't make out who was in the pictures. She needed a magnifying glass.

Back inside, she rummaged through her desk drawer and quickly found a magnifying glass. On her way out to the deck, she grabbed the pitcher of tea, clinking ice cubes into it. May as well have some chips, too, she thought. Both hands were full as she maneuvered out the door.

Laura hadn't noticed the breeze when she went inside, but now she found the photos scattered across the deck floor. Had Audrey put the photos in any particular order? Stacking the pictures on a side table, she began sorting through them.

Pictures of children, parties, and yards didn't seem to hold any clues. Most of the pictures were taken in the governor's mansion. Holding the magnifying glass above each photo, she scrutinized every one carefully. Nothing. Several pictures were still in the box, unmoved by the wind. At least she could keep these in order in case the sequence meant anything.

About halfway through the box she found a picture that froze her heart. Jack Cummings was smiling engagingly at two men standing by a fireplace in a house she didn't recognize. Jack was in the next photo, too, helping himself to a drink.

Jack seemed to know the people he was with. Alarming, since the men he was talking to were Wally Kaiser and Martin Gardner. They were all looking away from the camera and Laura was sure they didn't know a camera was pointed at them. The next picture showed Jack with his hands on Wally's shoulder. Hadn't Jack said he didn't know any of the men?

Laura reached for her phone and clicked in Noah's number. He wasn't answering. She dialed the sheriff's department, but Sam wasn't available.

"Do you want him to call when he comes in?" asked the dispatcher.

"Tell him I called," said Laura. "Please have him drop by to see me as soon as he is available."

Next she dialed Rose Haugan.

"What can I help you with?" asked Rose after she'd made a few appreciative remarks about Laura's ability to subdue three men.

"I'm looking through the pictures you sent. Do you know the dates these photos were taken? Or anything about them?"

"Nothing," responded Rose. "Sorry. We've been so busy, we haven't looked at any of them. Is something wrong?"

"Yes. Jack Cummings is talking with two of the men that have been arrested. They look friendly. Are these the only photos?"

"As far as I know. You think the men were setting Jack up to get information about my parents?"

"I don't know. I thought Jack said he didn't know any of these people. He admitted that he knew Mary Wallace because of her employment at the mansion. It seems strange."

"Maybe the photos should go to the sheriff right away," said Rose. "I didn't know what they were."

"I have a call into Sam. I'm sure he'll get in touch with me soon. Then we can figure this all out."

"Do you want one of the family to come to Birch Bay?" asked Rose.

"Not yet. I'll talk to Sam. And Noah." Laura mumbled a wooden, "Thank you."

"Call if you need anything," said Rose and ended the call.

Laura clicked the cell phone shut, grabbed the photos, and went inside. The wind was picking up.

Lock the door, Noah had said. Thoughts flew through her mind, confused and questioning. Why was Jack Cummings being friendly with Wally Kaiser? Why had he lied? Had it been a chance encounter? Jack was great at moving through a room, grabbing a shoulder, and shaking a hand. It's the way he worked the room.

Laura stared out the window at the expanse of Big Canoe Lake. Such an incredibly beautiful sight. How could such dreadful things be happening? The ideas parading through her brain were grim and chilling.

There was no time to reason things through. Jack was coming through the door as she walked into the kitchen.

"Laura. I've missed you. Press conferences, staff meetings." Jack took her in his arms and felt her stiffen. "Sorry I didn't call, but when I found out you were home I had to see you. Are you feeling up to going out for dinner tonight?"

"I have a couple of meetings. I don't know what will come of them. Maybe another time."

Laura's arms clutched the box of photos close to her. Her ears were sending thumping vibrations through her brain. She didn't want to seem nervous, but she wanted to set the box down as inconspicuously as possible.

"Let me run this box to the bedroom and I'll be right back," she said. "How about some iced tea? Or a soda?"

"I can help myself. Can I take that box for you? Looks like things are spilling out?"

"It's fine. There are chips on the counter."

She didn't want to confront Jack about the photos. It was something she'd hand off to Sam and let him handle. But as she walked into the bedroom, another comment reached her that sent shivers undulating across her body.

"It looks like one of the pictures blew onto your yard. I'll grab it," called Jack as he went out the door.

Her thoughts became fragmented. Jack was one of the most powerful men in the state. Why should she even question his motives? She felt nervous energy washing over her.

Jack's expression was agonized as he waved the picture in the air and then threw it on the kitchen counter.

"What's this photo about?" he asked. His voice was hard, the words brittle on his lips.

Laura reached out and took the picture of Wally Kaiser with Jack.

"Why don't you tell me?" she said, trying to keep her voice level.

"Where did you get this?" This time he was shouting, anger pulsing at his temples and in his throat.

"I'm not going to talk about this right now. Why don't we talk about this tomorrow?"

Jack was standing closer to her, his voice lethal in its clarity. "We'll talk now."

Laura was groping for an explanation, searching for any plausible reason that would explain why Jack was getting so angry and that would keep him from being implicated in the deaths. How much did he know about the murders? Was he afraid of his approval rating or afraid of being discovered? The tension between them was unbearable.

"Then it's time for you to offer some information." Her emotions were raw and intolerable and she tried to keep from trembling.

"Who gave this to you?" Jack reached over and jerked the photo from her hand.

"It's an anonymous person. Period."

"Who have you talked to?"

"Lots of people."

"You're on dangerous ground."

"It doesn't matter. I have the photos; that's all we need to talk about."

"Where are the negatives?"

"It doesn't matter. Tell me about your relationship with Wally Kaiser and Gardner."

"Damn it, Laura, quit being cagey. How many copies of these pictures are there?"

Laura was silent. Let him talk. She could see the tightness building, anxiousness working its way through his body. Warning signals were going off in her brain, but she wanted him to talk.

"Answer me." Jack's voice was edged with an uncharacteristic iciness and his hands quivered as he caressed the photo as if it were animate.

Guilty, she thought. But of what and how much?

"You couldn't let it rest, could you?" asked Jack, a definite tone of intimidation in his voice.

"People have been murdered."

"I'll take care of everything. Just give me the negatives." Jack's enunciation was clipped, his eyes like two frosty cesspools, his voice frigid, teeth clenched. He was so careful, so meticulous in his movements that it seemed that every muscle, every tendon, was ready to strike out and destroy her.

Looking out the windows, Laura realized there was no protective squad car in the area. Jack waved the photo around, making circles in the air, thrusting it in Laura's direction in a threatening gesture.

"Maybe if you tell me what happened, we can find a way to work things out."

Laura's voice was calm, but her body was rigid, fear gushing into every pore. Her mouth felt numb, but she kept talking trying to get Jack to communicate with her. "Just talk to me, Jack."

"I've worked hard, Laura. I'm governor of the state. Think about that. I plan to be in line for the presidency."

"Are you involved in the assassinations?"

"That's so damn characteristic of you, Laura. Direct. Always on top of things."

"Talk to Beckwith. He'll help you."

"You should have let things go. I really didn't want to see anything happen to you."

"A lot of people know about these pictures, Jack. Too many eyes have fallen on these to keep them secret any longer."

"Bullshit. If anyone else knew about these, the FBI would have questioned me. Quit jerking me around." Jack raked his hand through his hair, then rubbed his eyes.

"You're involved over your head. Or maybe you're the leader. Whatever, Jack, it's all over. You'll have to talk to Beckwith."

"Hell I will. Somebody tried to kill you. It won't surprise anyone when you're found alongside the road in a ditch somewhere."

"But you don't have the negatives."

"After you're dead, whoever has them will be too damned scared to show them to anybody."

Dead?

Laura was incredulous. The governor was going to kill her?

Jack was resolute. No dancing around the issue. Laura didn't feel a surge of courage as she stood at the edge of the kitchen table. She was overwhelmingly tired of the whole mess. Tired of betrayal. Tired of seeing the town scared. Tired of people dying.

"How are you planning on killing me?" she asked.

"I can shoot you here if you'd like." He pulled a .38 from his belt, hidden by the light jacket he was wearing. "No one knows I'm here. My car is still down at the Inn. I told my staff I was going out for some fresh air. I'll tell them I was walking by your house when I heard gunfire. After what's happened around here, it will be very believable."

Her teeth were clamped tight and her hands formed fists. The man was insane. To Laura's right, two of her beautiful blue willow dishes were sitting on the counter, ready to put in the cupboard. She felt her car keys in her pocket. With her left hand, she reached into her pocket as she edged toward the plates.

"What are you after?" he asked.

"I thought I'd put the dishes away; have the house tidy when my relatives come to grieve."

Jack leaned against the wall. "There'll be blood splatters everywhere. Not very tidy at all."

In an instant, Laura pressed the horn alarm button on the car key, the loud, rhythmic pulsing covering the neighborhood. Taken by surprise, Jack jerked and momentarily looked outside. Laura picked up a plate and tossed it like a Frisbee toward Jack's head. She heard his cheekbone pop and shatter. The second plate struck him in his mouth and blood splattered across the room. She did a running side kick which landed on his stomach catapulting him backward across the table.

Propelling herself forward, Laura reached the front door and ran into the yard. She dialed 911 on her cell phone as she ran toward Noah's house. Siren's were blaring as a sheriff's car and two FBI vehicles whirled into view. Noah was bolting toward her.

"Make sure those pictures are safe," she shouted. "He might try to destroy them."

"Who's after you?" asked Beckwith.

"Jack Cummings. He's involved in all the killings."

Sam Mikkelson was speaking into the radio attached to the shoulder of his uniform; he was requesting backup.

Leo Nelson was getting out of his car, responding to the commotion. "You settle down Missy Mayor," he said. "What have you done now?"

"You stay out of the way or I'll drop kick you into the street. I mean it Leo. Don't you dare blow this one."

"What in the hell is going on?" bellowed Leo. "Shit. Bossy bitch."

CHAPTER FORTY-TWO

Raspberry Point Inn
July 1
Late Afternoon

Summer was rising in fine fashion, warmth surrounded the lake, no wind, clear sky, and the scent of wild roses filled the air. Molly had invited a large group for afternoon tea. Television sets were set throughout the sunroom so they could watch the newscasts without missing anything.

Molly, with her wondrous flair for entertaining and cooking, had filled a table with food and beverages. Gary and his mother were home and Molly was ecstatic.

Laura, Knut, and Emily were relaxed, thankful that the nightmare was over. Sam and Noah had energy blazing around them, confident that the case was finished and the evidence was being collected quickly and efficiently by the FBI.

Agent Beckwith was smiling as he walked into the room. The latest press conference had gone well, agents were collecting strong evidence, and Beckwith was sure an indictment would come quickly.

Hippie arrived chatty and hyper. Clara was with him, saying she hadn't slept. Last night she had stayed awake because of the excitement that the whole dreadful thing was over.

People began drifting in, helping themselves to food, joining in the conversation. Hal Marshall came into the room with an armload of newspapers that he passed around.

Neatly across the top of the newspapers, the pictures were lined up. Governor Jack Cummings was smiling. The press had retrieved one of his campaign photos.

Wally Kaiser's picture was grim, sent by the Chicago police department from a mug shot when he'd been arrested for burglary.

"I heard Wally was the one who killed Cindy," said Hippie. "The other guys squealed. They fingered him for killing Mark Brewster and Lisa Sinclair."

Cindy's picture was on the front page, too, the picture from her high school yearbook. Charlie and Audrey Dahlberg's official photo was in the upper right hand corner.

Molly turned on the television sets and everyone watched CNN and MSNBC. The major networks also were having special news coverage, flashing pictures and giving voiceovers of the arrests. USA had a reporter standing in front of the Minnesota Capitol Building giving a recap of the assassinations and investigation. The President of the United States held a press conference and congratulated the FBI on their handling of the case.

The networks bounced between Washington, St. Paul, and Birch Bay. Photos were flashed on the screen with the news anchors giving background, but after a while there was nothing new.

"FBI, CIA, and BCA moved in fast," said Sam. "As soon as they had those photos they were on a roll. Rose Haugen said she didn't know there was anything important. Thought they were just pictures her mom had saved. She was very apologetic. She was also pleased that Laura had acted immediately on what she had seen."

"There's no mention of Rose or any of the Dahlberg family in connection with the photographs," said Laura. "Will they keep them out of this whole mess?"

"Absolutely," said Beckwith. "The family is being extremely helpful. We're not about to send them to the media wolves. They've been through enough. All the agencies are reporting an undisclosed source. That's the way it will stay."

"What if Barry or the other guy deny kidnapping Molly?" asked Laura. "What kind of proof needs to be shown in court?"

Mikkelson ate the frosting off his cupcake and smiled. "For one thing, one end of the handcuffs was hanging from her wrist; the other end was still attached to the hoop on the fireplace. You only broke the chain on the cuffs to free Molly. Law enforcement got photos of everything at the cabin. Besides, the key to the cuffs was found in Barry's pocket. There were lots of officers on the scene who will testify to all the evidence."

"We'll be investigating for quite a while," said Beckwith. "This case has reached international proportions. A governor being assassinated by his lieutenant governor. Damn. How much lower can you get? The press around the world is on a major feeding frenzy."

"Any of the bad guys giving testimony for the prosecutor?" asked Knut.

"Absolutely," said Beckwith "These guys are scared. They're trying for any plea agreement they can get. They're all letting Cummings hang out alone."

"Is there enough evidence to put Cummings away?" asked Knut.

"We're collecting it," said Beckwith. "The .38 Cummings had matches the gun that killed Wally Kaiser."

"Mayor Kjelstad. Would you take me up to that cabin some time?" asked Hippie.

"I sure will. After the investigation is over."

"I'd like to know where it is," said Hippie.

Mikkelson raised his chin and furrowed his brows.

"Just curiosity," said Hippie. "Honest. I'm still heading to treatment as soon as I can. Cummings was a real jerk, wasn't he? One of those up your wild blue asters guys."

Knut interrupted. "They're repeating the story on Molly."

Channel Four began with the kidnapping story. News anchor Tim Rushton introduced the story while the television camera zoomed in on the cabin and the yellow crime scene tape surrounding the area. Sun touched the edges of the trees and wildflowers were blooming profusely.

"It was along this beautiful forest road that a woman was shackled to a fireplace after she was kidnapped in Birch Bay," said Rushton. "Local authorities are giving little information about the crime, but we know it was directly related to the assassinations of Governor Dahlberg and his wife, Audrey."

The television screen showed a panoramic view of the road and the forest. In the background a deputy was walking the ditch and FBI vehicles were parked nearby.

"Do you have the identity of the victim?" asked co-anchor Lynn Hargrave.

"We have no information. We only know it ties directly to Governor Jack Cummings, which is the major story of the day."

"We will continue the assassination coverage and the involvement of Governor Cummings. CBS news in St. Paul has the story," said Hargrave.

"Information is flowing in rather quickly," said CBS news anchor, Sheryl Chavez. We have learned that Governor Dahlberg was not going to back Jack Cummings in the next election for governor. Sources tell us that Cummings wanted to be governor and then fall in line to be President of the United States. At the time, we don't know all the details, but law enforcement is gathering reams of information."

"Scary," said co-anchor Brad Lewis. "Can you imagine someone like that in any position of power in the states or country? It's a major tragedy for Minnesota, but the whole country will long feel the loss of the Dahlbergs."

"This story will hang on," said Sam.

"Lots more coffee," said Molly. "I'll get a fresh pot from the kitchen."

"I'll do it," said Laura.

Mikkelson was right behind her.

"We have to have a discussion," he said.

"About what?"

"About what we're doing this weekend."

"What did you have in mind?"

Sam took her in his arms. "Doesn't matter," he said. "Just so it's you and me together."

With his arms around her, he led her outside into the gardens, leaving everyone else inside.

ABOUT THE AUTHOR:

Andie Peterson was born in Fort Dodge, Iowa. Her family spent vacations in northern Minnesota where they moved permanently when Andie was in ninth grade. She attended college in Duluth and began a distinctive teaching career in Minnesota. Andie was Minnesota's Teacher of the Year and a finalist for the National Teacher of the Year Award. She received special awards from two Minnesota governors, was the recipient of an award from the National Education Association, and has received many other awards. She has received three Minnesota School Bell Awards for editorial writing and has published over two hundred columns and articles.

Andie served four terms as mayor of a small town in Minnesota. She lives near Duluth.

CPSIA information can be obtained at www.ICGtesting.com
Printed in the USA
BVOW031908130613

323265BV00001B/103/A